CHARM THE GEEKS

SPUNKY WITH A GEEK SIDE BOOK 1

ALLYSON LINDT

ACELETTE PRESS

ONE

Jordan

If a picture was worth a thousand words, any image of Chloe was worth at least double that. I couldn't take my eyes off her, as she worked at the desk in our hotel suit.

Her hair was swept into the same messy braid she put in before we got on the plane from Salt Lake to L.A. this morning, and loose tendrils of black hair with blond roots cured around her long neck.

She was one of my favorite subjects to draw, and had been since I met her more than a decade ago. Smutty fan art didn't hold a candle to Chloe in any way.

A knot formed in my chest at the thought. We needed to fix things on this trip. Whatever else happened, business, pleasure, sight-seeing... She and I needed to fix whatever the rift was between us.

"If you draw a picture it'll last longer." She didn't look up from the last minute prep she was doing on her laptop, but teasing lay under her words.

That was a better response than I expected, I'd take it. "I thought you liked to be watched." I'd keep the mood like as long as I could.

She'd seemed... off since we left the apartment this morning. Not angry, but not quite here. "I do, I'm just..."

Then again, it felt like that more and more in recent months. We'd been dating for more than ten years, and here at E3—one of the largest trade shows in the world for video game companies—for almost as long.

But this was the first year it felt like Chloe and I were falling apart.

Or maybe we'd never noticed the cracks in our foundation before. I wouldn't—couldn't —believe that. "What's on your mind?" I crossed the room to brush her hair aside and dance my fingers up her neck.

Even though this trip was business, we'd agreed that while we were we'd take a little time for ourselves, to figure out where we wanted to go next as a couple. Even a hint that I might lose her hurt like fuck, but that hadn't brought me any closer to figuring out what was at the heart of one spat after another.

Maybe she was just sick of me putting the toilet paper on the roll in the *wrong* direction, but I suspected there was more to it.

She leaned into my touch with a light sigh, tilting her head enough that I saw a ghost of a smile on her gorgeous lips. "Nothing's wrong. But everything is. I can't stop thinking about everything this weekend, running it all through my head, looking for possible failure points, figuring out what we need to do to fix them. There's just too much—"

"Stop," I said kindly. This was a tension I could deal with. "We've got this. We always have this. No one is better at this than you and me."

This show was a huge deal for any video game company, but Rinslet Enterprises had turned it into a ritual. Chloe and I had turned it into a ritual.

Years ago, when our employer had a different company name, a presentation gone bad led to a hostile takeover that cost us our flagship game and intellectual property.

Our owners rebuilt from the ground up, taking those of us with them who were loyal to the people not the money, and the next year, Chloe and I spoofed the failed presentation here, as a way to announce to the world Rinslet was back and better than ever.

Since then, we were expected to have a better showing every year than the year before. We'd tried to ease off a few times, but the industry wasn't having it.

This year, it was our turn to deliver again. Chloe and I would be in the spotlight and reminding the world how epic our titles were. Our presentation was solid and rehearsed dozens of time. Stressing about it now wouldn't make things go more smoothly.

I wouldn't tell Chloe *chill, we've got this*, but I was happy to distract her. I dipped my head and kissed along the soft skin of her neck, loving the way her chest heaved with a sudden breath. The faint honey of her shampoo teased my thoughts.

"I know the perfect way to take your mind off things," I murmured against her skin.

Her soft moan and the curve of her neck when she leaned into my touch made my blood roar with anticipation and tugged at my cock.

"What did you have in mind?" She asked breathlessly.

So many things. Words were her medium, the visual was mine, but I could dabble enough to draw her into a fantasy A little verbal foreplay with some interactive teasing.

"What do you think of the new sales rep at DM?" As I spoke, nibbled on her earlobe.

Most people wouldn't open a seduction talking about someone else, but some of our favorite fantasies involved a third person in bed with us. We'd never done it. Unlike our public personas, unlike most of the people we'd worked with from the start, we'd only ever been with each other, but the verbal play was a fun alternate universe.

"Can't say I've talked to him long enough to form an opinion." Her tone was light and playful, but her words implied her mind was still working.

I gilded my fingers along her collarbone to dip between her breasts and tease. "He's handsome. Kind of cocky, but I bet he's half talk."

"Rumor is, he's coming off a bad divorce." Chloe's response wasn't as enthusiastic as I'd hoped for.

I wasn't giving up, though. Desire coursed through me each time I touched her. Heard her voice. Tasted her. At least one of us was distracted. "Which means he's single."

"Yeah, but I'm not." She pulled away from me with a sigh.

One of the little hearts on my mental life bar flickered and vanished. I kept my hand on her shoulder, tracing my thumb over the exposed skin. "Of course not. You and me, forever."

She stood as she turned to face me, breaking all contact between us as she crossed her arms and settled her butt on the hotel desk. "I'm just wondering if you were thinking we—you and I—might have sex, oh, *any time* in the near future, without you needing to think about someone else in order to get off."

"The fuck?" I stared at her in disbelief and raced to catch up with the accusation. Why was she putting this entire thing on me? We'd both always been willing participants in the *let's share with someone else* fantasy. Unless she'd been lying about it all this time. "You know I'm here with you." I couldn't unclench my jaw when I spoke

"Do I?"

Seriously? "Where the hell is this coming from?" I was fine with talking through our problems, but an accusation out of left field? No.

Chloe dragged her fingers through her hair, growling in frustration when they snagged on braid. "I don't know. It's been there for a while."

Wonderful. How long was *for a while*? At least this argument was different from any other we had. "You should've said something."

"Maybe I didn't think I *should* have to. Why would this be okay?"

This—me being expected to read her mind—wasn't okay in any way. "Because you've said it is. Over and over, for years, you've said you enjoy the naughtiness in the daydream."

"What if I want something else?"

"Then *tell* me."

"What if it's boring and simple? What if it's something like just the two of us being here, with each other, and without needing someone else as stimulus. Or what if it's that I'm tired of pretending that my boyfriend, Mr. Master-of-Tentacle-Porn, is anyone other than a guy who's ever only seen one pair of tits in person."

I ground my teeth so hard I felt it in my ears. That was hitting below the belt. And two completely contradictory statements. Did she want more kink or less? I was slipping from *where did this come from* to *what the hell are we talking about* real fast. "Sorry to be so hands-on boring. Which do you want? Sex that's just us, or something wild and crazy and real-life kinky?"

"I don't know." Her sigh radiated frustration and mingled with my own. "I just know whatever we're doing now isn't working." She brushed past me.

I grabbed her arm and forced her to face me. "We don't walk away from each other. Not like this. We talk things through."

Except, apparently what we actually did was pretend to talk things through, leaving me thinking everything was fine with Chloe let the wound fester.

"*Talking* is all we do. We talk and talk and talk and talk," she said.

"And fuck. And have fun. And enjoy each other's company. And make an amazing team. How is that not enough for you?"

She yanked away from me. "It's not. I'm sorry, but... I can't be here right now."

I twitched my fingers as I watched her walk out of the room, and barely checked the desire to say *anything* to have the last word. I didn't have a response. I didn't know which frustration that she'd voiced was the one I needed to focus on.

And if she was so insistent on ending the conversation, I didn't have anything new to say if I chased her down.

The door closed behind her, closing me off from her.

She'd never done that before. More than a decade together and neither of us had ever walked away in the middle of a disagreement.

Fuuuuuuuck. The scream echoed in my head, clawing to be released.

This'd give people something to talk about when it came to Rinslet and E3. *Media Darlings Jordan and Chloe Finished?*

Chloe couldn't write a more viral headline than that.

TWO

Chloe

If I didn't wipe away the tears soon, they'd start falling down my cheeks instead of just blurring my view of the liquor on shelves behind the bar.

I hadn't wanted to pick a fight with Jordan. Once I started talking, the words just fell out. He must think I was nuts, going from zero to pissed in seconds, about the things I did. We were both a little odd anyway, but we were each other's kind of weird. He was the ham to my pineapple.

This swallow of cranberry didn't burn my raw throat as much as the last one. I rarely drank, but if I asked the bartender to add vodka to this, how long until I was numb?

I'd been trying to figure out for a while now what was bothering me. Yes, we were in high stress jobs, but they were our dream jobs. We'd come into these positions—Jordan with the visuals and me with the story writing—when we were barely more than kids. Even with the fresh talent, we were still some of the youngest in the group.

We'd shaped these positions. We had each other. We had most everything we wanted. Life was incredible.

And I was still unhappy. Still missing something. Did I feel a lot guilty and entitled? Yeah. Did that eliminate the dissatisfaction? Nope.

Then Jordan started into that familiar path of fantasy. One we took so often. And his words drilled straight to my insecurities. A set of contradictions I never had to vocalize, but today they became vivid and real.

Jordan and I were talk. So much talk. We joked about gang bangs and tentacles and tails and knotting... Then we went home with each other, and the most risqué thing we ever did was a little light spanking. Flat palm. Nothing more. I didn't know which one bothered me more—that we were all talk, or that sometimes it didn't seem like we could have sex without the talk.

Was I unhappy that we were boring in the bedroom or was I terrified that he thought so too, and he'd leave me for someone who wasn't?

I knew that last fear was unfounded. When I thought about it, I *knew* Jordan and I were good together. The fear still existed.

And instead of talking this through with him, I'd stormed away, wrapped in confusion and hurt, and most likely leaving Jordan with the same and wondering what the fuck just happened.

If this were a character arc in a game, I'd have known how to resolve the angst before I ever wrote a single word of it.

Too bad life wasn't that simple.

The bar was getting noisy and I wasn't in the mood to listen to the happy chatter, planning, and speculation about the show tomorrow. I should either find someplace else to clear my head or go back upstairs and.... what?

I couldn't face Jordan yet, as much as I needed to. I didn't have any idea how to put these thoughts into words without them sounding stupid. Words were supposed to be my bitch, damn it.

Someone took the stool next to me and I didn't even twitch in their direction. Most everyone here recognized me, but if I kept my head down and pretended I was busy with my phone, most of them left me alone.

"Are you all right?" A woman's voice disrupted my rambling journey through woe-is-me-dom.

I looked up to find a pair of gorgeous blue eyes watching me. Her hair was a stunning shade of violet that couldn't be natural anywhere but in an anime, but that didn't distract from her face. Kind. Concerned. Pretty. And a quick glance down at the school girl costume said she was a fellow short-girl.

I wasn't sure if I wanted to run my fingers through her smooth, purple locks, or lock lips and find out what flavor wine she was drinking.

I shook the random impulse aside and tried to summon a smile. *I'm dandy.* The sarcastic retort tried to force its way to my lips. *I'm sitting out here because my boyfriend and I are fighting over you. Well, not you specifically, but the concept of lusting after people who aren't us. How fucked up is that?* "I'm good."

"If you're sure..." She fiddled with her wine glass. Even in the dimly lit bar, wearing a costume made of flimsy fabric, she looked immaculate. The outfit was a deception because the small purse that hung from her wrist cost more than my entire T-shirt collection.

If she was here with the E3 group—which the costume and her presence implied—she worked for a company in such a different realm than Rinslet that we'd probably never touch them.

"I'm Liz, by the way. I'm not here to crash your night, but"—she gazed around the room—"I thought I was in the mood for company and I'm not."

If I stared at her much longer, I was going to make things awkward. "Chloe. And I get it. You don't want to go back to your room, but you don't want to have to talk to anyone, and if you're by yourself down here, people will approach you."

Liz's smile, perfectly shaped white teeth against the exact right shade of miraculously unsmudged lipstick, was a startling blend of sexy-sweet and adorable. "Exactly. But people are steering clear of you, and I can't figure out why. You're cute."

My cheeks heated. When was the last time such a simple compliment caught me off-guard? When was the last time I got one that sounded this kind of sincere? "I'm also scowling. And most of these people see me as one of the boys."

The reality of my reply soured in my gut. Liz was

adorable and just enough out of place that people wouldn't leave her alone if she was alone. I was the scowling tomboy in the corner making a glass of cranberry juice last longer than God ever intended.

"I see." Liz fiddled with her left ring finger, twisting though there was no jewelry. "Do you mind if I sit here anyway? We don't have to talk, but if you want to, I'm happy to listen. You look like maybe you could use a friend."

I had friends—an office full of guys who got my quirks and loved gaming as much as I did. And who were also Jordan's friends. Because my job a Rinslet *was* my adult life. Even my sister was married to one of the big bosses. Was I anyone without my job?

The last thing I needed right now was another sad path to diverge onto. "Not sure I've got much to say, but you're still welcome to join me."

"Do you want another drink? God, that sounds like I'm hitting on you. I just noticed you made that glass last a long time."

How long had she been watching me? And why did that intrigue me? I knew I was attracted to both men and women. So was Jordan. But we'd been each other's first real anything—yeah, the geeky fanfic kids who wrote and drew smut but had never even kissed anyone else.

Great. Now I was thinking again about regret and missed opportunities and wondering if I was holding Jordan back from the same.

"They don't have anything on tap that I like. My red of choice is fizzy, full of sugar and comes in twelve-ounce cans." If I was going to talk to her, I needed to talk *to her* and not to myself in my own head.

"They're all out of Code Red? Inconceivable." Liz's wink and accompanying smirk were enough to make me smile. She waved the bartender over. "Another glass of the house red for me."

Ah, fuck it. If I was in a slump, the best way to get out was to do things I didn't normally do. "I think I'll leave the same." Maybe it would knock loose whatever was stuck in my head, or clear out the stubbornness keeping me from going back upstairs or a least get me drunk enough I didn't care.

Seconds later, two glasses were placed in front of us. What came next? Suddenly I felt like a little girl completely out of my element. An attractive, confident woman sat next to me and was chatting me up as if this were the most natural thing in the world.

And I didn't know if I wanted to accept her offer of friendship or find out if girls really did kiss differently than guys.

Instead, I sipped my drink slowly, not daring to make eye-contact, as I racked my brain for words.

Jordan and I had actually discussed several times that we'd be okay with the other of us with someone else. If the opportunity arose. Testing that right after a fight didn't seem like a good idea.

"Are you here with them, then?" Liz's question startled me. "You said most of these people recognize you but I apologize that I don't. I'm new to the industry. Are you one of the voice actors or a developer or...?"

At least she didn't assume I was a booth babe. Not

that I was nearly tall enough or coordinated enough for that. "I'm Senior Vice President of Community and Writing for Rinslet Enterprises."

"Wow." Liz's surprise sounded genuine. "They make a lot of games."

Was I grateful or just a little wounded that she didn't recognize my name and title? Was I trying to impress her? Definitely. "And my people are the reason those games have award-winning storylines."

"I didn't realize."

"It's okay. I can't tell you who the rock stars of the investment world are, either." It had taken me a little bit, but the pieces fit now. She was money trying to fit into a group where only the higher ups cared about those things. Gaming might look like a bunch of trolls living in basements to the outside world, but big banks loved the right companies.

I took a sip of my wine. It was sweeter than I expected. Pleasant. I drained the glass before I realized what I was doing.

"My brother-in-law owns half the company, which has everything and nothing to do with why we're here." Why did I say that? She may not have recognized my name, but she'd know Zach's. Those same banks hated the gate our owners used to keep out investors.

"Oh." Liz's enthusiasm vanished in a flash. "You work for family."

Defensiveness spilled through me. I'd earned my job. Insecurities played no part here—I was in this position because I was the best at what I did, regardless of what rumors said. "It's not favoritism."

"What? No, I didn't mean that at all. I bet you're crazy talented, but working for family can be complicated."

Her rush to set things right warmed my cheeks. Or was that the wine? "He's been my boss longer than he's been part of the family. And I don't even report to him." I'd always worked for Scott, his business partner, but I'd still spent most of my career proving that I had my job because I could do it and not because I'd begged Zach for it.

"Then never mind my warning." Liz finished her drink.

"You can't just say *never mind* after something like that." Was I relaxing and enjoying this, despite the bumps and my mood? It might be that one tiny glass of wine, but it felt like more than that. It felt good to connect with someone who was talking to me *just because.* "Now you have to explain."

Liz shook her head, but she was smiling as she waved the bartender over. "More?" she nodded at my empty glass.

"Sure." Why the fuck not.

At Liz's prompting, possibly thanks in part to the extra twenty she slid across the bar, our glasses were filled almost to the top this time, and we were left alone.

She took a long sip of her drink, leaving a shine behind that I wanted to lean in and lick away. At least my imagination still worked. I shifted in my seat, and my head floated and bobbed. Had I eaten? It didn't matter. A couple of drinks weren't a big deal, and I was walking upstairs, not driving home, when this was done.

"Come on. I'll show you mine if you show me yours." I giggled, though the almost nonsensical request wasn't funny. I should stop at two glasses.

"I'd like to see that." Liz glanced at me. "It's not really an interesting story. My best friend and my brother... Actually it's kind of convoluted."

"Try me. You might think it's simple to plot a video game, until you have to figure out how many permutations there are for Character A to piss off Character B and still accomplish their goal." I took a large swallow of my drink.

"Here goes, then. My best friend hired me to keep her books. Then she became business partners with my brother and got engaged to him..."

I'd been there. Not quite like that, but close enough. *"Awkward."*

"More than you realize. When they were dating, I didn't want to see either of them get hurt. And I probably wanted to avoid it for myself, too. To keep them apart, temporary flash of insanity... insecurity, self-realization... whatever you want to call it... I kissed her and told her I loved her."

Okay, so I'd never done anything like that—I couldn't fathom making a play for Zach. "Do you?"

"I adore her more than almost anything, but not romantically. She's pretty. Adventurous. Amazing. The best sister ever.

"I want to be like that." The words came out sadder than I intended. "I mean, I already am the best sister ever." My attempt at humor felt flat. Lifeless. "I just...

Being the kind of woman who turns heads. Does whatever inspires her. Living impulsively."

"Aren't you already?" Liz sounded so sincere. "You're attractive. You're letting an almost total stranger hit on you in a bar. All of that has to count somewhere on the *adventurous* scale."

Hit on me? No. Was she? She just said she was. How bright red was I at this point? "I'm all talk." And not very good talk, apparently. If I were one of my characters, I would've said something far wittier.

"But talking is where it starts. Or maybe imagination is where it starts, but if you can't vocalize it, how does anyone know you want it?"

Finding words, at least on paper, had never been a problem for me. Putting those thoughts into action? This train of thought led back to the fight with Jordan… When had I finished my drink? "Anyway. Siblings suck, even when we love them. So do their partners. And your best friend? She missed out. I think you're anime-heroine beautiful." Open mouth, insert foot. Way to go, me.

Liz never flinched. "Thank you. The feeling's mutual."

"I can't believe anyone turned you down. I'd make out with you in a heartbeat." Damn it, wine.

Liz ducked her head. "It was just a kiss. It wasn't like I dragged her into a dark corner so we could grope each other."

Wow this got personal fast. How had we gone from talking about work to family to sexuality?

"You have to start somewhere." I leaned closer, using the bar top for support, and paused with my face near Liz's. The soft scent of lilacs mixed with liquor teased me, and I searched her eyes, unsure what I was looking for.

Fuck it. I closed those last few inches and pressed my lips to Liz's.

When she didn't return the gesture, my heart stalled, but then she kissed back. My pulse whimpered and raced through me, tingling in my fingers and toes and hitting every hidden coin on my body.

Liz settled a palm on my cheek, and I sank into the softness of skin on skin. Her smooth lips. Her hungry mouth…

Something clattered in the background and someone laughed.

Jordan.

I jerked back, eyes wide and heart slamming itself against my ribs. The sound wasn't him, but how had I let him slip from my mind at all? "I'm sorry." My tongue was like cotton and my brain raced too fast for me to grab onto all my thoughts. "I shouldn't have done that. I'm seeing someone. I should've said that up front. *Christ,* I'm sorry."

"No. It's okay. I mean, attached? Of course you are. I don't expect—" Liz caught her bottom lip between her teeth.

I needed to get out of here. When I stood, my world tilted and spun before righting itself. "Nice meeting you. I should get going. Enjoy the rest of the show." I snapped my jaw shut before I could ramble myself into another awkward—delicious, enticing, not-nearly long-enough—kiss.

"Can you make it okay?" And she was still worried about me.

I started to nod, but liked the room not spinning. "I'm fine."

Liz walked me to the elevator anyway. I didn't know what else to say. When we reached my floor, I mumbled, "Thank you."

Fortunately, my room wasn't far. As I slid the key-card into the lock, I turned and saw the lift doors slide shut, blocking Liz from view.

Guilt and sour wine churned in my gut. It didn't matter that Jordan and I always said *If the chance ever arises to be with someone, and you like them...* I still felt like a schmuck. I'd fought with my boyfriend of more than a decade, then made myself feel better by kissing a random woman who bought me a drink.

I slipped into the room and darkness enveloped me. Had I been gone that long? A glance at the clock on the microwave told me it was after eleven.

I padded to the bedroom off the main suite. When I stepped into the doorway, Jordan was already in bed. He rolled onto his side, back to me, and pulled the comforter tighter.

Sick surged inside. "Jordan?" I forced his name out. "Can we talk?"

Nothing.

Frustration welled inside, joining the parade already

doing its damnedest to make me puke. I undressed and slipped into bed.

Could we recover from this?

THREE

Liz

I stood next to the bed in my hotel room, shuffling through my bags for the billionth time. There wouldn't be anything new in them, and I'd had the list of things I packed memorized before the first look. But I needed to kill sometime and my *fidget* impulse was cranked to high.

When I'd agreed to an early breakfast with a client, I expected to need large doses of caffeine to get through the meeting. There was no universe in which I'd anticipated being up all night before, because I'd kissed a girl.

I hovered my fingers over my lips, close enough to feel their warmth, like I had so many times since last night. Approaching Chloe was a whim. I hadn't been in the bar to meet anyone, but when I realized I couldn't take my eyes off her, I had to introduce myself to the cute woman with the pixie-like face framed by black hair with blond roots.

It had taken me about two-point-five seconds to realize how out of my depth I was. I didn't know how to flirt—guys hit on me, frequently because of my family's money, and I got to pick and choose who to turn down. I didn't want to offend Chloe.

Apparently it hadn't matter. *Attached.* The word soured in my stomach. I'd been the other woman before, and had no desire to do it again. At least Chloe told me before I, oh, I don't know, planned an entire wedding around the affair and invited my whole family to watch me be humiliated when my boyfriend's wife showed up at the altar to yell at me, instead of him waiting for me in his tux

The only reason Chloe still teased my thoughts was because I'd never met anyone like her before. I couldn't define it beyond *fascinating* and a lot of other adjectives that meant the same, but didn't really hold any substance.

Chloe could probably put it into words. As part of my insomnia, I'd read up on her. Not that I'd do anything with the information, except be properly impressed if we ran into each other again.

Because Chloe was off limits.

My phone buzzed, pushing the circular thoughts aside. Was I late? No. I didn't need to be down there for half an hour.

The caller ID said *Kyle Ridge.* My lawyer. I could ignore him, but that would only postpone this round of *here's how your ex screwed you over this time.* Fortunately, Kyle was nice about it, and as much as I dreaded the news, being stuck in my own head thinking about what wouldn't be was worse.

"This is Elizabeth Thompson."

"Are you somewhere with a TV?"

I grabbed the remote. "Good morning to you too."

"Yeah. Morning. Turn on CNN." The edge in his voice was something new for me to fixate on.

I turned on the TV and flipped until I found the right channel.

"...*George Debson was arrested this morning at St. George Municipal Airport, trying to board a plane for Borneo...*"

My legs wobbled, threatening to give out, and I sank to the edge of the mattress. Sick relief flooded my veins, like the rush-crash that comes after an adrenaline high. They caught him.

"This is great." Fucking amazing. The police had found my ex-fiancé. The man I'd insisted my brother not do a background check on, because *I was in love.* The man who'd tied up half my assets in court for months, because I'd been an idiot and gave him access to my accounts. The man who was not only already married when he proposed, but who had conned at least two other women into similar engagements.

I was lucky we hadn't made it to the *I do,* but there were things I was still fighting to recover from him. I didn't think I'd ever get my dignity back.

And Kyle wouldn't sound so stressed if this was as great as I thought. "It is good news, isn't it?" I repeated.

"It's not the worst news, but it could be better," Kyle said. "He's been charged with securities fraud. That means all his assets—those with your name on them or anyone else's—are frozen. We can't get to them."

"Oh." Disappointing, but not the end of the world. George hadn't taken everything from me, and he hadn't touched my family's money. I wanted them back because they weren't his. "So... tell me how to feel." Because apparently relief wasn't right.

"Our office phones are ringing off the hooks this morning. People want a statement from you, and you don't want to talk to them anymore than I want you talking to them. Are you somewhere you can lie low?"

"I'm in L.A. for a trade show." I was from Salt Lake. "I doubt anyone here cares who I am."

"Good." Relief bled into Kyle's tone. "Keep your head down. Don't answer any questions if the press approaches you. I'll keep you posted."

I did all of that anyway. "Let me know. Thank you." I disconnected and let my arm go limp. Something new to fixate on beyond *her*. *Yay*. I'd rather be hyper-focused on that incredible kiss, still.

Screw this. I was tired of sitting in my room, trying not to climb the walls. At least if I headed to my meeting place, I could let the background noise drown out my thoughts until Jonathan arrived.

Stepping out of my room helped. The box pinning me in was gone, and I was free to roam.

Wow, sleep deprivation made me melodramatic.

My phone said I was meeting Jonathan at a place around the corner from the hotel. I'd seen the world when I was growing up, so the already crowded streets weren't new to me, despite being a start contrast to back home.

As I wove my way through foot traffic, the throngs of people drew me further from my own thoughts. I let noise and scents and body heat clashing with morning chill wash over me, and breathed it all in.

Better already.

It didn't make me long to find the bakery, and the amazing smells of fresh muffins and dark roast coffee replaced those of car exhaust and cologne.

The line of customers stretched back to meet me, and I had to squish into place at the back of the dining room in order for the door to close behind me.

Good thing I was early. I'd hold our spot in line, and maybe we'd have our food before our meeting time was up.

I was surprised I heard the bell chime above the door when it opened again, and a heartbeat later, Jonathan joined me in line. "Another thing I like about you," he said with a smile. "Better than punctual." He tugged a strand of my hair. "Love the purple, by the way."

This was far more pleasant than too-early calls from my lawyer and news my ex was trying to flee the country. "Good morning to you too. You didn't tell me this place was so popular."

"Best coffee within walking distance of the convention center, and they don't charge ten bucks for a muffin. They do all right." Jonathan was my contact for one of the companies I managed adverting for at my family's firm. His sandy-blond hair, brown eyes, and infectious smile made him a good breakfast companion anyway, but today his company would also serve to help me move past last night.

Before Mercy and Ian—my best friend and my older

brother—merged their advertising firms, they'd competed against each other for the same contract with KaleidoMotion. Jonathan had been furious about the merger, since he'd been wooed by both of them. He claimed the bidding process was rigged, and refused to work with almost anyone at the company.

I'd convinced him it was all timing, no matter how bad it looked, and talked him down from canceling the contract, and in return he told Mercy he refused to work with anyone but me.

"Did you get the newest art mock-ups I sent over last night?" I asked. Might as well start our meeting in line. His account was the reason I was swimming in this sea of tech without a life vest, and feeling out of place.

"I did. They look fantastic," Jonathan said. "The guy who set up our sound and video is testing everything now in the convention hall."

KaleidoMotion had animation software they sold to game companies, schools, and other groups who wanted to make drawings move and didn't want to write their own programs to do so. KM was debuting a new product here at E3, and our design team had spent hundreds of hours working with them to make some demo videos.

I was here as support, and to make sure there was an instant and open line of communication if KM needed any last-minute changes.

Jonathan studied me for a moment, his jaw working, then shook his head.

"Is there an issue?" I readied myself to call Mercy.

"What?" He frowned, then relaxed. "No. It's exactly what we wanted. Period. End sentence. No *but*."

"So something else is bothering you." I didn't know why he and I clicked so well, but it was nice to just talk random, small stuff with someone who wasn't a stakeholder in my life.

His smile was back, but tinged with something more somber. "I saw the news this morning. About your ex. You doing okay?"

I'd field this question half a dozen more times today, from Mercy, Ian, and anyone else I spoke to in the office. Seemed like a good time to practice playing it cool. "I'm good. He's where he belongs. Glad I got out of the relationship when I did."

"Me too." With his hand at the small of my back, he nudged me forward, then dropped the contact again.

We made small talk as the herd jostled us toward the register, and I relaxed more with each word exchanged and step forward. We gave the cashier our orders, and I handed her my credit card.

"You didn't even pause long enough to let me pick up the tab," Jonathan teased. "Now I don't feel like a gentleman."

I waved my hand in casual dismissal. "I'm expensing the cost back to you regardless." But this was a subtle way of showing I was doing my job. No one had asked me to prove anything to anyone, but I was almost thirty, this was my first job, and my sister-in-law gave it to me. I felt about fifty flavors of awkward about all of that. "If anyone asks, promise me you'll tell them we had a good time."

Jonathan chuckled. "No worries there. Speaking of, dinner is on me tonight."

I shook my head, but I was smiling. "I have plans." So did he. *Dinner* was a meeting with his convention crew.

"I'm-sorry-this-is-declined-I-don't-know-why." The cashier's quiet words ran together in a single blur as she handed back my credit card.

What? Even after I processed her words I didn't understand them. I kept my shock from my expression and slipped the card back into my wallet. "Crap. That's the expired card." The lie felt awkward, but admitting I couldn't pay a small bill was worse.

"Let me get it." Jonathan was already handing her a new credit card.

"I'm just letting you save face, by saving me." My laugh was forced, and I glanced in my wallet again at the offending card.

I'd accidentally handed over a personal one, instead of using my company account. But I should never run into an issue paying with a personal card. Tension cranked inside until I was wound tighter than a spring.

The declined purchase had to be a fluke.

So why was I certain the reality was far worse?

FOUR

Jordan

I shouldn't have ignored Chloe when she came in last night, and not only because it left me awake and staring at the wall until I finally dozed around three.

We needed to fix things between us. I needed to get to an early meeting. I couldn't do both at the same time, and my job rode on making the meeting. Then again, wasn't that part of our problem? Even the way the world saw us—the way we saw ourselves—was shaped by our jobs.

I brushed a strand of hair from Chloe's cheek and studied her sleeping face. Waking her up would be rude, at least one of us should sleep, but walking away this morning while we were still fighting gnawed a hole in my chest. This wasn't the first time we'd gone to bed angry at each other, especially in the last few months, but it was the first time we hadn't said anything else after climbing under the covers.

There was a little time until I had to be downstairs

for my breakfast meeting. I'd shower, make her coffee, and we could at least say *something* to each other. I climbed from the bed, careful not to disturb her, stripped down in the bathroom, and let the water flow over me.

Shower time was frequently great for creativity. I'd solved a wide range of artistic puzzles while I was soaping up. Today, I couldn't find the answer to the one thing that mattered more to me than anything—my relationship with Chloe.

We each headed different departments, so it was normal for us to keep mismatched schedules. Even here, traveling, we had different contacts to meet with. But today it was all wrong. It felt out of whack. This trip was supposed to be a chance to fix us, not turn a fracture into a clean break.

Chloe was tired of the verbal foreplay. Sick of the status quo of us.

I forced my jaw to unclench. There was more under her words—a frustration I didn't understand.

By the time I stepped from the shower, the bed was empty. The rich scent of coffee filled the hotel room. So much for waking her up with a nice gesture.

I yanked on my uniform for the day. If we were in the office, at least I'd be comfortable thanks to a *who gives a fuck* dress code, rather than this button-down shirt, tie, and trousers crap. But I got to keep the blue hair, even at trade shows. One advantage to being the company's trademark rebel.

Chloe was in the kitchenette, staring at the contents of the mug in her hand. Her hair hung loose around her shoulders and her tank top hugged her torso, stopping right above her panties and leaving her legs on display.

Fuck, I wanted to lift her onto the counter and spend the morning exploring her—who gave a shit about business partners. But first I had to figure out why she hadn't looked up yet. She had to have noticed me walk into the room.

A second mug sat on the counter. The coffee in it would have the perfect amount of cream, no sugar. I ignored the drink and approached her. As I drew closer, she stepped back, fiddling with her spoon and not making eye contact.

I didn't know what to make of her behavior. "Good morning."

A smile ghosted across her lips. "Hey."

"Did you get any work done last night?" I asked. Rather than force her another step back, I leaned against the counter, despite the suffocating desire to reach out.

"No."

Grr. "I'm sorry to hear it."

She was usually the vocal one. The writer. The person with all the right words. Her monosyllabic replies threw me off.

"I didn't mean to distract you from wrapping up your work before today." I tried a new angle.

Her spoon clanked against the edges of her mug as she stirred her drink.

This was like fucking pulling teeth. "Did you do anything fun instead?"

She'd been gone for hours, and wrong as it was, I'd

hoped she spent as much of that time staring at the wall, looking for answers, as I had.

"I kissed a girl."

What? Thank God I left my coffee on the table, or it'd be splattered all over me now.

When my mind kicked back on, every thought rushed in at once.

Jealousy.

Curiosity.

Fury.

Desire.

How the hell was this turning me on? Sure, Chloe and I had talked about being with other people, either together or separately. We'd even discussed that it may be spontaneous, especially given how much time we spent working the trade show circuit.

I'd still hoped for a chance to talk through either of our *first times* before they happened. A nice, calm conversation that started with *so I met someone cute...* Not something that was done right in the middle of a fight.

"And you liked it?" I filled in the missing song lyrics, not knowing what to say. "Are we playing name that tune?" I couldn't stop an edge from creeping into my voice.

"Yes to the first. No to the second. I'm sorry." Grief and guilt spilled into her voice, and she still refused to make eye contact. "I didn't mean to. It just kind of happened."

"Of course. That makes perfect sense. We fight about whether or not I actually want to be with you, you storm out of here without making things right, and...

What? You tripped in the lobby just as some woman was walking by, and accidentally locked lips and made out with her by mistake?"

Ceramic *thunked* against Formica, and Chloe closed the distance between us, hurt etched in her face. "There was no *making out*." Her voice cracked and she swallowed. "I had a little to drink enough to relax, and it was just a kiss. Doesn't this give you more fodder for your fantasies?"

She cringed and shook her head. "I'm sorry. I didn't mean that. I feel like shit about the whole thing, and I wanted to tell you last night and apologize but..."

But I'd ignored her when she came home. I heard her despair and frustration, but I was processing my own emotions. I could say anything if I couldn't figure out how I felt.

She stared at me with wide, sad eyes. "If you tell me you don't want me—us—to do things like that again, I won't. Not that I have plans to, but we can take the option off the table."

"It's fine." Was it? It might be, once the numbness spilling inside wore off. One thing it wasn't—fair of me to hold this against her. We were free spirits. Didn't let standard roles define us.

That and my imagination was already creating intricate images of how scorching it would be to watch Chloe with someone else. The visuals warred with every other emotion I couldn't identify.

"I have to get to that meeting with the swag vendor from New York." Wow. Way to be a dick and just brush the whole thing off, me.

"Wait. Please?" Chloe's tone made me turn. She raised her hands, hesitated, then rested them on my chest. The heat of her palms seared through my shirt, speaking to every bit of me that wanted this to just be all right. "I won't ask you to tell me we're okay. Not yet. But *God*, please don't brush me off."

I pressed pause on my swirling thoughts long enough to stare into her brown eyes. To study the dusting of freckles across her cheeks, and watch as she worried her lip with her teeth.

I really did love her.

Inviting another person into our relationship, even just for a night, didn't seem like the right way to solve *us*. Except if part of the problem was pretending someone was there, wanting the experience, but not acting on it.

Christ this was confusing.

"Well talk as soon as my meeting's over. I promise." I brushed my lips over hers, pouring all my reassurance into the kiss.

I should have saved some for myself, because the empty pit behind my ribs grew as I walked out the door.

FIVE

Chloe

I was used to the non-stop activity of trade shows. There was always something to do and someone to meet with, and I was always checking my phone to make sure I didn't miss my next appointment.

Today was no less hectic, but I swore every time I looked at a clock, only a few minutes had passed. My schedule didn't sync at all with Jordan's.

"Do you want to reschedule?" The kind voice reminded me I shouldn't constantly glance at my phone while I was in a meeting.

The smile I gave Grayson felt more tired than I wanted it to. "I'm sorry. I'm good. Did you have any questions about the NDA?"

He scanned the document again.

People streaming themselves playing video games was becoming a bigger thing every year, and like every gaming company, we wanted streamers saying good things about our games to their audiences.

I was talking to some of our most vocal fans about heading up our new Community Contributor program. Grayson wasn't just one of the most engaging streamers out there, he had also won our last two competitions.

"How are you enforcing if anyone breaks the NDA?" Grayson asked.

"You planning to fuck us over?" I made sure my teasing was clear. It was nice to be meeting with someone I didn't have to filter myself around.

He laughed and shook his head. "Not me. I don't shit where I eat and sleep. But you know as well as I do that a series of exclusive, consecutive reveals don't mean anything if someone else scooped it first."

I knew it better than almost anyone. "You're a *very* carefully vetted group, so I don't expect issues. But"—I added the word quickly when he opened his mouth— "we'll deal with it the same way we always do.

"Take-down notices, spin, and some of the best fucking PR in the industry?"

I gave him a dry smile. "You know it." We'd survived our CTO's dangerous lack of a filter, his stint in rehab, and a hostile takeover that cost the company the game at the core of its business. We'd live through a streamer talking too soon about our new program. "You're covered by that umbrella by signing on with us. We won't just brush it away from Rinslet, we'll take care of all of you as well."

Rinslet always looked out for their own.

As I wrapped up the conversation with Grayson, my mind drifted without my permission. Again. Taunting me with memories of *the kiss*. Guilt mingled with desire.

It had never been that intense with anyone except Jordan.

Not that I'd had a lot of experience before him, and none after, despite all our discussions about how much we'd each like that.

I sent Grayson on his way. The instant I closed the door behind him of the small meeting room, I sank back into the nearest chair and slumped.

How fucked up was I? I wanted to make things right with my boyfriend. I wanted to open our relationship. I wanted him focused on just me. I wanted us to be with other people.

The circular and contradictory thoughts weren't getting me any further than they did last night.

Except now, Liz was part of the *let's experiment* side of things. Jordan and I both knew we were bisexual, but neither of us had ever...

And now Liz was taking up residency in the part of my mind that wrote out scorching and vivid fan fiction. Clothes were coming off. We were exploring each other. Hell, Jordan was there for at least half the fantasies.

Did I understand that a couple looking for a woman to love them both—unicorn hunting—was an abhorrent thing in polyamory circles? Absolutely. But I didn't want her to move into our guest bedroom and be our love pet.

I just had so many fantasies of being with another woman, of being with a third person and having Jordan there, that my imagination wanted to indulge all of them in a non-stop stream.

Another team member needed this room in five minutes, and I had a different meeting to be in. I gathered up my laptop and made sure we hadn't left any paperwork laying loose around the room.

After Jordon's reaction this morning, I was hesitant to bring any of this up with him again. We were supposed to be able to talk, but my confession had pushed all the wrong buttons.

I wove through trade show crowds, cutting a fast and direct path to my next meeting, on the other side of the convention center.

Fantasy was one thing, but this was real life. Last night I'd been tipsy, frustrated, and feeling a bit melodramatic when I thought of Jordan and me as over. Losing him wasn't an option.

I'd let him lead the next conversation around where we went from here, and actually listen and try be rational rather than running hot and cold. No bringing up other people until—unless—he did.

Making that decision blanketed me with some reason. Not a lot, but this was better than the alternative, and I could use the resolve to ignore the gnawing in my gut at the idea of never getting to explore more of what I'd tasted with Liz last night.

My mind registered a new site, and the acid in my stomach shifted to something more intense and nauseating. The guy with the press badge cutting a line straight for me.

I didn't have the time or patience for Stew Knapfer. He was rock bottom on my list of things I wanted to deal with on a good day. It was too late to pivot and pretend I hadn't seen him—we'd already made eye contact.

Fuck.

I tried to cut in another direction anyway.

"Chloe. *Dude.* Wait up." Stew approached with a smile wide enough to show his teeth. "You have to give me the inside scoop."

"I'm late to a meeting. Catch up with me later." I never slowed.

He fell into step beside me. "We can talk while we walk." Years ago, he was a game review blogger. As the market grew more saturated with everyone sharing their opinions, in any media format possible, he split his priorities. He spent as much time writing gossip posts—ninety percent his speculation spun as *fact*—as he did reviewing games.

The money wasn't in the posts themselves, it was in referral sales from links to affiliate sites. Stew had the most click-baity headlines in the industry, and he didn't care who fell because of them.

Because I was the face of one of the top gaming companies in the world, it was frequently me who got covered in his bullshit.

"We're not talking because you're not getting an inside scoop." I increased my pace and found tighter spots in the crowds to weave through. "You watch the big reveal in Thursday's panel, like everyone else."

"Not even a hint? This is for you. To hope you feed the hype. Bro, come on."

I cringed, and more of Liz's words bled back in. *People keep trying to talk to me. No one's approaching you.*

Because they knew me. But it ran deeper than that. I was *one of the guys*. Most of the time, the fact that the men around me didn't see me as a pair of tits made it easier to get my job done. Every once in a while though —regardless of how not feminist it was—I had an irrepressible urge to be objectified.

Would I hate it? Almost definitely. Did that stop me from wanting to experience it just once?

Nope.

Except last night with Liz was something different. She wasn't there to talk shop with me, but she also wasn't hitting on me because I was some woman. She seemed genuinely interested in me, but also attracted to me.

Was that one of the reasons I couldn't get her out of my head?

I stopped a few doors down from my destination and turned to Stew. "No hints. No clues... Wait—I've got one for you. *Big Reveal.* Can you picture it?"

"That's not news, it's the same vague bullshit you've been spouting for a month." Irritation flowed from Stew. "If you don't tell me, I'll make something up."

As if my interaction drove his decision to do that. "And when you're wrong, people are going to call you on it."

"Unless I'm right. New game franchise?"

"No comment."

"New sexual for The Hoarde?"

Rinslet didn't even own the rights to that game anymore. "No comment."

"We get to see your tits in a secret Easter egg?"

Nope. Didn't like the objectification after all. I

clenched my jaw to keep my growl from escaping. "No comment."

"Fine." He turned away. "If I make it up and I'm wrong, I'll say you changed things last minute, to avoid being scooped."

"That doesn't even make sense." My protest hit his retreating back. Not that it would matter if he heard it.

A demo like the one we'd scheduled took months of planning, and couldn't be swapped last minute because a single blogger did or didn't guess right. Hell, I knew of at least three people, including Grayson, who had already figured out what we were up to.

None of that mattered. As much as I hated Stew's headlines, they made up the truth as much as reality did.

I was five minutes late to my meeting, and wasted another three apologizing. My day didn't pick up from there, and I didn't stop counting the hours until I could stop and breathe and see Jordan.

I'd never been so anxious for a trade show day to end, and that included the original stunt that put us on the map.

"Hey, gorgeous." Jordan's breath brushed my cheek at the same time he wrapped his arms around my waist.

His warm greeting—a stark contrast to the last twenty four hours—warmed me as much as the surprise of seeing him earlier than I expected. How did two simple words chase away so much tension?

I leaned into his embrace, resting my weight against his chest, and pulled his arms tighter. "You done rubbing elbows for the day?" I asked.

"Rubbing elbows. Is that a euphemism?" His question rumbled through me.

"I'm sure we could make it one." This was good. Right. Until I remembered this morning. I wanted to sink into his touch and pretend nothing was wrong. If I asked about his change in attitude, I'd ruin the moment. "I'm supposed to be on the vendor floor, but I'm sure no one will notice if we duck into the live demo booth and talk."

"I'd rather kidnap you and do this upstairs. But responsibility." His eye roll was audible in his words.

I smiled at the fake disdain. "It's only pretend adulting if we're hiding in back."

Jordan kissed the edge of my ear, drawing a line down to my earlobe to nip lightly. "You're the boss." He guided us skillfully through the evening crowd—fortunately Rinslet was one of the booths at the front of the convention hall, so it didn't take long—and behind the curtains that hid our demo room from the main floor.

He twirled me to face him, the nudged me backwards until my butt rested against a table.

An irrational fear spiked inside. I'd waited all day for this, and now I wanted just a little longer to prepare myself for something going wrong. If I let him talk, and didn't say anything, I'd be bitter that I felt I had to keep my mouth shut. If said the wrong thing, we'd fight again.

"I'm sorry for the way I reacted this morning." Jordan's apology tumbled out.

I tripped over the words as relief nudged my senses.

He squeezed my fingers. "I want to make us right, and you didn't do anything wrong."

"I kind of did." Why was I disagreeing? This was starting off better than my best case scenario.

"No. We've always said it was okay if one of us wanted to explore. I mean it, and I believe you do to."

Why was I surprised that we were talking about this like reasonable people? Of course we were. I swallowed past the lump in my throat. "But I had this expectation—not that it was reasonable, but it was there—we'd talk about it first."

"And that wasn't an option. We're talking now."

"No." Wait? What was I saying? I didn't even know what that meant, and his frown didn't help. "That is... we could just let it go and not risk another fight." Bad Chloe. Why was I shutting this down when it was going well?

Because I was terrified things would take a right turn at any moment.

Jordan brushed a thumb over my cheek as he searched my face. The touch and attention were soothing, but they had a lot to work their way through to make me feel better.

"I'm listening, I swear." He was pure sincerity. Like always. "I won't judge. I can't promise not to be jealous, but that's instinct and I can think my way past it. You said this morning you liked it. The kiss, I mean. Not the jealousy."

"I did." So much that the memory rushed back to tease me the instant it felt like I had his permission. "I'm not so big on the guilt that came with it."

"Do you want to do it again?"

Yes. Yes. Fuck yes. Suspicion joined my already jumbled emotions. "Is this how the fantasy starts? Because that's what provoked the fight last night."

"No. This isn't fantasy, it's a conversation about real life. Do you want to do it again, and not just talk about what it would be like to do it?"

The final announcement that the doors were closing echoed over the loudspeakers, and half the lights in the room dimmed. Jordan's gaze never left my face.

If I didn't speak my mind, I'd be bitter. I'd also be contrary... again. If I wanted this, I had to say so. "Yes." A damn broke inside at the simple confession. "I'm curious—you know I am—and I've had a taste, and you know I love you more than anything, which is why I'm terrified of doing this wrong, but that doesn't stop me from wanting to—"

Jordan silenced my rambling with a soft kiss. "So let's make it happen."

A movement in the background caught my attention, despite the fact I didn't want to be distracted. I looked again, but couldn't figure out what it was.

Jordan settled his palm on my cheek and drew my gaze back to him. The way he watched me was so open and adoring.

"Sticking someone between us won't fix *us*." I didn't want to argue, but there was another part to this entire thing that I couldn't ignore now that we were laying our cards out.

"If this is part of the issue, then it will help. You want to explore, and I'm good with it."

I liked that answer, and somehow he managed to address my contradictory fears at the same time.

I realized what I'd seen seconds earlier. *Stew and Liz.* "Shit."

"Not what I expected you to say." Jordan turned and followed my gaze, to where the two were talking. "Did you have to deal with him today?"

Even at a distance and with a clearer head, I didn't mind watching Liz. But right now, arms crossed and shoulders hunched forward, she looked the opposite of the open person she'd been last night. "He was a pain in my fucking ass," I said. "And the woman he's talking to?"

"Is pretty in an *I get my casual clothes at Ann Taylor* kind of way. Should we introduce ourselves?"

Jordan's open admiration tugged at my envy, despite echoing my thoughts. "I've met her. Liz is my partner-in-kissing from last night."

"Ah." Jordan's tone was one of happy surprise rather than disappointment. "She looks like she wants to be anywhere but there. Not that I'd expect otherwise with him."

"Yeah. And she's not in the industry so she probably doesn't have any idea what she's getting herself into. Want to meet my not-quite-fling?" Suddenly rescuing Liz was far more important than worry about what was and wasn't appropriate about our meeting. "Let's go inject ourselves into their conversation."

"Stew won't talk to me." Jordan tangled his fingers with mine and we headed toward the pair. He and Stew had almost come to blows more than a couple of times, typically when Stew pointed his sights on making me look bad.

"That's okay," I said. "Liz may not want to talk to me, either. I'll run interference and pull him away, and you rescue the fair maiden."

SIX

Lɪᴢ

I could be wearing a one-of-a-kind gown, worth thousands of dollars, and mingling with people who drove cars worth more than a lot of houses, and I'd be completely comfortable.

But, apparently, stick me in a convention hall full of tech professionals in anything from suits to foam costumes and body-paint, and I was completely lost. I'd spent all day at the KM booth, trying to absorb the language enough to participate in conversations. Mercy knew a lot of this stuff, why couldn't I keep up?

It wasn't the tech talk that got me so much as the attitudes. I kept reading quiet versus gruff versus terrified of anyone wrong, and that was only the tip of the iceberg. Root of the server? No, that couldn't be right.

The day was almost over, though, and I'd survived. Tonight would be social and fun with Jonathan and his team, and tomorrow I'd adapt even better. By the end of the week, I'd be a pro at this.

"Excuse me. Elizabeth Thompson?" The man who approached showed too many teeth when he smiled, but he sounded polite and looked open and friendly.

"Yes?"

"I'm Stew Knapfer. I'm covering a lot of vendors here. Do you have a moment?" He showed me his badge.

Media. Something I was familiar with, and not fond of. He wasn't a gossip mag, though. He was here covering tech details. I didn't imagine there was much gossip at all in this industry. "I'm not sure I'll be much help." I looked around for Jonathan or anyone else from KM, but everyone else was busy. "I can put you in contact with someone more technical than me, if you'd like to leave your card."

His smile grew, and I found myself crossing my arms before I realized my own reaction.

"Thanks, but I have a wallet full of business cards. I'm looking for you specifically," he said.

That couldn't be right. "Are you sure you're not looking for a different Elizabeth Thompson?"

Stew pulled his phone from his pocket just enough to click the screen. A beep sounded. "Almost certain. I won't take much of your time; I promise."

"I'm sorry, are you recording this? I don't consent to that." Now we were in familiar territory.

His toothy smile flickered for a heartbeat, and was back. "Of course. I should have asked." He repeated the same motions as a moment ago. "You were engaged to George Dobson, correct?"

My irritation spiked at the mention of my ex-fiancé,

and I summoned the words to tell this individual where he could stick the phone I was almost certain he hadn't stopped from recording. Poise in everything, though. If he was looking for a rise, or anything, he wasn't getting it from me.

"I can't help you." I moved to step around him.

He blocked my path. "I'm looking for a statement about how this morning's arrest impacted you."

"No comment." I didn't like this bit, but I could do it all day.

"Not the first time I've heard that today."

Big surprise there.

"He's right." Chloe wedged herself between us, and my heart skipped. Her smile today was plastic compared to last night, but she still looked beautiful, confident, and perfectly kissable. "I've already told him *no comment* more times than he can count today. Spoiler alert—that's not a high number." She winked at me.

The man accompany Chloe squeezed her hand before letting go. That must be the partner. Boyfriend? Husband? Neither he nor Chloe wore a ring, but that didn't mean anything. He turned to me. "I've been looking everywhere for you. Legal wants your sign-off before this contract goes to the vendor, and it needs to be tonight."

Language I understood. Thank God.

"We're not done," Stew said.

Chloe stepped toward him and he moved back. "The woman said no comment." Her tone was icy and professional.

Like Mercy in a negotiation. That was sexy. I searched for my voice.

Stew's smile vanished under a scowl. "But I—"

"No comment." Chloe never raised her voice, but Stew didn't try to go around her or take his attention from her.

"If you'll come with me, Liz." Chloe's partner pointed me toward the exit. "Those documents won't sign themselves."

"Ms. Thompson." Stew's call landed against my back.

"We're not done yet," Chloe said. "You wanted to talk to me earlier. I'll tell you *all* about Ms. Thompson."

My feet froze to the floor.

The man with the shocking blue hair who was leading me away bent his head close. "Trust her."

"She's a gymnast." Chloe's voice was all false cheer. "Russian circus. Escaped last week."

What the...? I'd ask what they were up to when this was over. I didn't care about the nonsense. My non-existent desire to talk with a stranger about my stupidity and failed marriage were enough to get my legs moving again.

Behind us, Chloe's ridiculous story faded as she continued to talk over Stew.

Once we cleared the convention hall, the stranger stopped and faced me. "I'm Jordan. You looked like you needed a hand in there."

I leaned against a nearby pillar, struggling to put my thoughts in any sort of order as he studied me with bright blue eyes almost the same color as his hair, concern etched on his face. *Sexy.*

Apparently I was Alice, and I'd stepped through some sort of looking glass where tech people traveled in sexy pairs and rescued naive girls from media worms. "I did. Thank you. But..." How did they know?

"It was pretty obvious you didn't want to talk to him. We've had a lot of practice dodging the media."

Yup. Looking glass land. If I searched around me, would I need to avoid Jabberwock? Come to think of it, I was pretty sure Mad Hatter and Dormouse had stopped by the KM booth earlier, decked out in full steampunk gear. "I thought Chloe worked for a gaming company."

"We both do. And our jobs come with a lot of knowing what to say to bloggers and when to walk away." Jordan sounded as though that should explain everything.

It didn't, but I wasn't sure what to ask next. What was I supposed to say to the boyfriend of the woman I'd shared an impulsive kiss with? Did he know? He couldn't, or he wouldn't be this friendly.

It wasn't my place to tell him, especially since I could already see how he and Chloe fit together. Two different kinds of confidence and sparks that probably glowed when they were side by side. Even their rescue effort was a flawless and beautiful thing.

Time for me to leave this strange looking glass world behind. "Right. Of course. Thank you for saving me. Both of you. I'll let you go do the same for her."

"Chloe's got this." Jordan leaned next to me against

the same pillar. "I know about last night." He glanced sideways at me, his tone as casual as his posture. "She told me this morning. I assume all of it. Just a kiss."

Did his voice catch on those last words? It was the first sing of hesitation I'd seen from him, and it helped take the edge of my *lost* feeling.

His words also stung a little. It wasn't *just* a kiss. It was incredible. And I shouldn't be thinking that if she didn't. "Yes. That's all it was." Mostly.

"It's not a big deal." His casual tone was a stark contrast to the way he raked his fingers through his hair, leaving already chaotic blue strands sticking in a million different directions. "She and I aren't hung up on things like monogamy."

Chloe's reaction last night said otherwise... Unless she really didn't like the kiss. I couldn't be the only one still thinking about it. And none of the mental back and forth kept my hope from grabbing onto his words and wanting them to be true.

Months ago, when I threw myself at Mercy, a desire was knocked loose in me to explore my sexuality. At this moment, admitting I was attracted to both men and women was going to make things double awkward with this attractive and compelling couple.

"I'm glad you're both good with it. I should be on my way." I didn't have a problem making the words sound believable. I was raised to fake it, no matter how wrong it felt.

"Chloe will be done with Stew soon." Whatever hesitations Jordan had a moment earlier vanished behind confidence again, but this time I recognized the mask for what it was. How did that make him more attractive? "It doesn't take long to twist him up. You free for dinner tonight?"

"Uh…" What? Way to sound intelligent, me. "You were here for the part of the conversation where we talked about your girlfriend kissing me, weren't you?"

His laugh lit up his eyes. "I was. My offer stands."

"I'd love it." No. I was supposed to say *thanks, but no thanks.*

"But…? I hear a but in there." He was good.

I still felt like I was chasing the white rabbit, but so far it was fun. "But… I have plans tonight." That sounded like a brush-off. Which it needed to be, but I didn't want that. "Legitimate ones," I added quickly. "With a client. I'm free tomorrow, though."

"It's a date. Chloe will see you then."

It was just a phrase. Wait. "Just Chloe?" What was I doing? Tumbling down that rabbit hole so fast… I wanted to be the bottle labeled *Eat Me* at the end of the tunnel. And I wanted to know more about both halves of this fascinating couple who *didn't get hung up on monogamy.* "Not that I have an issue with that, but you… I'm going to stop talking before I make things bad."

Jordan's smile grew. "Both of us then." He handed me a card. "Email, text, call, whatever, and let me know what time, and I'll send back details."

"I will." And I'd also work overtime to keep my imagination from running rampant…

Not that I expected to be successful.

SEVEN

Chloe

"And then, when she was seven, Liz toured the world by herself in a zeppelin she built from broken cereal bowls." I danced an effective blockade with Stew, side stepping every time he tried to move around me to follow Liz.

In the office, I reigned in my imagination to keep things *marketable*, but any chance I had to let it run loose, I took.

"Don't do this, Chloe. She's *real* news." Frustration bled into Stew's plea.

Liz was fascinating news to me, but it didn't explain why he was so interested in her. Not that I cared about whatever gossip he was chasing. "Right? I'll even give you a BuzzFeed headline—*Top Ten Facts You Didn't Know About Elizabeth Thompson.* Subhead—*Number Three Will Make Your Hamster Weep.* Guess what Number Three is?"

He sigh-growled and tried to get past me again.

"Almost married one of the biggest scammers in Salt Lake City? And didn't realize it?"

Whoa. What? No.

It didn't matter if it was true. I wasn't interested. "*Yawn*. Number Three is discovering the secret to cold fusion, using a glass of Alka-Seltzer and a popsicle stick." There were a lot of things I wanted to know about the gorgeous enigma that was Liz. For instance, was she local to where Jordan and I lived? Did she have any desire to hook up with the cute-but-awkward woman she'd bumped into while traveling, who always said I'd see a second person, if I met the right one?

Stew rubbed his face and another sigh escaped through his fingers. "Do you even know her?"

"Nope. Never met her before this week."

"She's Elizabeth Thompson."

I raised my brows in disdain and disbelief. "So we've already established. You keep saying that like it should mean something."

"Heiress to the Thompson Advertising fortune?"

No shit.

The thing about being from big money in Salt Lake City—as in, the kind of money most people couldn't fathom—was that everyone in the valley knew those family's names. I wasn't one of the wealthy elite, but I worked for someone who was.

Knowing Scott for as long as I had meant I was familiar with the family trees that connected everyone to everyone. It turned out there was a twisted kind of financial incest when it came to keeping wealth with the people who already had it.

If Liz was who Stew said, her brother owned Thompson Advertising, and had a lot of clout associated with the large number of zeros in his net worth.

I hid any notion of being impressed. "Heiress? You make her sound like royalty. You realize she's not even running a courtesy suite here. She's wandering through E3 like another of us drones. Have you stopped to consider how common the last name *Thompson* is?"

"If you don't know her, why do you care if I talk to her?" Stew pocketed his phone and leaned against a nearby pillar, arms crossed.

Because… Because…

Fuck. I'd wanted a nice, quiet evening. To finish one of the most useful conversations I'd had with Jordan in months. Rescuing Liz? I was good with that? Talking to Stew? *Gag.*

I kept the looming exhaustion from my posture. "Maybe it's because she's my story and I don't want you scooping me. Maybe Jordan's getting the inside deets right now, and we'll have our Top Ten list in place before you walk out of here."

"You think you're funny. You're not."

"Then it's probably because I'm human and she looked like the last person she wanted to talk to was you. Why does she matter, again? I'm not sure I'm getting the real news part of this thing."

His irritation vanished in a smirk. "She agreed to marry this guy, who was already married to one woman and engaged to three others, and now he's been arrested and everyone's talking about them. If I had an actual story, with actual quotes from her, imagine the clicks and views."

"*She* did?" I nodded toward the exit Liz and Jordan had vanished through.

"Yes."

"So, one of the Thompson children, their family princess even, agreed to marry some dude. She's worth millions. Billions? When people get up that high, the zeroes only matter to them. He says *be mine* and she says *okay*, without ever running a background check on the fucker? It never occurs to her he's already taken? Her family—her lawyer—let her get away with that?" I let the disbelief ooze from my words.

"Exactly."

"Uh-huh. Did they exile her to L.A. as some kind of punishment?" I patted him on the arm with as much condescension is I could. "I was wrong. You don't need my help making up ludicrous bullet points for your little list. You've already got ridiculous and implausible covered. At this rate, why do you even need to talk to her? To confirm your weird fantasy story?"

"I—"

"Leave her alone." An edge crept into my voice. I wanted this to be over.

"You can't stop me."

Fucker. "I can write you into my next game as a love interest." I hated using *I'll write a fictional you falling in love with another man* as a threat. Despised the fact that Stew was so phobic that he'd recoil at the notion.

His smugness flickered. "No one will recognize it as me."

He'd reamed me more than once in reviews for my *queer storylines no one asked for*. Now that I had the idea, it was tempting to go through with it regardless. "You'll know. I'll make him swoon over X. Fall at the big guy's feet. *Beg* to be loved."

"You can't stop me from finding Elizabeth later." His bravado was gone, and his attention darted between me and the exit.

It was true, I couldn't stop him, but I wasn't conceding. "Are you sure about that?"

"You suck." He turned and left.

When I was certain he was out of sight, I sank into a nearby seat. The entire conversation was deceptive rather than fun, and that drained me. At least Liz got out of here.

I was used to a good verbal spar with the media, and even fending off Stew wasn't usually a big deal. This it me harder than normal. Why?

Because I stayed behind, and Jordan left with Liz. Sure, we'd agreed on that exact plan, and we'd done similar things in the past, since talking to the press was my job and being charming was an unspoken part of his, but tonight felt different.

Next time, Jordan was fending off the bullshit questions, and I was whisking away the fair maiden to save her day. Or maybe I wanted to be the one who was saved. Just once. Jordan hadn't swooped in on my behalf since…

A fake marriage proposal that never became more, after at least a decade, in front of the audience at this same show.

My phone chimed with a text from Jordan. *You okay?*

I hesitated, thumbs hovering over the screen, wanting to type *No. Come save me?* I couldn't do it, and instead sent him a nondescript *I'm good. Where are you?*

Second star to the right, and straight on till morning.

My smile forced its way out without permission, and I headed to find him.

The first few years we were here, there was a coffee shop in the foyer called *Pan's Brew*. Their claim was their coffee would grant eternal youth. We were sitting at their tables, completely buzzed on too much caffeine and the high of another amazing demo, when we decided to move in together. How long had it been? Seven years?

So many of our happy memories were built here, because this was where we dared to let loose.

And there he was, standing near a new, far more generic coffee shop, looking as incredible as ever. The instant his gaze met mine, he smiled.

He crossed the distance between us. Before I could say anything, he cradled my cheeks with his palms and kissed me hard, nudging me back at the same time.

The intensity stole my breath and thoughts. My back met the wall, and he dove his tongue into my mouth, drawing a whimper from me. This was…

The thought vanished in favor of focusing on his hunger. I fisted his shirt in my hands, needing the anchor before I floated away, and our bodies molded together.

When Jordan broke away, he didn't let go. "You

okay?" His voice was deep and low, his gaze never straying from me.

"Better now." My voice barely reached my own ears. This was what we used to have. Sharing kisses that sank inside me and made my stomach flutter and lit my senses on fire. I didn't want to lose this.

"Good." He nipped by bottom lip and glided up my jaw to my ear, his mouth hot and tempting. "I hated having to leave you back there."

This was better than being rescued. "I'm here now. Which is good. So very good."

Jordan's light laugh was intoxicating. He traced his hands down my arms to intertwine our fingers. "Your plans for tomorrow night haven't changed, have they?"

The shift in subject, to something that required my brain, yanked the clouds from under my floating thoughts. "As in, *my nights are yours*? Hasn't changed. They still belong to you." We'd promised each other we'd make this work, and that we'd specifically make sure we weren't working evenings, in order to help that happen.

"Good." Jordan kissed the tip of my nose and my lips. "We have dinner plans."

Okay…?

"With Liz."

What? "No. That's not… We promised."

His frown was faint. "We promised we'd save our evenings for working things out. She's part of the plan."

I pulled away from his touch, unable to give a name to the mess of swirling emotion inside. Confusion was there, but so was hope. "Why?"

"You said you wanted to experiment. She was the catalyst. She's free tomorrow. We'll never see her again." Jordan's tone implied this all made perfect sense to him.

"I didn't mean with her."

"Why not?" He was genuinely curious.

Because… Because— "I don't know." I was scared.

"Okay." Jordan's expression shifted to impassive, but sympathy filled his words. "Not her, then. I'll have the hotel desk send a note up to her room, telling her never mind."

That was that. He gave me what I wanted, and then spun and gave me the opposite the moment I asked for it. It wasn't Jordan's fault we were stuck in this place I wanted to leave but didn't dare, it was mine. Was I going to back down from every opportunity because I was afraid? That wasn't me.

"Don't do that. I'm just… I'm nervous." It felt better to admit it aloud, but I couldn't ignore the nervous flapping that churned my insides. "Dinner sounds good." Please don't let this be a mistake. Or a disappointment. Or absolutely incredible.

EIGHT

Lız

My attention should be focused completely on the KM presentation I was in.

Instead, as I stood at the back of the dark panel room watching their rep bounce through launch news I'd heard in fifty iterations during prep, I was comparing them to E3 demos I'd never seen. Had no idea existed in such a way until last night.

When Jordan said he and Chloe were used to media attention, I just knew he had to be exaggerating. The families around ours dealt with gossip mags on a regular basis. Gaming was nothing compared to the rumors people loved to start about the wealthy.

Then I looked them up.

The rabbit hole ran so much deeper than I realized. There were videos of some of their stunts. First, second, and fifth-person accounts of their exploits. Both praise and loathing.

One thing was certain, though. This industry knew exactly who they presented themselves to the camera as.

If Chloe and Jordan were doing the presentation I was in, how would they draw attention? I couldn't even imagine. Probably some sort of way that would scandalize Ian. I shouldn't smile at the idea, but I couldn't help it.

My phone vibrated, and I pressed *Ignore* without so much as a glance. The damn thing had been going off all day, with calls from 800 numbers. I swore every credit card company on the planet must have picked today to do a marketing push. When I finally had time to listen to my voicemails, I suspected they would all be reminders about how I wasn't fully utilizing all the *benefits* that came with my cards.

As the demo wrapped up to a wave of applause, Jonathan slid into the seat next to mine.

"They love you," I said.

He was all smiles. "We've got great marketing behind us." He leaned in enough to nudge me with his shoulder. "We'll be back for more."

"Of course you will." I gave a fake scoff. "No one's better."

"It's true. Speaking of how amazing you are, do you have plans tonight?"

Weird segue. It knocked loose the wave of uncertainty I'd been trying to ignore since talking to Jordan last night. The doubt tumbled with a *thunk* and landed heavy in my gut. "I do. I'm sorry."

He waved a dismissive hand. "No worries. I'm glad

you're taking the time to see the city while you're here—that is what you're doing, I assume."

I'd seen L.A. several times in my life, and it lost its sparkle after a few visits. "No sight-seeing for me. The Rinslet team invited me to dinner." That sounded far more professional than *I'm going on a maybe-date with the cute couple everyone here knows but me.*

Jonathan's smile vanished behind a flat mask. When the corners of his lips pulled up again, the joy didn't reach his eyes. "Be careful with that group."

"Why?"

"Their thing, marketing-wise, is making a spectacle. Don't let yourself or your company get sucked into that."

Public opinion was driven by drama. It was almost certainly why that Stew guy wanted to talk to me yesterday, and given Chloe's job, she knew that. "I'll keep that in mind, thank you." I kept the bristle from my tone as I replied, because how one presented themselves in public was rarely a true indicator of the depth underneath, and I was bothered that Jonathan either didn't know that, or didn't think that applied in this situation.

He shook his head and stood. "I'll let you go, so you can beat the rush of *every panel just let out at once* crowds. See you in the booth tomorrow morning."

"I'll be there." I shook his hand, then strolled into the hallway. I had to blink a few times to adjust my eyes to the sudden brightness, and when I paused, the full force of nervousness about tonight rushed back. It didn't matter how many times I told myself it was dinner and nothing more; I couldn't stop hoping it would be a lot more.

How deviant was that? I'd only admitted my bisexuality to myself in the last year or so, and now I was fantasizing about burying my face between a stunning woman's legs while her gorgeous boyfriend slid inside me.

Overachiever Liz, that was me.

I'd married my high school sweetheart right after we graduated. He and our baby were taken in the same accident that killed my parents, almost a decade ago.

The memory clenched and cramped my already churning insides. The pain was dull compared to intensity in the past, but I still had to force myself to focus on the now, to keep from lingering in grief.

After their deaths, I withdrew from people, from any relationships, for years. I'd thrown myself into the college education I skipped by my marrying so young. I volunteered for groups who needed my money and connection more than they needed me to be warm. Anything that distracted me from what I'd lost.

Thanks to my family's money, I had a lot of options.

Then George came along. Suave, sweet, and sympathetic. He *got* me. Or I thought so. What he'd actually understood was how to tug my heart strings and make me believe true love trumped all...

Including background checks and prenups. Untangling his lies led me back to those I'd told myself. For instance, that my attraction to women was a passing phase. I still liked men too. Why choose, right?

Someone jostled me and grumbled as they walked

past. I should probably move out the middle of the flow of traffic, rather than parting it like a stone in a river. As I started walking again, I boxed up my rambling thoughts.

Dinner wasn't until seven. Three hours. That was way too much time. And not nearly enough. What was I supposed to wear? I brought plenty of suits and skirts, all pressed, button-down, and silk or high thread-count cotton.

Did dressing down make sense? Did I really just wonder that? It may be the first time in my life I'd done so. Not that I owned anything *that* casual. There was the school girl skirt and top, but Chloe already saw me in that.

Did I really care this much about impressing them? Of course I did. I didn't want them to look at my clothes and think I was a rich little socialite who had no clue that there was a world outside of money. I didn't want them to see how naive I was when I asked about the nature of their relationship.

We don't get hung up on things like monogamy. That was what Jordan said, and it mingled with my memories of kissing Chloe. *I'm attached.* She'd looked so mortified. That didn't make sense in combination with his words.

Shopping. I had enough time for that and spending money always helped distract me. Not that they would judge me for not owning any trendy clothes—that was so high school and they didn't strike me as those kind of people—but I could at least try to look like I belonged in their world.

GPS pointed me to the nearest Hot Topic. I had no

idea how such a small shop took up so much time, but I spent the next hour sifting through racks and stacks of shirts with vintage game characters, references I was pleasantly surprised to get, and jeans not meant for someone with hips as wide as mine.

I made my way to the register, selections in hand and distraction gone, which meant my mind raced back to tonight. What was I doing?

The cashier gave me a total and I handed over my credit card.

She swiped it once, frowned, and swiped the card again. "I'm sorry. It says this is declined."

Excuse me, what?

This wasn't her fault. "Right. I'm sorry about that." I tried to look casual as I fished out my bank card instead. Yesterday morning, trying to pay for breakfast, nudged my thoughts. I'd never followed up on why the bakery refused my payment. I'd figured it was just a fluke.

"This one too." The girl handed back my debit card, her tone inching toward annoyed.

I promise I'm not trying to pull something over on you. Panic crept in. I had my corporate card, but I wasn't charging date clothes to my expense account. I had other credit cards, but now I was paranoid about going through each and having them all refused.

What were my options? "Give me a minute." I smiled politely at the cashier. I could call Ian and ask permission to use his card—the one I'd sworn to myself over and over that I was going to stop carrying. "Make that two minutes. I'll be right back, I promise."

Her *Okay* dripped skepticism.

I didn't blame her.

I called the credit card company, and then the next, and the next. Every single automated system gave me a version of the same reply—"We're sorry, this account has been closed."

Maybe I shouldn't have ignored the phone calls and emails today. When Kyle told me some of my accounts may be frozen because of George's arrest, I didn't think he meant every single bleeping one.

Then again, George had access to all of them. We'd shared everything, and I'd never stopped to think that for me that meant putting his name on all of my accounts, and for him that meant I got to drive his car when I needed it.

Fuck.

At least my investments and trusts were safe, but I didn't have access to those without going through a lot of paperwork.

Great. I was stuck in a different state with no money of my own.

Mercy had lived like this for years, and she didn't have a company card to take care of business expenses. I'd be okay for a few more days.

I just had to swallow my pride and call my brother.

"Hey, How's L.A.?" Ian's friendly greeting was undercut with his standard stress.

"Smoggy. Crowded. As one expects." I didn't have the focus for small talk and he likely didn't have the time. "I need a favor."

"Always." Like that, his tone shifted to concerned.

"It's nothing big. I just... Can I use your AmEx while I'm here?"

"Sure." He didn't hesitate. "If you tell me why."

The last thing I wanted from him was another *I told you so* sigh around my relationship with George, but hesitating wouldn't get me anywhere. I gave him a brief run-down about my currently frozen funds, wrapped up with, "But Kyle's team is on it. I should have anything back soon."

There. Brief. Reassuring. I had this under control.

"Did Kyle say *soon*?" Ian asked.

I scowled at my phone. "No. I did."

"I'd check your expectations on that timeline, but yes, the card's yours. Just let me know if you make any big purchase. Are you sure you're okay?" Like that, his concern was back.

"I'm fine." I really was. None of this was life-ending, it was simply annoying. "I'm having a blast besides the money thing." Also true, though I wouldn't give him any details outside of the work stuff. "Thank you."

"Any time, you know that. I have to run. Call me if you need anything else."

"I will." I was pretty sure he disconnected before I finished talking.

At least George wasn't using my money any more than I was, and now that he'd been arrested, it would be a lot longer before he had access to anyone's funds.

The thought didn't comfort me the way I wanted.

NINE

JORDAN

It wouldn't matter how long I stared at the clock, it wouldn't magically skip backwards to give us more time. "You almost ready?" I called to Chloe.

She'd been in the bathroom for more than an hour, and we had to be downstairs in less than ten minutes. Chloe was never late to anything. Why wasn't she answering me?

"Chi?" I tried again.

The bathroom door opened, and Chloe stepped into view. "You haven't called me that in ages."

At least, I was pretty sure that was what she said. My brain had frozen when I saw her. Instead of pulling her hair into a low ponytail, the way she normally did, it fell in loose cures around her bare shoulders.

Thin straps were the only thing holding up a dress I'd never seen before. The bodice hugged her torso and flared at the hips, a row of tantalizing buttons leading all the way down. If I sketched her right now, I'd give her red wings and matching horns, turning her into a stunning succubus.

"What are you wearing?" Crap. That probably came out wrong.

She frowned—yup, definitely the wrong thing to say—and crossed her arms. "I didn't bring anything nice with me that doesn't scream *business,* so I grabbed this in between meetings. You did see her, right? All coifed and put together and perma-pressed. Do you think someone like Liz even owns a free T-shirt with a company logo on it?"

I hid my wince at the combination of defensiveness and insecurity in Chloe's retort. I wanted her to have fun tonight.

"I did see her. And she saw you, and she knows who she's spending her evening with."

Chloe smoothed her hands over her dress, pausing to tug the hem. "Should I change? You look all casual and comfortable. I should put something else on."

I grabbed her fingers before she could vanish back into the bathroom. "You look gorgeous. You always look gorgeous, no matter what you wear." There were few things I believed more sincerely than that. "I promise everyone in the room will be watching you for all the right reasons."

The corner of Chloe's mouth tugged up and she leaned into my shoulder, lingering for a moment.

"Okay, let's go." She straightened, smoothed out her skirt, and let me lead her from the room and to the elevator.

I knew exactly how lucky I was to have Chloe, and

not just because she was stunning. She had a sexy as fuck brain and she *got* me.

In high school I was the gross computer club nerd who drew the kinky-nasty pictures that everyone sneered at me for. The art was my escape from reality, and the first time I ever found people who appreciated it was in the forums where I posted fan art, mostly of the tentacle variety, for various games.

When Cord—who later became Rinslet—offered me an artist job at eighteen, I thought I'd died and gone to heaven.

Then I met Chloe. Everything that came before her was cast in sepia. She did the same thing with words that I did with images. We clicked from Day One, and fell for each other hard and fast.

More than a decade later, and we were at the top of our careers and had epic levels of industry recognition. I was never going back to being the timid high school kid who was bullied or who cared what anyone else thought. This job, this life, Chloe, they all made me who I was and I was never surrendering them.

I wrapped an arm around Chloe's waist when we stepped onto the main floor, and pointed us toward the restaurant where we were meeting Liz.

As we rounded a corner, Chloe slowed then stopped. "I'm going back upstairs to change. Apologize for me, for being late?"

"You're not going to change." I tightened my grip on her hip and visually scanned the area.

Liz stood near the host's podium. The T-shirt that hugged her torso and showed off ample breast, and the jeans that did the same thing for her hips, were too vibrant and had creases in the wrong places to be anything but brand new.

"You look incredible," I assured Chloe. "And I'm not saying that to make you feel better."

"But you're dressed down and she's dressed down..."

I loosened my grip but didn't drop my arm. "I'll let you go change if you really want, but I guarantee she made the same call you did—she went and bought new clothes to impress you. That means she cares what you think, and you'll impress her by being you."

"Except this isn't me."

"It is you. You picked the dress. You're the person wearing it. We can spend all night going back and forth about the dress, or we can do this." I nudged Chloe forward, leaned in enough to brush the edge of her ear with my lips, and dropped my voice to a whisper. "Imagine how much fun it will be for her to undo those buttons. One. At. A Time." I was definitely picturing it.

"Only if she's interested." Despite the words, the argument vanished from Chloe's voice.

"Only one way to find out."

As we approached, Liz looked up and a faint smile ghosted across her lips. When we were within speaking range, she nodded at Chloe. "I almost bought that dress yesterday. Now I'm glad I didn't."

Fuck.

"Oh?" Chloe frowned.

"You look so good in it. I wouldn't have been able to compete."

Thank Christ.

Chloe relaxed against me, and her gait was more natural as a host led the three of us at a booth at the back of the restaurant.

More tension evaporated—I wasn't sure if it was Chloe's or mine—when Liz took a seat and Chloe slid in next to her. I took the bench seat across from them, not bothering to hide the fact that I was staring. Did I want to experiment? Yes. But inviting Liz tonight, that was for Chloe. But now, as I watched them sitting next to each other, my mind skipped ahead to the possibilities. These women were two sides of the same coin—refined flipped to carefree.

Then there was reality. What if we didn't all get along? Did we have anything in common with Liz? Did it even matter, if this was just sex? Was Chloe looking for a girlfriend, or was tonight simply about fucking?

A decision to be made between the two of them, but the longer my mind traipsed along the possibilities, the more vivid the fantasies became. Of watching Chloe make out with someone else. Stripping Liz down. Burying myself to the hilt inside her while she and Chloe explored each other...

My pulse roared in my ears and my cock strained against my jeans. I should probably dial back the mental visuals.

"Boop." Chloe reached across the table and tapped my nose, jarring me back to the now. "You're staring."

"I absolutely am." I gave them both another glass, and took a long drink of ice water to cool my heated blood.

TEN

Chloe

Welcome to Overthinking 101. AKA: my brain.

"So... you work together. Did you meet before or after you got your jobs?" Liz asked.

I could spin a story with the most intricate and vivid details, and as I talked to Liz, I didn't dare say more than a few words. Did she really want to hear me go on for hours? "After."

Jordan raised his brows.

"That's it?" Liz's question had a teasing lilt.

"If you ask a binary question..." Thank Christ for Jordan. "And seriously there's a lot of story to tell. How long do you want to be here tonight?" There's was only kindness and reality in his statement. He knew me so well.

Liz fiddled with her straw wrapper. "Start at the beginning and leave out the boring bits."

"There are no boring bits. Last warning." If I had an open invitation, I'd dive into things. "It starts with two young, starving artists, struggling to make our way in the world."

"Really?" Liz's awe almost made me regret the exaggeration.

Jordan gave a fake cough. "No. Not really. We were both fresh out of high school, still living at home, and sifting through college acceptances and student-loan paperwork."

"Spoiler alert," I teased.

Liz's laugh was light and soothing. I'd never thought a laugh could be cute before. I liked hers. "I want to hear it anyway. All the details, even if there's no starving involved. I assume there's still art," she said.

"There's a lot of art." I hoped Jordan would keep offering contributions. This was a lot more fun when he and I bounced off each other. "This little gaming company decided to step outside the box and ditch their distributor. They wanted to give censors the finger and were bringing on fresh talent—us—to make sure what they created was different from anyone else."

The waiter interrupted to see if we were ready to order. I could get something alcoholic, make me look sophisticated and calm my nerves. But regardless of what happened tonight, I wanted Liz's impression of me to be of me, not drunk Chloe. Not this time.

We all ordered drinks but no one was ready for food. The waiter left, and Liz shifted on the bench to lean halfway against the wall, letting her face both Jordan and I. It was such a casual, natural gesture that it put me more at ease. Maybe if I stopped looking at her as a princess just come down from her tower, this would be easier on me.

"That was Rinslet?" Liz asked. "Who hired you?"

"They were Cord at the time." The gaming industry was so different in 2006. It was amazing how much things had changed in a decade. I hopped through the highlights of those first few years.

Really the only important thing I skipped were the orgies. Jordan and I were never part of those, because for as much as we talked, even back then, we always had an excuse to not participate.

"And then one of the owners proposed to his girlfriend on stage." Even now, the memory of Zach's embarrassment, of what followed, made me cringe. "She said *no*."

Liz's wince reflected my thoughts perfectly. "Ouch."

"It gets worse," Jordan said. "She'd found out it was going to happen, and was an equal shareholder. She sold her stock right before, and that combined with her rejection... Cord was worthless overnight and by the following Monday, Digital Media had bought up enough stock that they owned us."

"Double ouch." Liz was leaned in slightly, and looked totally enraptured.

"They laid most of us off, they kept our top game, and they tried to steal Jordan," I added. "Then they forced Zach and Scott out."

"I know them. Zach Johnston and Scott Evans." Liz's answers were simple, but her engaged look, the fact that she looked so invested in the story, made telling it so much more fun.

"McAllister. Not Evans." I could do this. This was a normal conversation with a normal person, who just happened to be gorgeous and proper and rich and here because I'd kissed her then my boyfriend invited her to dinner, and—

Could I really do this?

I could. I would.

"Mercy's older brothers butted heads with them in high school. Dean hated Zach. Always lost to him in debate meets. My dad did advertising for Evans Motor Group," Liz said

Jordan set his drink aside and leaned in. "Question for you, Liz." His tone shifted. It was subtle. Most people wouldn't hear the light hitch, but after so long together, I knew he was hesitating over said question.

Liz's casual *sure* implied she didn't catch anything beyond what was on the surface.

"If all you rich Utah people know each other, how come you didn't know who George Dobson was?"

Horror and embarrassment washed over me. "Holy fuck, Jordan. What's wrong with you?"

Liz had paled to the point where she matched the napkin she tore tiny shreds from.

Jordan frowned and twisted his mouth to the side. "I'm not trying to be cruel." Sympathy bled into his tone. "If we get it out of the way now, it won't be distracting going forward."

"It wasn't distracting to begin with." I hadn't dwelled on Stew's questions last night, and I wished now that I hadn't shared them with Jordan. Except that keeping anything from him felt wrong.

A pile of paper confetti grew in front of Liz. "It's okay. I'd rather you hear it from me than from someone like that guy last night. None of it is a secret except my side of the story, and I feel like you actually care about that."

"We do. That's the only thing about any of it that matters, is your side of things," I said quickly. Yeah, yeah, there were three sides to every story. But experience told me the one side that held the most truth was frequently the last to be heard.

Liz ran out of napkin to shred and fiddled with her bare ring finger instead. "There are those people who are worth a couple million. They're the ones with houses on the sides of the mountains. And then there are those with their names on buildings and car dealerships. George's family was one of the former, and he wanted to become one of the latter. I didn't know any of that. I only knew I was madly in love with a man who said he felt the same, and there was no way in hell anyone was doing any background checks or drawing up any contracts, because that wouldn't be true love."

An ache grew in my chest at the sadness and resignation in her voice. "I'm sorry."

"It's okay." Liz drew in a deep breath and pushed out a smile that didn't reach her eyes. "Lesson learned, and with any luck, I avoided the worst of it. Besides, it's indirectly the reason I'm here tonight."

I nudged her arm playfully, hoping to chase away the threatening gloom. "Ooh, a sad story with a happy ending?"

The waiter chose that moment to interrupt with our

drinks and ask if we were ready to order. Jordan told him to keep the refills coming and we'd wave him down if we needed anything else.

I did love this man.

When the waiter was gone, Liz looked up, meeting my gaze. "The whole experience with George made me think..." She worried her bottom lip with her teeth. "It's like you and I talked about in the bar. I've spent most of my life doing what I thought was expected of me, even letting *him* become that voice for a while. Maybe it's time to do what I want. And then yesterday Jordan said..."

I raised my eyebrows, waiting for her to finish the thought, and turned to him when she didn't.

Jordan shrugged. "I asked her if she wanted to have dinner with you."

Liz's laugh was tight, but it made me think she was relaxing again. "Before that. He said the two of you don't get hung up on things like monogamy."

Verbally we didn't.

"So I figured tonight I'd get drunk, let down my defenses, and see what happened," Liz said.

Except that she'd ordered iced tea.

Jordan traced a finger along the back of Liz's arm, drawing her attention. "Does that mean you're interested?"

Liz's pause made my gut clench and twist in on itself.

"We're not unicorn hunters or anything, I promise." I spit out the assurance. "You don't have to date both of us or be with both of us or like both of us or—" I snapped my jaw shut at her wide-eyed look.

"I don't know what that means, but I'm pretty sure I'm more a princess than a unicorn," Liz said.

She really was.

And now I had to explain my rambling to someone who didn't ask for it in the first place. "I just mean… just because we're a couple doesn't mean that whatever happens has to involve all three of us. There's no expectation of that. Or of anything happening. That is, I really liked the kiss, and I want more, but you don't have to—"

Jordan covered my hand and squeezed gently, shutting me up.

"I have no idea what I'm walking into," Liz said softly. "But I'm not a total stranger to casual sex. I understand if the three of us hook up and there's nothing else the next morning."

Right. That made perfect sense. I was trying to put all these rules and reassurances in place about a relationship and she was here for a fuck. I could do that. I wrote about it all the time. I could totally live the fantasy.

Jordan squeezed my hand again, and took Liz's as well. "Fair warning, since we're laying so much of this on the table, including you later if we're lucky, we've talked about it before—fooling around with someone else. But we've never done it. Not that there are any expectations here. There's a little bit of hope, if we all get to know each other and like what we see."

Liz settled back. "See where the night takes us? I can live with that."

This was so surreal. Was this how most people approached casual sex? I guess it would have to be if they didn't want any understandings. Still, did this prim, proper society woman just basically say *I want to fuck both of you?*

The pulse between my legs and the hammering of my heart against my ribs couldn't believe how incredibly hot that was. Did we leave now, or talk some more first, or order dinner, or...?

"Now that we have that out of the way," Jordan said. "I have a hopefully far less controversial question, solely because I'm a curious monkey and depending on whose mouths are full of who later, you may not be able to answer."

I stared at him with curiously and a little bit of envy that he was rolling with this so smoothly.

Liz relaxed further. "Fire away."

"What are you doing with KM?"

That came out of left field.

"The advertising company I work for is helping them show off their individual package."

Did she mean the innuendo?

Her giggle and bright pink cheeks said she caught it, at least. "I can't believe I've never registered before how filthy that sounds."

Verbal innuendo was my freaking playground. "Jordan's been playing with that. He thought their commercial package was a bit much, but this smaller one is more his size." I adjusted my weight on the bench, nudging then resting my leg against Liz's. Warmth fluttered inside when she leaned into the pressure rather than pulling away.

"I'm a *firm* believer that what you do with a package,

how it works, is far more important than its size." Jordan grinned.

"Have you had a solid chance to explore?" Liz's tone was lighter now. Playful. "Stroke it. Fondle it. Run your finger over the tip to make it move the way you want?"

Jordan wiggled his eyebrows. "You know your packages."

"Not as well as I'd like to." Liz looked at me. "Maybe you could give me a few pointers on the best way to handle the packages you're familiar with."

My brain stalled. Had we passed from innuendo to something more serious, or were we still talking about the software? Why couldn't I stop overthinking things?

Because I was me.

"Jordan's turning his drawings into cartoons." The words tumbled past my lips before I could consider how completely conversation killing they were. Why couldn't I have overthought *that*?

"Chloe's being generous. Without her script they're not cartoons, they're just moving drawings." Jordan had my back. Like always.

Liz looked between us. "Don't you have animation software at work?"

And she'd rolled with shift like a pro. Things to be grateful for. "What we have at Rinslet isn't made for the kind of things he's doing."

"I'd love to see what you do with it sometime," Liz said.

"You want to watch me play with my package?" Jordan's wink was exaggerated. "For personal or professional reasons?" He managed to make the question sound creepy and seductive at the same time.

He was such a dork. A lovable, wonderful, sexy dork.

"I might tell Jonathan you thought his commercial package was too big." Liz quirked her mouth in amusement. "But this is between us. I'm genuinely curious."

"We have a copy upstairs." I winced when I realized how that sounded. "That's not a line. Not that you're not welcome upstairs. I— It's where the laptops are. We can show you after dinner." Not that I could eat at this point. The joking was fun, but it didn't untie my insides.

"If you two are waiting on me to order, don't. I'm not hungry," Liz said.

"In that case, do you want a sneak peek now?" Jordan slid from his seat and tugged Me up.

Liz stood too. "That sounds like fun."

Jordan snagged the waiter. "Bill this to room 512." He turned back to Liz and me. "Shall we, ladies?"

We were doing this. Now. We were all going back up to our hotel room. What next?

"Evening, folks." Stew blocked our path. Where did the asshole even come from? He focused on me. "I thought you three weren't acquaintances."

An irritated growl rumbled from Jordan's chest. He was thinner than Stew but a couple inches taller, and when he moved forward, the blogger retreated. "I'll catch up with you ladies in a minute." Jordan didn't look at us, and an irritated threat lined his words. "Stew and I are going to talk about Elizabeth Thompson and how uninteresting a story she is."

ELEVEN

Liz

When I called myself a *princess* at dinner, it was meant to be a joke, but Chloe and Jordan had rescued me twice in as many days, and I was starting to feel like the maiden trapped in the tower waiting for my knights in shining armor to pull my hair—

Not where that thought started.

"Is he going to be all right?" I asked Chloe as she let us into their room. Jordan hadn't caught up to us.

Chloe gestured to a table with two laptops, and a chair in front. "If you want to have a seat, he'll be right behind us." She didn't sound worried. In fact, it was the most confident she'd sounded all night. I liked both Chloes—shy *and* assertive. "So Stew is looking for the story you told us downstairs?"

"I guess." I still didn't understand why a tech blogger wanted gossip about me, but he certainly seemed to.

As I sat, Chloe pulled up another chair, putting her close enough for her arm to brush mine. I didn't know if

85

the contact was intentional or not, but it seemed be, and I liked the softness of it.

"It's not a super interesting story," Chloe said. "No office—I'm truly sorry you went through it. The whole thing must have hurt like hell. But I know what makes a good, dramatic story, and that's not it."

"No, it's not." I'd never been so grateful to have my life—my mistakes—diminished.

The door swung open again. "Sorry to keep you waiting, ladies." Jordan joined us without hesitation. "Problem is solved. You still want to take a look?" He flipped reached between us to open one of the laptops and logged in.

"Yes. Definitely," I said.

If Chloe was a stunning and enviable lesson in duality, Jordan was fluidity, sliding from one thing to the next with zero effort. I'd never met people like them before, not that I knew. Who were open and true to themselves and so very compelling.

When I accepted the invitation to come up here, I didn't know what to expect. Despite the bravado, not-at-all veiled innuendo, and flirting, I didn't know if I was ready to take things a step further. I'd kissed two women in my life—sweet, first base kisses—and my experience with men was barely more.

Did the idea of sleeping with these two—sex—do wonderfully yummy things to my insides? Hell yes. Did I know if I was ready? Absolutely not.

And here we were, looking at animations, just like they'd promised. It was reassuring.

Jordan started the video, complete with subtitles at

the bottom, and made the image full screen. He leaned one arm on either of our chairs, as the cartoon played.

It was stunning artwork. A blend of hand drawn style and a more digital feel, but here they blended flawlessly. "You drew these?" I let my awe show. "You're so crazy talented."

Jordan's smirk seemed semi-permanent. "You didn't think I got where I am based on my looks alone."

Chloe shook her head, but her smile never faded. "He certainly didn't sleep his way to the top."

"I hear that's harder for men, anyway." I tested out the joke, hoping it wouldn't fall flat.

Jordan placed his hand over his heart and tossed his head back with a dramatic lilt. "You wound me. Looks like mind transcend traditional labels."

"Drama queen." Chloe tossed a hand in his direction in a half-hearted slap, but he caught her fingers mid-air and kissed the tips, one at a time.

Heat flooded my face at being on the edge of the intimate moment. At least I didn't have to worry about either one of them being jealous of me if this went further—they were so obviously in love with each other.

I reached for the volume, to distract myself, but it was already turned up. "How come there's no sound? Like, talking."

Chloe slumped in her seat with a sigh. "We don't have anyone to do the girl's voice."

"Uh, you?" I must be missing something. Chloe had a beautiful voice.

"No. Nope. Nuh-uh." Chloe shook her head emphatically. "I couldn't. I can't."

"Why not?" I read the lines as the subtitles scrolled past. I'd pretty much been groomed from day one to follow a script when needed. "Just like that. Easy peasy."

"Not for me. I hate the sound of my voice. But you're amazing. Do some more," Chloe said.

Jordan picked up the hero's lines, and I slid in with the heroine's parts. It was awkward at first. He knew where he expected the pacing to be, and had obviously done this dozens of times, at least in his head if not out loud.

But within a few minutes, I'd found my pace and was bouncing off him as if we were having a conversation along with the animations on screen.

"Figures." Chloe's tone was playful.

I glanced at her, one eyebrow quirked, curious.

She laughed lightly. "I knew you were too good to be true. You're actually an anime girl."

"Busted."

"I *knew* it." Jordan grabbed a nearby pen a hotel pad of paper.

Chloe gave an exaggerated sigh. "It's a tale as old as time."

"Beauty and the Beast?" I thought we were talking anime.

"Pft." Chloe waved a dismissive hand. "*Way* better, and without the potential copyright lawsuits. You're a space princess, from a far away galaxy."

How cool would that be? "Do I really have to worry about copyright in that case?"

"When it comes to Disney, *everyone* in the universe has to worry." Jordan's tone was serious, but he kept his focus on whatever he was drawing. Short faint lines at first, that he darkened and elongated as he went.

"It's more comfortable over here. Easier to talk." Chloe grabbed my hand and tugged me toward the sofa.

The simple gesture felt natural—two friends hanging out and chatting—and terrifying at the same time. Because we weren't just two friends, I'd told them I was up for a night of no-strings sex.

"I figure it's like this." Chloe's tone shifted to have more *oomf.* "You're a space princess. You've been sent to search the galaxy for a husband. Your family line must live on, and you must find suitable stock for that to happen. It's expected of you."

"Suitable stock?" I giggled. "Like a soup?"

"That's exactly what you've been asking yourself, for years now, as you come out of cryosleep on each new planet that's supposed to have intelligent life, only to find none."

Chloe gave me a far more interesting story than my own, but there were snippets of truth buried in there that ached from their reality.

"Will I have to go home empty handed?" I asked with false dismay.

"See, that's what you're afraid of. It's why you've let yourself become distracted from your primary objective. Months ago—decades in light years, but you've been frozen through most of it—a pair of space smugglers helped you out when your ship broke down. Fun, sexy couple. You want to find them again. Maybe they can smuggle you away from your responsibility."

I stared at her with amused disbelief. "Are you two

space smugglers?"

"No." Chloe scoffed. "We're just normal, boring earth humans. But we do remind you a bit of them."

Jordan perched on the arm of the couch on my other side, and handed me a piece of notepad paper. He bowed as he handed it over. "Your highness."

"I disagree. You're anything but bor..." I forgot what I was saying when I saw the sketch. It was a pen drawing of me, in a flowing ballgown, and I was holding a long, curved blade. "Wow. Is there anything you can't do?"

"Advanced mathematics," Chloe said.

"Profit and loss projections," Jordan added.

Chloe nodded. "Really, anything involving numbers... not our thing."

Mercy would love them. "Numbers are easy. The answer is always the same. This... You two... you're like inspiration brought to life." Was I gushing? Maybe a little. I didn't care. I'd been worried about how little I'd have in common with Chloe and Jordan, but it didn't seem to matter. I didn't remember a time in the recent past when I'd had so much fun.

No way was I spoiling it tonight by bringing up the sex again. I was going to enjoy whatever this moment was, for as long as it lasted.

* * *

I woke up to the teasing scents of jasmine and musk. My room didn't smell like this.

I opened my eyes and last night fluttered back when

I saw Chloe laying face-to-face with me, Jordan behind her. We fell asleep talking last night, and that was it. All that build-up and stress for a simple evening of carefree tangents. I'd never experienced something quite like that; not even with Mercy.

Both of their eyes were still shut. We'd fallen asleep in our clothes, and Chloe's dress has twisted around her during the night. Propriety said I should look away, but I couldn't stop my gaze from traveling along her figure— over round breasts struggling to free themselves, down to a narrow waist, along pale, slender legs exposed almost to the hip in places…

Chloe's skirt slid higher as she shifted, and my pulse jumped into my throat as I forced my attention back up.

They weren't asleep any more. My cheeks heated under their gazes.

"Morning." Chloe's face was pink and her voice shy.

Okay, so the talking was fun last night, but they were both still gorgeous, and now that we were all so close… Christ, I wanted to kiss her again. And him. And more. "Hey."

"So… Last night. Lots of fun." The uncertainty in Chloe's tone spoke to the hammering of my pulse in my ears.

I nodded.

Screw this. I didn't want *what now*. I wanted *this is next*. I propped myself up on one elbow and slanted my mouth over Chloe's. When our lips met, a jolt ran through me, staring at the source and sliding on sparks to my fingers. My toes. My core.

She kissed back, and I leaned into the sensation,

hungry for more of what I'd had in the bar. But this wasn't the same. It was more intense. More vivid.

Jordan's groan reminded me we had an audience, and sparks became a flame of need.

I dropped my hands to Chloe's hips. I swore I could feel my own touch as I glided my palms up her stomach to brush the bottom of her breasts. "Is this okay?" I asked, breathless.

Chloe tangled her fingers in my hair and crushed her mouth harder to mine.

I was vaguely aware of the mattress shifting, but I was too focused on Chloe to care what Jordan was doing. When I'd kissed Mercy, months ago, it was awkward and stilted. The other night in the bar was rushed with an underlying wave of guilt.

But this… Chloe's mouth was softness propelled by a hard need, and she tasted like Mt. Dew and sparks. I was so tired of second-guessing myself. I wanted this. I wanted *them.*

When I undid the top button on Chloe's dress, she sighed against my lips and pressed closer. I trailed my fingers down the front of her dress, removing each button obstacle along the way and letting my mouth follow. When I reached her waist, I pulled the fabric apart, putting her gorgeous figure on display.

Hesitation flitted back. Daydreaming about being with another woman was one thing, but the realness of this was suddenly too vivid.

From behind me, an arm lay along the length of mine, and Jordan's breath caressed my cheek. He covered my hand and glided us up Chloe's ribs. "Start with what you'd want, if you were her." His low voice drilled into my senses, amplifying everything further—the brush of cool air on my skin; the hum of the fan; the smooth, tempting skin in front of me.

I cupped one of Chloe's breasts, marveling at the way it molded to my palm, and flicked a thumb over a pink nub that was bigger than my own. Brighter. Tempting and yummy like bubblegum.

Chloe arched into my touch when I pinched and tugged. "Use your mouth?" Her plea was breathless.

I wrapped my lips around her nipple and flicked my tongue as I sucked on the swollen flesh. I swore I could feel each brush and lick on my own skin. I kissed along Chloe's chest and finished unbuttoning her dress. I was so wet, and my jeans pressed into me, amplifying my desire. This was such a delicious build-up.

When I pushed aside Chloe's panties, my fingers slid along slick skin? Waxed? And as wet as me. My fingers were already coated.

Stroking Chloe, drawing my fingers along her slick skin, was like playing with myself, but better. Every rasp and sigh that slipped from Chloe cranked my anticipation higher. I needed a taste. I dipped my head and trailed my tongue along the same path as my fingers.

Every fantasy I'd had about going down on another woman paled in comparison to the reality. The moment. The flavor. The way Chloe squirmed under me… If I squeezed my thighs together tight enough would I come?

Not yet, but I wanted her to. I eased two fingers inside her and hooked them up to hit her Gspot as I sucked on her clit. She pressed into my face, grinding, stealing my breath. Her moans became cries and I sucked and pumped harder.

Chloe's hips raised off the bed, and she tangled her fingers in my hair. She clenched around me when she came. *God* this was incredible. I didn't ease up until she shuddered away from my touch. She pulled me up and crushed her mouth to mine again, diving her tongue in. Nipping. Teasing. Demanding as she licked herself from my lips.

"I think he wants to join us," Chloe murmured against my lips. She pulled away enough to glance behind me.

Could we? Could I…? "Yes, please."

Jordan tugged me away long enough to pull my shirt off and unclasp my bra. He trailed his lips down my spine as he undid my jeans.

I helped him kick my clothes off the rest of the way, while Chloe dragged her hands along my bare skin. There were so many sensations, I didn't know which temptation to focus on.

Jordan pulled me upright, into him, breaking the kiss with Chloe, his bare skin and erection pressing into my back. He nipped at my shoulder. "That was scorching." His breath seared my skin. He guided a hand between my legs. "Fuck, you're so wet. I want to bury myself inside you. Feel you clench around me, while Chloe plays with you."

Yes, please. I couldn't find my voice. Chloe watched me with bright eyes and pink cheeks.

"Okay." I managed.

TWELVE

Jordan

I guided Liz onto her back, nudged her legs apart, and rolled on a condom. It took the last of my restraint to keep my thoughts from tumbling into *so incredible* over and over again.

Chloe looked gorgeous, glowing and freshly fucked. Watching while it happened was so different from being the other participant, but it was just as tantalizing. Seeing Liz make Chloe come. Hearing those familiar sounds, and seeing it all in a whole new light.

And now, Liz... I dragged the head of my cock along her gorgeous pussy, short curls of black hair teasing me even though latex. My control was gone. Watching was one thing, but being part of it... I nudged her opening and drove inside, unable to hold back. That first sweet, tight penetration shoved me toward the edge of ecstasy.

I bit the inside of my cheek, hoping to last a little longer, and copper hit my tongue. I wanted all of us to be a part of this. "Chi." I couldn't wrap my head around more words.

She lowered her head to Liz's breast to suck, her ass sticking in the air, teasing me.

I pounded with frantic abandon, spurred on by the rocking of Liz's hips and the way she hooked her legs around my ass.

Chloe glided her hand down Liz's stomach, and when she found Liz's clit, Liz clenched around me, milking my cock. Chloe teased and stroked, and Liz's motions became faster. She squeezed me tighter.

The sounds Liz made when she came were a beautiful song. Her sweet mewls and strong grip drew out my own orgasm. I slammed inside her, spilling, sparks dancing behind my eyelids, until I was spent.

The frantic grind slowed, and moans became pants for air and then tiny giggles. I didn't know which woman they belonged to, or maybe it was me. I collapsed on the bed and pulled Chloe close, between me and Liz. Chloe's chest pressed into myside, her heart hammering against my ribs.

A second set of fingers brushed my chest, and Liz pressed herself to Chloe's back. They both wore faint smiles.

"Fuck, you two are amazing." I forced the words through lungs still searching for breath.

"Crap." Liz bolted upright. "Yes. Definitely. And I didn't realize what time it was." She wobbled and grabbed the edge of the mattress as she stood. I couldn't help my satisfaction at the sight. She grabbed her jeans.

"I have to go. Meeting in half an hour. I had a fantastic time. I mean it. Thank you both."

After she left, Chloe cuddled closer. "Thank you from me, too."

"Sure. Because it was completely selfless on my part." I chuckled. This was better than any fantasy. What held us back for so long? Whatever it was that stopped us before, that had us fighting. I wasn't letting hang-ups or lost words get in the way again.

I MENTALLY TICKED through the high-level list of *why we're awesome* for the E3 demo I was doing with Chloe, while I paced outside the convention hall, waiting for the current group to finish, so our people could get in and set up.

Chloe stepped in my path—a welcome and beautiful obstruction to my wearing a path in the carpet. "Hey, handsome." She rose on her toes to brush her lips over mine. Her white T-shirt and jeans matched mine, as part of our visuals for our show, but she wore them better than I did.

Things between us had gone smoother today than they had in a long time. There were no miscommunications or barely-suppressed snarls. I refused to linger on the fact that we hadn't made future plans with Liz. It was clear what last night and this morning were. But I was grateful to have my Chloe back.

I wrapped my arms around her waist to pull her close. "Lighting and sound all squared away?"

"Mmm. You're so sexy when you talk shop." She molded against me. "And yes. Ready and set."

"Ready and set."

"Jordan Iverson?" A stern voice carried over the chatter of the crowds.

I looked up to see two police offers stopped next to us. "That's me."

"We need you to come down to the station with us."

People around us slowed and stared, and murmurs reached my ears.

"Is this for the show?"

"Is there anything these people won't do for publicity?"

"Disgusting."

Unfortunately for all of us, I had no idea what was going on. "Can I ask what for? The timing's not so great."

One officer thumbed the clasp on his holster. "I think you'd rather do this quietly, but we can cuff you here and escort you to the care forcefully if you prefer."

"The fuck?" Not the smartest thing I'd said today. "You can't tell me why?"

"We'd like to talk to you about the assault on Stew Knapfer last night."

Any thoughts of the demo vanished as I tried to make sense of their words. The guy was an asshole, but I didn't know anything about anyone beating him up. "Yeah. Okay. Whatever I can do to help."

"I'll call Legal and have them get us local representation," Chloe said. "We'll meet you down there."

The officers boxed me tightly as we walked outside to

a waiting car, and they put me back. When they miran-dized me, I swore my heart stopped for a beat. I wanted to protest. Point out I didn't know anything about an attack on Stew, and I certainly hadn't been involved.

I kept my mouth shut, and the protests devoured me from the inside out. One of things Zach had drilled into our heads after the fake marriage proposal, was that if for some bizarre reason we ever got in trouble with the law, we weren't supposed to say *anything* without a lawyer present.

This was the first time I'd ever had to put the rule into action.

"It's a simple assault case." The officer in the passenger seat glanced back at me as we crawled along with traffic. "We have witnesses and proof. Do you really want to jump through legal hoops for the same inevitable outcome?"

How was it possible to have witnesses for an incident that didn't happen? I understood it was easy enough for someone to lie, but proof? Whatever led to me being picked up wasn't real, and that meant I absolutely wasn't opening my mouth. I shook my head. "My lawyer will meet me at the station."

The policeman shrugged and turned away. "We get paid either way."

When we reached the station, I was processed into holding and placed in a small room with a table, a couple of chairs bolted to the ground, and what I assumed was a one-way mirror. I couldn't see a clock, but there was nothing to do in here besides wonder *what the fuck* and count. Based on how I got, over and over, I waited several hours.

The longer I waited, the more my irritation and anger simmered and grew. Why the fuck wasn't anyone talking to me? Chloe would have gotten me representation minutes after I left, and that meant someone should be here consulting with me. I was tempted to slam my fist into the table as an outlet or to get attention or just to give my brain something new to do.

Keys rattled in the lock and a uniformed officer opened the interrogation room door. "Mr. Iverson, you're free to go. The charges have been dropped."

Oh thank God for that. I kept the sarcastic retort to myself, for fear of earning another few hours of isolation, gave him a tight-lipped smile, and stalked into the lobby.

Chloe stood next to a man wearing a suit that probably cost as much as my high-end graphics laptop. She ran toward me and hugged me tight. "I'm sorry it took so long." Her words were muffled by my shirt, where she'd buried her face. "I wish I understood why. Dave took the demo. He said it was a hit."

I rested my lips on the top of her head and squeezed her. At least something went right.

"Mr. Iverson." The suit approached, hand extended. "I'm Dean Twents. I represent the firm retained by Rinslet. Mr. Knapfer has dropped the charges against you. Not that he had anything beyond circumstantial evidence anyway. Well done, keeping your mouth shut."

"Not my preference." But I was a good trained dog. The bitter thought came from nowhere and settled in.

"It doesn't have to be, and I do have some news for you."

Chloe pulled back to look me in the eye. "You're not going to like it. I hate it. We have to go straight to the airport from here."

"Bullshit." I spat the word with more venom than I intended. "I didn't do anything."

"And once you're on the plane, that trend will continue," Dean said. "There's a car waiting."

Fuck him and his blatant lack of a personality. I kept my attention on Chloe. "We have things to wrap up." We didn't really. The show ended tonight and the rest of the team could handle clean-up, but it pissed me off that I was being punished for something I barely had any information about.

"Zach made the call." Chloe frowned. "He says I have to make sure you're on that plane."

"Fuck." Fuck-fuckity-fuck-fuck-fuck. I wanted to whine that it wasn't fair, but that wouldn't improve the situation. "Fine." I didn't trust myself to say more.

This was such complete and utter crap. I had to leave the biggest event of the year with my tail tucked between my legs, because some asshole blogger had their panties in a bind. Over something I didn't even do. I should be grateful I wasn't spending my night in a cell, but that didn't make me any less pissed off.

THIRTEEN

I found a seat at the back of the room where the Rinslet demo would start in about fifteen minutes. It was a good thing I hadn't had intense plans today, because memories of Chloe and Jordan occupied my mind. It was okay that I hadn't exchanged numbers with them. One-night stand meant exactly that, and we'd agreed.

Besides, I knew where they worked.

Wow, that sounded stalkery. *Dial it back, Liz.*

I wasn't here because of any of that, though. I had to see what the hype was about when it came to a Rinslet Demo. Even now, waiting for things to start, I was surrounded by whispers around the afternoon's big reveal. Not only the *what* but the *how* of it.

I'd waited in line for several hours to get this seat, and that was another reason to be grateful for my clear schedule.

The lights dimmed, and the low roar of muttering

voices reached a crescendo, and then fell silent when the room went dark.

"Gals and guys. Geeks of all persuasions." An announcer-style voice spilled through the speakers. "Are you ready for something spectacular?"

The room erupted in cheers. Rinslet knew how to work the crowd. This kind of hype and anticipation must be hard to live up to. Black lights flashed across the display, illuminating first the screen then the person strolling toward the middle of the stage.

The flashing display made it difficult for me to identify the person, but after this morning, I was certain neither Chloe nor Jordan was that tall or broadshouldered.

More whispers rolled around me. I wasn't the only one curious about the last minute presenter swap.

"You expected our notorious troublemakers to present this afternoon." The voice boomed over the speakers. "We've got your favorite community manager, Grave Dave – The Inquisitor, instead. And that's just one epic surprise among many you'll see over the next hour."

Well, bummer. The show should be good anyway, and I was going to stick around to get my answers, but it didn't hit me how much I wanted to see Chloe and Jordan again—even from a distance—until I realized I couldn't.

Definitely stalkerish.

I sat back to enjoy the show.

The light display was pretty. The games they

demoed were neat. It was another media display among the dozens here this week.

I probably didn't know enough about gaming to appreciate what I'd seen. Either that or missing the one thing I'd been hoping for was enough to color my view.

Forty-five minutes later, I strolled out of the room surrounded by a wave of excited chatter and blinking away the sparkles left by the bright against dark in the room.

"...*arrested...*"

"...*right outside the stage door...*"

"...*positive. Jordan Iverson assaulted...*"

Was he okay? I tried to follow a thread of conversation long enough to catch more information, my concern for Jordan growing with each new snatch of his name.

My phone vibrated with a call from Mercy, and my focus was shattered.

I found the quietest corner of the convention center that I could, which meant the background noise was still there, but had been reduced to a dull roar, and answered. "Hey."

"Hey, love." Mercy sounded cheerful, but hesitation ran through the words. "You doing okay?"

Odd question. "Last time I checked. What have you heard that I haven't?" I teased.

"Lots of stuff. The best film speed and aperture for shooting in low light with a tripod and high-motion subjects, for instance."

"You're hilarious." I was comforted by the humor, though. "Seriously, what's up?"

"Ehhh, Ian told me what happened with your accounts, and I'm worried about you."

"Thanks." The concern warmed and embarrassed me at the same time. A downside to Mercy and Ian being together was that, for some reason, I was a favorite topic of theirs. It had been a lot easier to face their clashing versions of sympathy when I got to tell each of them in my own way when something was going on. "You didn't just call for that."

"I might have. I *am* worried."

I believed her, but her tone said she had more than one motive, and she'd waited almost a full day to reach out about the accounts. "Are you going to ask me to do something horrible? You don't want to set me up with someone, do you?" Because I'd found the perfect—

Nope. No I hadn't.

"No more blind dates. Cross my heart. But are you still flying back tonight?"

As a matter of fact, I needed to leave for the airport soon. "Yes. Do you need me in-office tomorrow?"

"Yes, but not ours. Any chance you got to see the Rinslet presentation? Or meet any of their people?"

Holy hell, had I. The memories sent heat coursing over me. "Yes."

"What did you think?"

Life. Altering. Experience. Okay, maybe that was an exaggeration, but was it really? That wasn't what Mercy meant, though, and while I'd tell her later, I wasn't doing so in the middle of a crowded convention center. "The presentation was pretty. Lots of lights and flash. Why?"

"We're talking to them tomorrow about licensing exclusive artwork and video. Or rather, you are, if you're up for it."

My heart leaped into my throat, and I took a few deep breaths to calm my racing pulse. "Sure. Of course." Rinslet was a huge company. I wouldn't be meeting with the two people I already knew. They were important people, who definitely had far better things to do than take sales meetings.

"Thank you." Mercy sounded relieved. "My brother pulled some strings to get us on their calendar, and something came up that I absolutely can't cancel. You're only a few miles from their offices, so... I'll email you the meeting details."

We tried to talk a little longer and catch up, but after I asked *say again* for the fiftieth time, I decided to let Mercy go. I had a plane to catch anyway.

I let the events of the past few days jumble and roll through my head as I made my way to the parking garage. I'd already checked out and had my luggage in the car, so I could go straight to the airport from here.

It had been a weird week. Amazing, but weird. I loved this exploring-my-sexuality thing. After last night and this morning, I was far more willing to do temporary hook-ups again. Especially if a certain couple was involved.

Which didn't make any sense, because if I went back to Jordan and Chloe, it wasn't temporary.

I'd go clubbing tomorrow night instead. Could I get a recommendation from Mercy without telling her why? Something to figure out later.

I grabbed my phone to send Jonathan a quick email.

Thanks for letting me crash your booth this week. The experience was fantastic. I'm on my way out, but you know how to get a hold of me if you need anything.

- Liz

When I'd started working with clients, the less formal correspondence went against everything I'd ever been taught, but most of Mercy's clients preferred the casual tone, so I adapted.

I was surprised when a text came through from Jonathan, second later. *You okay?*

Why did everyone keep asking me that? *Last time I checked.*

Good. Have a safe flight.

A URL sat at the end of his note. I sent him back a quick *thanks* before clicking the link.

I let the page load as I situated myself in the rental car, and scanned the headline before sticking the key in the ignition.

Assault at E3. You'll Never Believe Who Was Involved.

I grimaced at the horrible click bait. It was probably easy to believe.

And then I saw Jordan's name, not as the victim, but as the perpetrator. No. No fucking way. He'd never hit someone, not even that Stew guy.

Okay, so all I really knew about Jordan was that he was a great dinner companion and the sex was incredible, but he'd been with us. And I trusted both him and Chloe.

I'd been an idiot about my trust with George, but this didn't feel the same.

I hoped whatever this was, they got it sorted out quickly.

FOURTEEN

Jordan

I was back in the office, and embracing my inner Warhol as I sketched on a whiteboard with three different colors of dry-erase markers. I needed my artists to have a rough idea of their next project.

A good night's sleep with Chloe wrapped in my arms had chased away most of my resentment about yesterday's arrest. The whole thing was a mistake, but it was also done and in the past. I was still pissed I went through it, and Dave didn't pull off the feeling we'd planned for so long for in our demo, but I was moving on. Making things better with Chloe ranked higher than knocking the media dead with a demo, and now the bar wasn't so high for E3 next year.

"I'm thinking something like this." I let the loose lines flow, keeping them generic on purpose. The three guys who worked on my marketing art team shared this large space because when they needed to collaborate—

like now—they got loud, and when they needed to concentrate, no one else could be.

I switched been markers for skin, fabric, and shadow. If I had my way, I'd pencil this, scan it, then 3D render it. But my job wasn't creation these days; I was responsible for direction. If I took this design past this rough, erasable concept, I'd end up putting my own flare on it, and hunch down over the computer, focused until it was near perfect.

When I stepped back, a rough sketch of our flagship curvy heroine and muscled hero filled the board. "Posed like this. But—you know—the way you guys do."

"…ass shot…?"

"…torn leather to the cleavage…"

"…give him scars and a bullet wound…"

I hid my eye roll. These guys were over the top, but they knew what the market wanted—it was why I'd hired them. I left them to do their thing, knowing they'd have mock-ups for the limited edition T-shirts by the end of the week, and finals not too long after. Now that E3 was over, it was time to start planning for RinCon in December.

Damn it. I couldn't let *all* their comments go. I opened the door again. "No ass shots."

"Full frontal?"

This time I rolled my eyes. "Only if you mean for both characters."

"Really?"

I'd be fine with it. There were some things even our management wouldn't put up with though. "No, not really. Strategic rips are fine, but don't show more of her than him. She's as much the star of the fucking game as he is."

That was enough warning. They had plenty of time to make their deadline so I left them to it. Clicking off dates in my head left a gate open for more of my calendar to slide in. Who was I meeting with next? And if I walked back into that room and spent the next thirty-six hours doing those images myself, the way I pictured them, how many people would I piss off?

I didn't know if I cared, as along as Chloe joined me. We'd stay up all night plotting, creating, eating too much pizza… Being eighteen again and realizing we'd just been hired for our dream jobs by a software company with bigger ambitions than their bank account.

Sigh. This wasn't the time to get stuck in the past. I had a work to do. I loved my job, truly, but some days I missed the freedom and creativity I'd surrendered to climb this high.

"Jordan." Scott's sharp voice snagged my attention. "What are you doing for the next half hour."

"Catching up on email if I'm lucky."

"You're not. We've got a vendor coming in at…" Scott glanced at his phone. "She's in the third-floor conference room now. I've got a crisis to deal with. Will you talk to her?"

"About what?"

"Check your email." Scott was already walking away.

Whatever. I headed for the stairs and jogged down one floor, trying to find that balance between not keeping this person waiting, and me waiting on the information from Scott. The message showed up right as I reached the conference room.

When I saw Liz waiting, I didn't give a fuck what it said. Her suit—matching jacket and skirt with a light-weight top—was out of place in the casual Rinslet offices, but she looked gorgeous.

And she was staring back at me with wide eyes. She pushed a smile into place as she stood. "Scott McAllister?" she teased.

"I wish." I shook her hand and forced myself to not hold on longer than was professional. I took the spot across the table from her, wishing I could be closer and knowing that was a bad idea. "Actually, I really don't. Dude's gotta be pushing an ulcer and he's not even forty." Plus, he'd completely lost the passions that led him to start this place, and I never wanted to be there. "But I wouldn't mind the bank account."

"It's overrated, I promise you."

"Easy to say when you're the one who has it." My tone was light. I wasn't bitter. We were more than comfortable.

"Is Scott joining us?" Liz asked.

With any luck, not at all. "He had a crisis and asked me to fill in. Which means… I have no idea why you're here." Looking for Round Two? "Give me thirty seconds to read the itinerary."

"I'll fill you in."

I'd prefer that. Staring at her was so much better than staring at my phone. I couldn't pull my gaze from her clear blue eyes.

She looked away first, cheeks bright pink. "Is this some sort of conflict of interest?"

"Oh. Right. We don't do that here." What I wanted to do here, right now, was drag her up to Chloe's office and see what the three of us could get up to in this half hour timespan. "Besides, we all agreed it was only a one-time thing." I didn't like the sound of that at all.

Her brow flicked toward a frown before an impassive mask slid into place. "Exactly. And it doesn't impact what happens in this meeting."

"Not at all." Though I was still tempted to ask if I could personally oversee this partnership. "So we're good?"

Her smile returned, cooler than before and not reaching her eyes, and she gave me a brief rundown of what she was here for. "I didn't even know you dealt in licensed assets."

"It's a new market for us." And it had been my idea. "I wanted my people branching into other things, so I set up an independent group that works directly with advertisers and marketers."

"Wow."

Her genuine awe cranked up my smugness. "It's some amazing work, too. You won't find anything like it anywhere. Do you want the standard sales pitch to go with this?"

"I'd lo— appreciate that." She sat rigid in her seat, gaze flitting everywhere but in my direction.

I gave her the spiel, including contract highlights, licensing, showing her some samples, and letting her know what to expect from the partnership.

Each time something that could even vaguely be construed as innuendo slipped out, she clenched her jaw. So much for the fun we had the other day.

"Enough." I dropped my dry erase marker and it clattered in the dust tray before falling to the ground. "I won't do this if it's going to be awkward."

"What else should it be?" Liz asked.

A chance to figure out what else the three of us could get up to? "We all had fun Wednesday night, even before the sex."

"We did." Her reply was so quiet I wasn't sure I heard it right.

We're still the people who made the funny voices."

She looked up. "True."

"Problem solved, then." Not really, since I still wanted Round Two, but this would do for professional purposes. "What other questions can I answer for you?"

She worked her jaw, then shook her head. "I think I have my answers. I'll take this to Mercy and we'll be in touch."

I showed her to the lobby, neither of us really speaking in the elevator. We exchanged painfully polite goodbyes, and she turned away.

Fuck it. "Liz."

When she paused, I grabbed a business card from my wallet and a pen from the front desk.

I scribbled mine and Chloe's personal numbers on the back, and handed it to Liz. "So we can do more not-awkward stuff, someplace that isn't a Rinslet meeting room."

"Sounds like fun." She smiled as she tucked the card into her purse, and headed out to the parking lot.

Speaking of Chloe… I had three minutes until my next meeting, and a fresh store of fantasy staring her and the things she could get up to with Liz. Not enough time for anything, but I'd make it work.

I strode toward Chloe's office as fast as I could without breaking into a run. When I reached the room, she was gathering a stack of papers and standing.

Her twin braids gave her a deceptively innocent look, and cranked my desire higher. Her frown… not so much. "I have to be somewhere." Apology filled her words.

"Same place I do." I kicked the door shut and closed the distance between us. "You have two minutes, and if anyone cares that we're late, they can go fuck themselves."

"Okay?" she said with an uncertain laugh.

I set her paperwork back on the desk. Before she could respond, I grabbed one braid in each hand, and tugged while I kissed her hard. Her whimper drilled into my thoughts, and I nudged her back onto the desk. When we broke apart, her jagged, needy breaths drilled into my soul.

"I don't want to look track of the peace we found in L.A." My voice came out more gravelly than I intended. I moved one hand to her hip and gripped tight. "Whatever we need to talk through." I nipped her bottom lip. "Whatever it takes to keep you." I pushed up the bottom of her shirt.

She dug her fingers into my chest. "One minute."

"You and your schedules." I glided a finger under her waistband, toward her navel. "We'd fall apart without you."

"That's a given, but I appreciate the sentiment." She squirmed against me with each teasing touch. "Did you lock the door?"

"No." Why did she want me to think? I unbuttoned her jeans.

She bit her bottom lip when I slid under her panties. "What if someone walks in?" She pushed closer rather than away.

"They can watch." My erection dug into my zipper—a nagging reminder that the location and timing were less than idea. But the flush on Chloe's face and the way her chest heaved with each breath overrode common sense. "Not sure if you realize this, but the whole office already knows we're fucking."

"You're wicked." Her teasing reply faded in a gasp when I shoved her jeans halfway down her hips, to dip my fingers between her legs. She ground into my touch, making it easy to find my target.

I stroked her swollen clit. "You're so wet." I crushed my mouth to hers.

"Not until you got here."

I stroked faster, my pace matching her moans. God, I loved that sound. She was holding back, trying to keep quiet, and that made it tempting to yank her jeans to her ankles, bend her over the desk, and slide inside her.

There wasn't time, so I focused on her responses instead. The way her face scrunched up as she drew closer to climax. Her nails digging into my arms. The gasp and hold of her breath—the way the entire world paused—before climax spilled through her.

Her hips bucked and her legs wobbled, and she finally pulled away from my touch. She leaned her head against my chest, hot breath searing me through fabric. "Where did that come from?" she asked breathlessly.

"You inspire me."

Her giggle was light and airy. "I won't argue with that. Minus three minutes."

I tugged one braid to lean her head back and look her in the eye. "Tonight, after work, we'll do the forming-of-the-words thing. I'll pick up sandwiches. We'll talk and we'll screw around."

"Tempting. Two naked, dirty minds on display for each other to see? Pull an all-nighter plus a little smut, like the old days?"

"You've got such a way with words."

"Damn straight, I do." She smiled, nudged me back, and did up her jeans. "Don't be late tonight."

I kissed her again. "Cross my heart."

FIFTEEN

Chloe

My face was hot, and I was pretty sure one of my braids had come loose. Not that I minded.

I walked with Jordan to the conference room, my mind distinctly on what we'd just done, rather than the planning meeting we were stepping into.

As we entered the room, someone made a light quip about us being late, and a few others exchanged *looks*. Then the spectacle was over and everyone turned back to the itinerary.

No one knew. No one cared. Jordan and I were the only people who felt the impact of his fast, hot fingering. The rush still fluttered in my chest. I almost felt like I was getting away with something. The one time in this office I was actually the sexually adventurous person I pretended to be, and there was no impact. No reason to even bring it up.

Which was fine with me.

The meeting droned on, and I kept half an ear on

the conversation. I was only here because my managers were here. Our copy was already written, and our demo was the same we'd shared at E3, so my team's list was small.

Not that I was complaining. This was a rare moment to catch my breath, and linger on what just happened in my office.

We'd never done anything like that before. Before the other morning with Liz, the most risqué not-at-home sex Jordan and I ever had was in a hotel room. Just the two of us. That wasn't all on him. It had taken me a while to realize I wanted more. I was grateful he understood, but I wished it hadn't taken months of us snipping at each other, to the point of almost falling apart, to find this common ground.

So why did it feel like something was still missing? The harder I reached for the thought, the further it slid out of my grasp, until it evaporated.

"I'm going to say what everyone else is thinking." Dave's brash voice drew my back to the now. "The whole *kinkier than thou* thing is only for shock value. No one wants to see the tentacle-porn innuendo in our teasers."

I rolled my eyes. This was Standard Dave, and he was within his rights to dislike some of our concepts. He preferred his half-naked to be a bit more traditional, and barely on the right side of questionable-age-of-consent.

Ugh.

If I made a concession, he'd drop the complaint and we could move on. He'd saved us with our demo yesterday, and I wouldn't give him grief in return.

"All right. We'll cut the sexy Cthulhu joke. Not everyone's up for novelty-sized." When I started working with all these guys, being so vocal about giant, tentacle-shaped dicks turned me beat red. My reputation required it of me, though, and I was much better at pretending this didn't faze me. "We'll change it to alien probes instead. Add in a little seventies porn music."

"Why do you keep subjecting us to your fucked-up fantasies? Not getting enough at home?" Of course. Not only didn't he drop it, he also made it personal. Maybe he wasn't as cool with taking over the panel as he said.

A mile-long list of retorts spun through my head, starting with *maybe you prefer the unemployment line?* That would terrify and infuriate rather than draw laughs, and I wanted this to drop so we could move on.

"She wasn't complaining ten minutes ago," Jordan said before I grasped a reply.

The room erupted in a wave of *nice one bro* and *dude, no way.*

And now my face was red hot again, for entirely different reasons this time. Off-color jokes were one thing, but this room of people didn't get to know our actual private lives. I forced a smile past the scalding heat. "Fine. You and your repressed world views can have Catholic school-girl skirts." I glanced at my phone, pretending it had buzzed. "I have to take this. You boys keep fighting the good fight."

"Don't be like that." Dave's tone softened. "We're fucking with you. That's all."

"Enough." Again, Jordan cut me off before I could speak. Was he shutting me down or looking out for me?

And was I really about to fake a phone call to walk away from this bullshit? Yes. "Don't worry." I smirked at Dave. "No hard feelings, but your girlfriend is on the phone asking if I've got what you don't." I shouldn't have said that. The unemployment *line* joke would've been less abrasive, but I wasn't going to lose face here.

The chorus of *ooh, burn* backed me up.

I didn't like it. I whirled away from Dave's clenched jaw, and strode from the room with my back straight, and my head high, despite the frustration clawing at my chest.

Moments later, I was back in my office, fingers poised over the keyboard. Hey, unexpected free time. I could get some work done.

If my mind would stop replaying that meeting. What was wrong with me today? An exchange like the one with Dave wasn't uncommon, and to him, to all of them, it really was harmless teasing. A variation on the same conversation I'd had with this entire group for as long as I worked here.

And I had to go and get all emotional and wreck the fun. I could've laughed it off, redirected the jokes to something that didn't attack anyone, and then moved on.

But then Jordan brought *us* into it, and never even batted an eye.

When a knock dragged me out of my own head, I realized I'd been stewing for nearly half an hour. So much for checking anything off my to-do list. My ambivalence surged when I saw Jordan in the doorway.

"We needed you in there." He stepped into the room

and closed the door behind him, the tone very different from when he'd done the same earlier.

And now I felt guilty. Fuck. "You seemed to have a handle on things."

"You're hung up on…?" He crossed his arms and leaned against the wall, as far from me as was possible in the small space.

I'd be rational about this, the way I should've been in the conference room. "*She wasn't complaining ten minutes ago,*" I spat out in a false baritone. *Damn it,* that wasn't what I meant to say. But it was what I was trying not to focus on. "Is there a reason you undermined me in front of half our managers?"

"I was backing you up. It's what we do. Part of the show we put on."

Fuck, he was right. When I was recruited, it was because I wrote fan-fiction where the characters didn't hold back. My talent got me the job, not the fact that my sister was best friends with one boss, and had some sort of complicated relationship with the other.

I'd pushed hard to prove I belonged here—that my advancement through the company was all on me—not only in sharpening my skills, but by never backing down, even when the jokes got too personal or embarrassing or infuriating.

My history here had been my decision.

I sighed. "Do these masks we made for ourselves ever come off?"

Jordan's scowl shifted to sadness. "I'm starting to wonder."

We'd become adults wearing these disguises for the

people around us. Were we even ourselves with each other? Was the quickie with Jordan because he'd been caught up in the moment, or because it was expected of him? Did he invite Liz to join us in L.A. because he wanted to take that next step, or just to smooth things over with me?

God, was over-thinking things, and I couldn't stop. I *knew* Jordan. What we had was genuine.

My phone rang, and I instinctively went to hit *Divert* until I saw Zach's name on the screen. Couldn't ignore the boss-slash-brother-in-law. I hit *Speaker* instead. "Yeah?"

"Your other half in there?" Zach's question was clipped.

Jordan's frown deepened and his slouch vanished. "I am."

"My office, *now*. I don't care what else you're doing." Zach disconnected.

Eep. "Any idea what that's about?" I asked.

"Scott mentioned a crises, but I don't have details." Jordan stepped close enough to kiss me on the cheek—how could such a simple gesture be so bittersweet?—before he moved back to the door. "We'll figure this out. I promise."

"I know." I hoped.

With him gone, I needed to get some work done, regardless of my jumbled thoughts. I'd almost convinced myself to get back to my tasks, when another knock interrupted. My sister entered the room and closed the door behind her.

Apparently it was going to be one of those days.

Rae controlled the company finances, but she was technically an independent contractor, so it was rare to see her in the office for more than a few hours at a time. What were the odds she was here to take her baby sister to lunch and just catch up?

She sat without waiting for an invitation. "I need to talk to you."

"You and everyone else in the fucking building." My retort came out with more of an edge than I intended. I rubbed my face. "Sorry. Long day."

Rae clenched her jaw and exhaled loudly through her nostrils. "It's about to get longer."

SIXTEEN

JORDAN

I didn't have any more of a problem interacting with company executives than I did anyone else. Hell, Zach was basically family. Or I was. Whatever.

But the atmosphere in his office made my skin crawl. Especially the way he closed the door the instant I entered, and the flat way he said, "have a seat," as he gestured to the chair across from his desk.

"What up?" I wouldn't make assumptions. Not that I knew where to start.

"You're familiar with the phrase *no such thing as bad publicity*?" The bite in Zach's words and the fact that he still stood, combined with the molasses thick tension in the air, told me I needed to take this seriously.

Bad luck for me that I was already pissy about how things went down with Chloe. "You mean our unwritten company mission statement?"

"Yeah, well, it has its limits." Zach rested his weight against the desk, next to me, putting only a few feet between us. Without looking, he reached behind himself and grabbed a few sheets of paper from where they lay on his keyboard. He handed them to me. "Assault charges? Are you *fucking* kidding me?"

Jesus. Of course that bullshit arrest hadn't gone away as easily as I wanted. "I didn't do anything."

"Read it."

A glance told me it was a printed webpage, and I resisted the urge to ask who the hell printed a blog post in order to read it. I scanned the article by Stew, skipping the wordy filler and zeroing in on the highlights as I tried to ignore the low-quality images of Stew's bruise-covered face.

Despite legal counsel's attempts to intimidate me...

...Can't keep quiet anymore...

...was assaulted by a member of Rinslet Enterprises senior management...

...won't be silenced, no matter the empty threats.

Wait. What? He was accusing me of beating him up? He had *photos*? How the fuck did he get photos? Was he really lowly enough to pay someone else to hit him, in order to get a headline and make me look back?

I tossed the papers on the desk. "It's not true."

"You know what is true? You were arrested outside our hall at E3, in full view of half the attendees. You were all but hauled off in handcuffs."

"But the charges were dropped. Because *I didn't fucking do anything.*" I was starting to feel like a broken record. The protests sounded childish, as if I was throwing a tantrum, but I didn't have another defense. This was the truth.

"And if we issue a statement saying exactly that, to an internet full of people insisting this time we went too far and someone at Rinslet needs to grow up and be held accountable, how well do you think that goes over?"

Fuck. Fuck. Fuck. *Fuuuuuck.* I sank in my seat. "Not well."

"I'm sorry." Zach finally sat. "I don't have to ask if you see how bad this looks. It doesn't matter that you didn't do it."

Of course it didn't. "Because no one is going to buy my denial while he has a potent headline, complete with photos." Frustration swelled inside. "So I'll issue a generic apology, distance myself from the press for a while, and behave." Everything I normally got paid not to do.

Zach sighed and pinched the bridge of his nose. "Not this time. *Rinslet isn't responsible for...* won't cut it on our side."

"No." My insides twisted as reality threatened.

"You know how hard we fought to keep you here, always. You have to know we don't have another option. The only way this plays out well for the company is if we let you go."

"You're firing me?" I almost choked on the words. "How about instead, you stand by me, because—"

"You didn't do anything. I get it. I'm not saying otherwise. Who do you think they believe, though? The asshole who always pulls obnoxious stunts for the cameras, or the *poor blogger* everyone knows you can't stand, who has photos of a battered face?"

"I thought we were a software company, not a public relations machine." I knew better. I understood this all too well, but I wished I didn't. Not that it mattered if I got it. Trial by public opinion was one of those things that didn't always operate on logic.

Rage spilled in, overtaking self-pity and trying to claw its way out. "Fine. It's not like anyone but you will ever hear this, but I'm going to do it anyway. At the risk of sounding cliché, you can't fire me; I quit. I'll clear out my office."

"You won't." The emotion was gone from Zach's voice. "I'm not cold enough to have Security escort you to your car, but I'll see you out if I have to, to make sure you leave the building when we're done here. Chloe will clean out your desk. Your department will be transitioned under her until we can make other arrangements. Rae is talking to her right now."

"Must be nice to know people on the inside." I was having trouble thinking past the red that clouded my thoughts.

"I didn't want to do things this way."

What-the-fuck-ever. "Must suck for you. No, wait, it really doesn't." I kicked back from my chair and summoned what little restraint I had left to paste on a blank mask before leaving the room. The screaming rage that echoed in my thoughts wouldn't stop, but I refused to let anyone in this building see it.

SEVENTEEN

Chloe

"Call Jordan," I said, for the billionth time. My phone, which sat in its cradle attached to my dashboard, dialed the number again. Like every other time, my call went straight to voicemail. "Hang up," I said, and resisted the desire to push the car to ninety, to get home faster.

When Rae had broken the layoff news, I was floored. Dumbfounded. An entire thesaurus of words tied to disbelief.

I'd argued, but it was like talking to a tablet with a dead battery, for all the good it did me. Rae was sorry. Rae couldn't do anything. This was out of Rae's hands.

You're fucking the CEO. Go give him a blowjob and get my boyfriend his job back.

That didn't go over so great.

I'd texted Jordan as soon as Rae left my office. *I'm sorry. It's not fair. Let's talk. Lunch?*

He didn't answer.

I'd told myself it was no big deal. He was brooding, and he deserved to. I gave him a few hours to process.

I didn't hear from him by lunch, and tried calling.

Concern set in when I still couldn't get a hold of him, or find anyone who knew where he was. It quickly blossomed into almost-suffocating panic, and I took the rest of the day off.

I pulled into the parking garage of our condo complex, and relief trickled in as I parked next to Jordan's car, already in its spot. My heart hammered against my ribs as I sprinted up the stairs to the second floor. Concern and exertion stole my breath, leaving me panting as I stepped into our place.

Jordan's job meant as much to him as mine did to me. I didn't question that. That'd taken it from him today, and I couldn't guess where his mind was at. I'd probably be sobbing in a corner, and growling at him if he came close.

He was more vocal. More likely to take action. Was he doing something rash right now, either with the media or himself? He wouldn't. "Jordan?" I called as I moved through the condo.

No answer. His keys were on the table by the door. "Jordan?" There was a good reason he wasn't replying. He had his headphones on and was lost in a game or a project. Something not-bad.

I didn't find him in the kitchen, our bedroom, or the master bath. My concern spiraled out of control as I approached the back bedroom we used as an office.

When I saw him seated at his computer, relief flooded me. "Jordan?"

His dual monitors displayed multiple browser tabs and windows. The ones I could see were various articles about the assault—some with pictures of Stew, face bruised and swollen, and others with images of Jordan being escorted from the convention center by police.

I joined him and settled a hand on his shoulder.

He jumped under my touch. "Holy shit, you scared me."

"You're one to talk." Irritation swirled inside, tempered by a surge of gratitude that he was all right. "I'm freaking out because I don't know where you are, and you're… I'm so glad you're okay."

"But I'm not. I can't just roll over and take this."

"So you'll polish résumé—or create one—so you've got work when your severance runs out. Sorry. That came out wrong." Money was the furthest thing from my mind right now. Why did I say that?

Because I didn't know what else to do.

Jordan's laugh was bitter. "Severance? Right. That's a pretty huge assumption, considering they didn't offer any."

"Or you stormed out before Zach got to that part." I set an envelope on the desk next to him, and pulled my own seat closer so I could seat nearby. "It's six months, including benefits. Plus they'll make sure you're eligible for unemployment." Six months. After he'd given them his entire adult life. Fucking insulting.

But Jordan got offers weekly to go somewhere else. He'd be in a new office in no time.

He stood and paced to the edge of the room before heading back. "Why bother with a résumé? Who do you think is going to hire me after this?" He gestured at his screens.

"Someone who's more lenient about public image." Which was no one. "Someone who recognizes your talent." Why hadn't I realized how badly Stew's news would rock Jordan's world? "What are you working on?"

"Those images are photoshopped, or something. I'm going to figure out how Stew pulled off filing assault charges for something that didn't happen, and undo the damage." Even when Jordan leaned against the wall, he didn't stop moving. He tapped his toes, drummed his fingers on his leg, and focused on nothing long enough to keep his head still.

The knots tying up my insides tightened. How much longer until I snapped? "You have to be careful." And so did I. I needed him to know I was sympathetic. "This could backfire fast."

"So you're on Zach's side? It's okay to lay me off until things blow over, and then pretend it didn't happen? This isn't only about my job. Do you realize that?"

"I do. I also don't think, even for a second, that you should just drop it. You've got every reason and right to try to fix things. But you have to remember, you're already the bad guy. If you don't tread as though your life depends on caution—if we don't plot every single step to the tiniest detail—this will backfire and make things worse." I approached him and covered his hand with mine, to stop his fingers from wiggling. "But no matter what happens, I'm with you on this. Whatever you need."

He relaxed under my touch and his shoulders slumped. "I almost asked you to quite, too. As a show of solidarity."

Acid rose in my throat, and I couldn't summon an answer. Especially not an, *I would, if you did.*

"I wouldn't do that. I won't make you choose." He rested a hand on the back of her neck. "And thank you."

"Wednesday night, when we were with Liz and you left to talk to Stew, what happened?" I didn't want to ask, and shatter this near-calm, but I needed to.

"Do you think I did it?" His jaw barely moved when he spoke.

I didn't hesitate. "No. Not even for a second. But other people will ask me, and I need details beyond *he didn't do it.*

"I guess." Jordan sighed an scrubbed his face. "But nothing happened. I told him to back off of Liz, and to find someone else to gossip about."

"And boxed him into a corner to remind him of the height difference?"

"Maybe." Jordan kissed me on the nose, the chin, and the lips. "Thank you for standing by me."

I couldn't hide my stress with my smile. If only the road ahead were as simple as this conversation. It wasn't a matter of having proof that Jordan didn't do it. We had to convince the world to listen, now that they'd already formed an opinion.

It was going to be a long weekend.

EIGHTEEN

Liz

I hesitated on Mercy and Ian's porch, knuckles halfway to the door. For half of my teenage years, the Park City property was my home, and now it felt wrong to walk through the door without being invited.

But I wasn't in the mood for Mercy to remind me I didn't need to knock or ring the bell—that this was still my place, too. I stepped into foyer. "Hello?"

"Kitchen."

I followed Mercy's call and found her seated at the desk built into a nook by the fridge, scribbling in a notebook. She looked up. "Had an idea. Didn't want to forget it. How was L.A.?" She stood and gave me a quick hug.

Her question triggered an avalanche of amazing memories. I so desperately wanted to tell her about my adventure. "It was incredible. Where's Ian?"

"Study. Client call. Speaking of—whatever you did for KM, Jonathan won't stop singing your praises."

I didn't do anything. "Thanks?"

Mercy grabbed two bottles of sparking water from the fridge and handed me one. "Fine. Don't tell me. Just keep doing it. So… *amazing* week? What happened to *L.A. is all smog and traffic?*"

"It still is"—I fiddled with the cap on my drink, unable to hide my smile at thoughts of Chloe and Jordan—"but the company made up for it."

"You're not talking about Jonathan." Mercy leaned in. "Spill."

Where to start? "There was a woman in the bar, and something about her… I can't describe it. I sucked up my courage and approached her. Turned out she and her boyfriend were in the market to explore, too."

Mercy grinned. She'd traveled the world when she was younger, and had all sorts of stories to tell about the people she'd met, hooked up with, and loved. "Liking it so far. Plus, there's a distinct advantage to a couple."

"Oh?" I could think of more than a few things I'd enjoyed about this particular pair, but they probably weren't generic enough details to be on Mercy's list.

"They're easy to walk away from. Everyone knows they're separate from you, so there's no fussing about if it means more."

Oh. Right. "Totally. Took all the doubt of it for me."

Ian rested a hand on my back, startling me, and took a swig of my drink. "Took the doubt out of what?"

"Client management." I didn't have a problem sharing explicit stories with Mercy, but my brother didn't need to know the details of my sex life. "Where are we going?" The three of us set aside Friday nights to hang out. Every week, one of us picked a new place to try, and tonight was Ian's choice.

He raised his eyebrows, probably at my less-than-subtle change of subject, and walked up behind Mercy. He wrapped his arms around her waist, and she leaned into him to steal a kiss. They were so right together. Two halves of a whole. That must be nice.

"There's a new Indian place on Main," he said. Supposed to be authentic."

"Sure is." Mercy shook her head and pulled his arms tighter. "But I'm in."

"Sounds good to me," I said.

Mercy tilted her head to the side, studying me. "Are you all right?"

Where did that come from? "I'm fine." Had my tone shifted? My expression? I didn't *feel* off. The faint gnawing in my gut was because I'd skipped lunch to catch up on work. The nagging ache in my chest was most likely the same thing. "Who's driving?" Dumb question. It was always Ian.

Mercy's phone rang, and she had it to her ear before the first chime finished. "This is Mercy. May I help you?" Professionalism replaced all hints of teasing in her tone, and she stood straighter.

"How'd the meeting with Rinslet go?" Ian asked.

I would've rolled my eyes, if his question hadn't happily whisked me back to thoughts of stunning blue eyes and matching hair. "You both know how this works. I'll confiscate your phones if I have to." When we started getting together like this, it took me about two dinners to realize if I let the two of them talk business, they'd go all night. The rule was, once the evening started, no one took calls or brought up anything work related.

Normally it was just something we teased each other about, but tonight I wanted the excuse to not give Ian a glimpse into exactly what I thought about *Rinslet*.

All right, grump, we won't talk work." Ian's sigh was exaggerated. "Did Kyle give you an update on when you'll have control of your accounts again?"

I'd almost rather talk about work. "Getting there. I closed all the old accounts—they can stay frozen as long as the SEC wants—and shifted funds from investments George didn't know about."

"All set." Mercy's announcement interrupted our stilted conversation.

Had it always been this weird talking to Ian?

The three of us climbed into his SUV, and we were on our way. I settled in the back seat as Ian and Mercy chatted up front. Apparently, there was a Mystery Science Theater 3000 marathon running, and they were one-upping each other with their favorite one-liners. I didn't have anything to add, so I listened to them chat and stared at the scenery outside, rather than watch the constant smiles, soft touches, and frequent innuendo.

I didn't realize they had stopped talking, until I turned away from the window to find Mercy staring at me. "Are you sure you're all right?" she asked.

"I might be a little jetlagged. Catching up on the time zone difference. Something." The flight had only been two hours, and the time difference was only one, but I couldn't find a better explanation for the ennui settling inside.

As we reached the restaurant, ordered, ate, all of it, whatever had settled inside me refused to leave. Mercy and Ian tried several times to draw me into the conversation, and eventually gave up.

What was wrong with me? I loved our Friday nights and spending time with my two favorite people. But I wasn't feeling it tonight. When we got back to their house, I made my apologies, hopped into my car, and headed down into the valley.

The green of the canyon, so vibrant it almost glowed and mirrored the stars, was a pleasant distraction. I was back at my condo too soon. Loneliness sank into a pit I hadn't felt in months, when I unlocked the front door and stepped into a dark room.

I didn't turn on any lights. The city shone through the balcony windows, casting the room in long, sad shadows. I opened the door of the fridge and blinked at the harsh light. There was half a bottle of red wine, calling my name.

I shut the door without grabbing it. Fogging my mind might be a pleasant distraction tonight, or it might trigger memories I didn't dare lose myself in.

I padded into my bedroom. As I grabbed the remote, a single business card, glaring in its bright whiteness, taunted me. Jordan's handwriting scrawled across the back, with two names and numbers.

There's a distinct advantage to a couple. Mercy's words mocked me. *Everyone recognizes it's not going to last.*

I flicked the card toward the trashcan and turned my attention to the TV.

Nothing grabbed my attention, until the familiar strains of *All I Ask of You* greeted me. *Phantom of the Opera* would do nicely. A twisted love story to distract me, and by morning, my funk would pass.

FEELING BETTER THIS MORNING?

Brunch at Silver Fork?

It's after 10. You've been awake for hours. Just tell me you're all right.

I scrolled through the series of messages from Mercy. I'd stepped out for some air and coffee, and left my phone behind. I should call Mercy back. Join her and Ian for brunch, to make up for being a wet blanket last night. But I wasn't in the mood to live on the fringes of their happiness.

The bitter thought made me frown.

I replied to Mercy. *I'm good. I have plans. We'll do brunch another day.*

Oh. Okay. Mercy's disappointment actually carried through the text.

I needed a distraction so my brain could set itself straight in the background. My gaze landed on a white rectangle on the floor, next to the trash can. I grabbed the card to throw it out, but paused, turning it over and over, before tucking it into my pocket.

Jordan's offer was out of politeness, nothing more.

But I wasn't ready to surrender this tie to those memories.

I wandered into the kitchen, scanning the headlines on my phone. Because I'd spent so much time looking up E3 news in L.A., everything I saw was about hot and new game trends.

Jordan Iverson Arrested for Assault

I stalled, feet frozen in place, at the reminder that his trip didn't end nearly as well as mine.

He'd seemed fine yesterday, but this article was new. I clicked through to a story about accusations, photos, dropped charges, and how his former employer, Rinslet, released a statement saying they didn't condone his actions.

Former employer.

No. Jordan didn't do those things.

Was it possible that the people I met were monsters in disguise? Sure. George had fooled me.

I didn't believe it with Jordan and Chloe, though. Not them.

I fished out his card and dialed before I could talk myself out of it. His voicemail picked up without a single ring, and my insides did a topsy-turvy thing at the sound of his voice, as well as at not being able to reach him.

Mercy's comment about couples flooded in again. Careless, not meant to harm, but distracting. The words didn't care the same weight as earlier, and I pored over them to figure out why. Sure, fooling around with Jordan and Chloe had been—and would be—fun, but what led up to it was too. Like Jordan said yesterday.

Besides, when I'd told them about George, about my mistakes, they didn't judge me. That was a first. They'd been supportive, and they probably needed the same kind of friend right now. I dialed Chloe.

"Hello?" The hesitant, familiar voice pushed away the cobwebs inside.

"Chloe? It's Liz. Thompson. We met at E3."

"Yeah. Hey." Chloe's tone shifted to cheerful, but tension ran through it. "Not to be rude—I'm glad you called—but how did get my number?"

"Jordan gave it to me when we met yesterday."

"When you—? Right. Of course." The lilt vanished from Chloe's words. "What can I do for you?"

My resolve evaporated. "I… Uh…" This was stupid. What was I thinking? Too late to back out now. "I saw the headlines this morning, and wanted to make sure Jordan and you were okay. If there's anything I can do to help, I'm here." That wasn't so hard.

Chloe sighed. "I don't know what to do. Jordan didn't do this. It'll sound stupid, but we're trying to figure out how to dig under what this Stew guy did and get on top of it."

"I actually can help with that." It was nice, being able to make the offer. "That is, if you need me to. I have advertising experience, and if I'm reading this in the news, so is everyone else. I can help you spin this. You might already have this information, but—"

"We could use the help. Whenever you're free." Chloe rattled off an address a few miles from my condo, and I agreed to be there in a couple of hours. As I hung up, adrenaline spilled through me at the thought of seeing them again. The circumstances weren't ideal, but at least this way my reasons for visiting were friendly, and nothing more.

NINETEEN

Who was Chloe talking to? Someone she trusted with information about our situation, but who didn't have our address? That didn't make sense.

She finished the call and focused on me. "Did you leave something out of our conversation yesterday?"

Leading question. Great. That was what I was in the mood for. "Odds are high. Wanna give me a hint?"

"That was Liz. Said you met with her?"

Fuck, that was a lifetime ago. "I did. Took the appointment for Scott, as he was helping figure out how to fire me, because her company wants access to our—your—licensed image options." My idea. My success.

Not anymore.

"I meant to tell you that I gave her our numbers. Guess I've got a lot on my mind," I said.

Circles hung under Chloe's eyes, and her frown hadn't faded since yesterday. "I know. But she says she can help, so it's a good thing you did."

"How?" I was too tired to manage more.

"She's got experience with **PR**, and access to resources you—we—just lost. She can help…"

"Redeem me?" I didn't want to pick a fight, but I was a lot bitter that I had to prove I wasn't evil, because some asshole didn't like me. "Yeah, okay. Sounds good." It would be nice to have another support structure who didn't think *I* was the jerk with the agenda.

Chloe and I had been spinning our wheels since last night. It didn't matter how I looked at the images of Stew's bruises, they looked real. So we'd gone searching for any whispers about what actually happened. Who were the witnesses? Who took the police report?

It didn't matter how many trails we chased, they all led back to a giant pile of shit with a *Bite Me* sign on it. The Reddit thread on my screen was a great example.

Did you see that cocky, talentless hack from Rinslet finally got his?

Right? Who puts a dick like that in charge of anything, let alone an entire art department?

Not surprised the fucker snapped. He's wound up tighter than a broken spring.

That last one didn't even make sense.

It had been hours since I obliterated the desire to respond. It faded about the time the eyestrain set in— too much rolling. I couldn't bring myself to look way from the trash-talk, though. There had to be someone here who would let something slip about what really happened.

And then there's that bitch he says he's fucking.

My rage soared.

Bull-dyke alert. Doesn't know what a real dick is.
She needs a good, hard—
Something *cracked* and pain rocketed through my knuckles. I looked down to see ink running down my fingers, from the pen I'd just snapped. I closed the tab before Chloe could see the thread in question.

"You all right?" she asked. "I mean, other than..." She gestured broadly.

"I need to wash this off." I cut a straight line for the bathroom before she could ask me.

This was going to devour our sanity. I sure as hell hoped Liz had a better idea. If Chloe stumbled on a post like that one, the assault charges against me would be legit next time.

I cranked on the cold water, gripped the edge of the sink, and stared at my reflection in the mirror. What were we doing? Nothing helpful, that was for sure.

"Hey." Chloe's soft voice tunneled through my rage and frustration. "You're staining the porcelain."

I smiled in spite of myself. The sink was already a rainbow of colors from the countless times one or the other of us dyed our hair. I shoved my hands under the icy spray and let it shock away the cloud in my brain.

When the globs of ink were gone, and nothing but splotches stained my skin, Chloe handed me a towel. "Maybe Liz will have something good," she said.

I ignored the towel in favor of pulling her to me. Her palms where fire against mine. "Maybe we're wasting our time." I didn't want to let hopelessness bleed in, but I couldn't help it.

Chloe molded against me and settled her cheek on my chest. "Since when are you a quitter?"

Since I didn't want her finding anything like what I'd just read. Shit-talk was a hazard of our job, but over the years we'd become masters at avoiding it. Last night and this morning, we'd dived in headfirst. I rested my forehead on top of her head. "I'm not giving up. This is my life. You're the only thing that means more to me."

"What if we apologize to Stew?" Her question was quiet.

I didn't want to disrupt this fragile calm. "For what? Telling him no?"

"If he understood the fallout he caused…"

"This isn't the kind of thing someone does by accident."

"I could try talking to him anyway," Chloe said.

"And if it backfires?" I could see the headline now. *Rinslet Tries to Buy my Silence with Bullshit and Tits.*

Nah. Stew was too smart to use a headline that would piss off the bots. He'd be thinking it, though.

Chloe leaned more weight against me. "Good point. What next?"

"LinkedIn?"

She pulled back to look me in the eye, her brows furrowed in question. "You're going to do better reaching out directly to contacts."

"I'm not talking about my job prospects." Which were shot to hell. "Maybe Stew has a connection who's a really good makeup artist." I was reaching, but oh well.

Chloe tugged me back to the office. "Might as well give it a shot."

She was putting everything aside for me. Why were we fighting earlier in the week? It was so insignificant now.

The next couple of hours passed in a haze of more-of-the-same, until I was certain we were pantomiming insanity—doing the same thing over and over and hoping for a different result.

When Chloe stood and stretched, I was obvious about watching her. "That's my kind of distraction," I said.

She smiled—the best sight I'd seen all day. "Happy to be here for you."

Someone knocked at the same time her phone rang. She grabbed the device. "It's Rae."

"I'll get the door." I headed in that direction, and Chloe wandered into the kitchen. I was happier than I expected to see Liz, and I let her in.

She met my gaze with sympathy. "How are you holding up?"

"It sucks, but whatever doesn't kill you…" Gives you a series of unhealthy coping mechanisms. "Chloe said you might be able to help."

"I hope. You've already written your apology, correct? When are you posting it, or did it already go up?"

Maybe I wasn't happy to see her. "Why would I apologize? I didn't do anything."

"I know." There was no hesitation or doubt in her reply. "You don't apologize for being responsible; you say you're sorry something so horrific happened. Chloe told me you were working on something, so I assumed..."

"We're trying to find the truth." I nodded toward the office. "I'll show you."

Liz joined me, and I pulled out a chair and scooted it next to mine. "We're looking at Stew's connections; who he might have told; if there are any rumors about fist-fights..."

Liz stared at me, lips pursed and expression otherwise blank.

"What?" I tried to keep my question kind.

"You can't start there. That happens later."

"Why?" I shouldn't snap at her, but I needed an outlet and she'd dismissed a night's worth of work with a few short words. "You're not in PR. Advertising isn't the same. While the story is trending, people care. As it fades from their minds—which only takes a day or two —the last thing they heard is what they remember." Which meant I was out of time to tell prove I didn't do this.

"Exactly. And no, I'm not in PR. I work for an advertising company that specializes in brand recognition."

She thought she was giving me an answer, and I felt like we were having two separate conversations. "I'm not a brand."

"You are. Every time I heard Rinslet's name at E3, everything I found about you online, it was accompanied by a comment about how they hold themselves in the public eye. Some people admire it, and some people hate it, but regardless, you and Chloe are at the center of it. When you start job-hunting, are you going to sell yourself based on your skills or your reputation?"

My skills, of course.

But I knew better. "So what am I supposed to do? I won't imply I was involved. Any statement I issue is either going to sound like *the man doth protesteth too much* or include an unspoken admission of guilt. Or both."

"Hey, Liz." Chloe's greeting interrupted the conversation and my mounting frustration. I let the sight of her calm me enough to have this irritating-as-fuck conversation. Chloe turned her attention to me. "Rae's inviting us to dinner Wednesday night."

After the conversation I had with Zach yesterday? *Jesus*, family dinners were about to get tense. I didn't want to say *yes*, but I refused to keep Chloe from her family and friends. "What just her?" Probably not.

Chloe winced.

It was going to take time for me to forgive Zach for the decision, but I understood it. Mostly. This wasn't his fault. As long as I didn't think about the Rinslet side of things too much… "Sure. Wednesday is great."

"Thank you." She kissed me on the cheek, then turned her attention back to her phone and wandered from the room.

I watched her until she was out of sight.

"You love her a lot, don't you?" Liz's question was soft.

"More than anything. I wish——" Sex with Liz was one thing. Exposing the cracks in my relationship with Chloe, that felt scandalous.

Liz looked concerned and curious rather than judgmental, though. "Wish what?"

"That I could make her smile for more than a couple of minutes at a time."

"When was the last time you did something random and out of the blue for her, just because?"

"You mean besides lose my job and add another layer of stress to our lives?" I meant the words to be a lighthearted joke, but the bitterness in my voice disturbed me.

"I mean besides that."

Friday morning in her office? The memory was enough to flood my skin and tug at my cock, and wasn't the kind of thing I was willing to share.

"If you're hesitating that long for an answer, it's not a good sign." Liz interrupted my thoughts. "Little gestures go a long way."

Did little gestures include watching next time Chloe kissed Liz? Probably not. I didn't know if I was turned on, or just relieved to have something less strenuous to think about. "Like what?"

"Flowers. Candy. That kind of stuff."

"Chloe's not really a buy-me-flowers kind of girl."

Liz raised her brows. "It's one example. What does she like?"

Easy. "Whips. Leather. Alien lasers."

Liz blushed and turned her gaze to her hands. "Leather's an option if you do it right." She cleared her throat and jerked her head up. "Anyway. She writes."

"Sexy, intricate, vivid stores that come to life on their own."

"Do her characters ever fall in love?"

"All the time."

Liz leaned closer. "What kinds of things do they do for each other?"

"Buy whips. Leather. Alien lasers..." My flippant retort faded as her question sank in. "Oh." There was always something small in Chloe's stories, whether she was writing for work or fan fiction. Sometimes it was poetry. Frequently it was a sketch. It was almost always a creative expression of love.

"Lightbulb moment? Liz asked.

"You could say that." I needed to process, and I wanted to keep the thoughts to myself. I frequently drew Chloe into my art. How did I never manage to vocalize she did the same with me? With us? "You're not here to offer relationship counseling. Though, thank you. Tell me more about this Jordan-as-a-brand concept."

"I can show you."

"Sure." I rolled my chair back so she could slide up in front of the computer. I watched in fascination as her fingers flew over the keyboard.

She'd type a few sentences, delete half of one, copy, paste, and tweak another, then move on.

I tried to keep up, but I surrendered when I stopped being able to tell where one thought ended and the next started. She was writing some kind of letter, which appeared to be from me, but it was too fractured to make sense.

"These are all jumping off points for you to build from," Liz said. "The goal is to say you're sorry Stew was assaulted. That you hate seeing something so horrific happen to anyone, and that you hope whomever is responsible is brought to justice. You never get close to yourself or any involvement or accusations. You keep away from your animosity about him or that he's making this all up."

"But I still have to imply that he's making things up."

"Yes. You have to lean into it without ever touching it."

Silence settled between us as she went back to work. Should I be helping? I could go and check on Chloe. I liked the view here, but it felt creepy to stare.

A faint tune drew my attention. Liz was humming. She carried a tune well, and after listening for a moment, I recognized the song from *Phantom of the Opera*.

The tune tugged at my memories, pulling strands of the past to the surface. One of the first times Chloe and I traveled for work, *together*, we managed to get tickets on Broadway to see *Phantom*. It was the first night we'd slept together.

Because, of course, the entire office was fucking each other, and we were sweet and chaste and monogamous. And terrified.

I missed those days. Maybe not the being afraid of sex, but the rest of it. Life wasn't so demanding, and we had miles and galaxies of creative freedom.

While Liz hummed, I sketched on a nearby pad, and mouthed the lyrics, my voice growing in volume the longer she went on. I wasn't sure when, but at some point she started singing as well, offering Christine's parts as I sang Raoul's. She hit every note. I'd never heard anyone off-stage do that.

I heard Chloe approaching, but I was enjoying the music too much to break the tune. Liz turned to me, flushed and smiling as we hit the crescendo, and let the music fade off.

That was fun.

A steady clap broke the silence, and I tore my gaze from Liz's face. Chloe stood in the doorway, watching us with an unreadable expression.

No, that wasn't quite right. She was looking past me, and was… tired? Wounded?

Whatever it was, I wanted to hold her and kiss it away until she was better.

Better felt so far away.

TWENTY

Chloe

I was conflicted.

Jordan singing was one of my favorite sounds and the duet with Liz… Her voice was the perfect complement to his.

But the way they were looking at each other when I walked into the room—the nearly tangible tension stretching between them—made me question so much.

The way they both stared at me now, curiosity etched on their faces, helped me push my doubts aside. "You're amazing together," I said. "Singing. I mean," I added quickly. "Sorry for taking so long." Rae was a nervous talker, and she was extra worried right now about what happened with Jordan.

"Welcome back. We were just working." Liz nodded at the screen.

That was a funny word for it.

I hated my own creeping envy. "On what?"

"Ms. Thompson thinks I'm a brand. That you and I

both are. So she's going to make me all sparkly and clean." The upward quirk of Jordan's lips counterbalanced his words.

"Not quite what I said. I'm making him say he's sorry." Liz explained the theory behind it all.

Her plan made sense, and was obvious once she laid it all out. Why didn't I think of that? My only excuse was it had been a long twenty-four hours.

Liz pointed at the document on screen. "And I'm glad you're back because I need your eyes on this. Both of you, of course, because this is supposed to sound like it's from Jordan, but mostly Chloe, to make sure it's got that *oomph*."

Something I could do. Finally.

We made sweeping changes at first, taking out entire sentences, then moved on to swapping individual words and tightening punctuation. It had to look clean and professional, but still sound sincere, while leaving as little room for misinterpretation as possible.

People would take this the wrong way no matter what it said, but we needed to narrow that margin where we could.

By the time we were all satisfied, the sun had dropped low enough in the sky that it looked like it was resting on the western mountains.

I forced my gaze from the computer, and faced Jordan and Liz, blinking until I could focus on them again. "Now he sends it?"

"Now we let it sit for half an hour, give it another glance, and then he sends it." Liz rolled her head, stretching her neck.

I liked the simplicity of the next step, but at the same time it felt too easy. "Are we doing the right thing?"

"I can't guarantee it; I can only guess what the internet is going to say. Keep in mind though, once it's out there you can't take it back. There's no backpedaling on this, because retracting anything here is going to look worse than not saying it at all." Liz looked at Jordan. "That's your one saving grace right now. You may have stayed silent, but that means you haven't said the wrong thing. If you're not comfortable with the idea, don't pull the trigger. Is this what you want to do?"

Jordan sought out my hand and squeezed. The way he searched my face, he might be expecting to see the answers to the mysteries of the universe. The best I could offer was a reassuring look, regardless of how heavily this weighed on me. We were fucking creatives. How was a single letter so important? "Whatever happens next, I'm here," I said.

"I know." Jordan puffed out his cheeks with a noisy exhale. "I'm sure. Half an hour, we'll give it another look, and I'll send it wherever Liz tells me to."

"That's that, then." Liz slouched in her seat. "And with any luck, it should go better than trying to be spies."

What? "Who was being spies?" I asked.

"The two of you. Secret agents, digging up any dirt you could find on this Stew guy?"

I laughed at the comparison, as much as out of relief that was over as anything. "I guess we were. Agents double-oh-six and nine. That's us."

"Nice. Working on top secret enemy penetration?" Liz rolled her eyes, but amusement sparkled in them.

"Nah. Enemy penetration sounds too James Bond," Jordan said. "I prefer the friendly variation."

Liz raised her brows. "Doesn't that make you a double agent?"

"I'm digging for a pun about double penetration, but it's not coming to me." Things almost felt normal if we were making dick and sex jokes.

"If you actually had the double penetration, there would be plenty coming to you." Jordan frowned. "Wait. That didn't sound right."

I grinned. "Sounds perfect to me."

"Okay, but seriously." Liz held up her index finger, as if to pause the conversation. "Huge guilty pleasure for me."

Jordan didn't hesitate. "Double penetration?"

Not with the three of us, not without a strap-on. The moment the thought popped into my head, memories of the other morning rushed back, flooding my skin with delicious heat.

"Maybe. But no. But maybe. I've never tried, but I'm open to it." Liz bit her bottom lip and ducked her head. "Seriously-seriously, though—James Bond movies. Huge guilty pleasure."

It took me a moment to register what she'd said, because fantasies of Liz and penetration were short-circuiting my brain. I wouldn't get anything else done tonight, including conversation, if I dwelled there, so I focused on the term *guilty pleasure* instead. I'd never liked that concept. "Why?"

Liz looked at me. "They're action packed and a little over the top."

"A little?" Jordan asked.

I nudged his arm playfully. "Not why do you like them. Why do you feel guilty about it?"

"They're action packed and a little"—Liz paused—"a lot over the top. They're sexist. They're illogical... Do you want me to go on?"

Jordan shook his head. "Guilt is for things that cause others pain. Like this bullshit Stew pulled. If you like the movies, like the movies. You can recognize their flaws, but own your enjoyment, don't qualify it."

I couldn't have said it better.

"All right. No qualifiers. I love James Bond movies." Liz rolled away from Jordan's computer and gestured for me to slide into her spot. "One last glance, and then Jordan publishes this to his website and shares links on every account he owns. Chloe, you back him up. Nothing extravagant. Sharing the links with a comment that says you support him and agree with everything he has to say."

"Why does she get off easy?" Jordan asked.

Liz twisted her mouth in amusement. "Fresh batteries in the vibrator? I doubt this is easy for either of you."

She had that right.

We followed her instructions, and with each new site Jordan and I published to, the knot in my gut tightened a little more. How long until my insides resembled a pretzel?

I was coiled too tight to think as I shared on my last social media account. "Done."

"Good." Liz grabbed our phones from where they sat on our desks, and hot-keyed our computers into sleep mode.

I was impressed with the quick click-work, but confused. "What are you doing?" Having my computer off and my phone out of reach amplified my buzzing tension.

"We're walking away. Both of you. Me too." Liz slapped Jordan's hand when he reached for the mouse, then moved out of reach when I lunged for my phone. "Turn them off." She handed the devices back. "Because if you spend all night obsessively refreshing for responses, you'll drive yourselves insane, and one of you will break and reply before the sun rises tomorrow. Like I said, you can't undo this now. It's out there, and it's the best solution we could come up with. If we were wrong, you can hate me, but I wouldn't have done it if I thought it might fail."

Cutting myself off from the online world this way felt like severing a limb.

Okay, so I was exaggerating a little bit—I was offline half the time when I flew—but this was no-computer as well. Liz's logic made sense, though, so I 'd give it a try. "What do we do instead?" I asked.

"Order pizza and watch James Bond." Jordan sounded as if it was the only logical conclusion.

Smart man. I moved to his lap and draped my arms around his neck. "I love the way you think. Liz has to order, though, since she cut us off from the rest of the world."

"That's fair." Liz pulled out her phone. "What are we having?"

A few hours later, half-finished pizza stuffed in a box in the fridge, we'd made their way through *From Russia with Love* and were watching *Skyfall*. There was no reason to watch them in order, so instead we picked from whatever was we had access to stream.

I sat with my back and weight rested against Jordan's shoulder and chest. At some point during the first movie, I'd moved my feet to rest on Liz's lap.

On screen, Bond swam through the dark waters, while the baddies moved about on the boat. Séverine disrobed and stepped into the shower. Moments later, Bond joined her.

"See? That's what I'm talking about when I say guilty pleasure." Liz pointed at the screen. "I know this is going to happen in the movie and the kind of message it sends—societal impact and all that—but I like the films anyway."

She had a good point, but I stood by what I'd said about not feeling guilty for liking something. Especially if Liz recognized that it was problematic. "You're over-thinking it."

"It doesn't take much thought." Liz displaced my feet when she turned to me. *"Mr. Bond, I was sent to kill you."* Her voice shifted an octave, to something smooth and seductive. *"But please, I'd prefer you assume we'll have sex first."*

Jordan squeezed my arm, kissed the back of my

neck, and then shifted me aside enough to stand. He extended his hand to Liz and pulled her to her feet. "But my dear"—he adopted a flawless English accent—"*no* means *yes*."

"Oh, my." Liz's words were exaggerated. She swooned, spun, and fell back into his arms.

I laughed at the antics despite the nagging shards of jealousy.

No. I wouldn't get sucked into something negative. Seeing Liz and Jordan like this was fun, and I wanted more of it. When him and her. With her and me. With all three of us.

The words felt good rolling through my head, rather than like some attempt to delude myself.

Liz straightened and whirled to face Jordan. "No, Mr. Bond, as in, *no* means *no*." She fluttered one hand near her chest and rested the other on his arm. There was that tangible tension between them again, like when they were singing. They fell into this so easily.

It was fucking alluring, and I wanted to be part of it rather than sulking over it. I stood and brought my face close to Jordan's, licking my lips. "Perhaps they should issue you a dictionary to go with your secret-spy training."

Jordan seemed to consider my words. "Or perhaps" —his accent was still in place—"you need a better offer." He looked at Liz, and tugged me closer. "Is my counterpart more to your liking?"

"I'm not sure." The way Liz studied me sent heat rushing over my skin. "I hesitate not because I want to say *no*, but because I'd like to say *yes*."

Me too. "You have to choose."

"Why?" Liz asked.

I stalled, not knowing why I said it. If I talked fast, I could take it back. "I suppose if agents double-oh-six and nine worked together, maybe they could seduce the assassin."

"How does that work?" Liz looked intrigued.

"Our agents have their target." The story nudged its way into my mind, and the words spilled out, fueled by inspiration. "And they realize she's watching them, as well. Counter intelligence and all that. Ms. Spy is supposed to distract the villainess, while Mr. Spy sneaks into her room and secures the top-secret documents."

Liz watched me, her blush growing but her gaze unwavering. "Distract me how."

Should I keep going? The lighthearted mood and Liz's attention pushed aside my hesitation. "Ms. Spy is going to put on a show. I move in front of the window, darkness outside and enough light inside to make me an easy study."

"I'm watching." Huskiness melted into Liz's fake spy voice.

"You're wondering where my partner went, but stop caring so much when I strip off my shirt. I try not to think about the details of my task." Should I do this? The two sets of eyes watching me, movie all but forgotten in the background, told me *yes*. Anticipation tingled inside. My nipples strained against my bra, and desire flowed through my gut with anticipation, humming between my legs as my brain leaped ahead several steps. I pulled off my shirt and tossed it onto the nearby chair.

"I know I'm the distraction, but I can't ignore the arousal at the thought of you watching my every move." This was fun. And a rush. And even better with Liz here than it would be with just Jordan and me. He stared back at me with open lust.

Liz was harder to read, but the way she trailed her finger along her neck and to the edge of her ear was enough to urge me on.

I pushed my jeans to the ground. "I'm disrobing, a piece at a time. I need to keep your attention captive long enough for my partner to get in and out, but now that I've started, I'm not sure I have the patience to take things slowly."

"Fuck." Jordan stood behind Liz. He dropped his hand below his waist and shoved balled fists into his pockets.

If this went like it had in the past, I'd need to carry most of the story. That was fine with me. "You like what you see." I held Liz's gaze. "Curiosity and desire fill you, as I remove the last bits of my clothing."

I stripped off my bra and panties and tossed both aside. Standing naked in front of a still fully clothed Liz and Jordan amplified my arousal. If I dipped my fingers between my legs, I wouldn't be able to stop until I got off, and my story wasn't done, so the intimate self-love would have to wait.

"I lower myself to the bed and run my hands over my torso, cupping my tits and pinching my nipples. You can't pull your gaze away and mirror my gestures." I sat on the couch and mimicked my words with gestures.

When Liz groped herself through her T-shirt, playing with her breasts, I let out a breath I didn't realize I was holding. Her lips parted with a soft sigh. *So captivating.*

"You get wetter the longer you watch." I kept my hands above my waist, despite the pleading from lower for attention. "And you start to rub yourself. Stroking through your jeans at first, and then gliding your hand inside your pants and rubbing your clit through your panties."

Liz dipped her fingers down, and her moan mixed with mine as she rubbed more intently.

"Our spy plan is working." I couldn't hold back any longer. I leaned my weight into the cushions behind me and spread my legs. The hungry gazes focused on me almost made me come before I touched myself. I stroked my bare skin, then dipped a finger inside. "You don't hear Mr. Spy enter your room. The distraction worked too well, though. He's enthralled by the sight of you touching yourself. Enough that he forgets his primary goal."

Liz jumped when Jordan slid behind, then she relaxed against him. He undid her jeans and covered her hand with his. I couldn't see it, but I swore I felt his cock digging into Liz's ass. The jealousy that had surged earlier was absent. This wasn't something to envy; I wanted to get off to the sight.

I just had to find my voice long enough to finish the story. "You're enthralled with watching me. With Mr.

Spy's heat against your back, his hand forcing you to pleasure yourself. You can tell from the way I'm moving that I'm close."

And I was. I wanted to finger myself until I screamed, but we weren't to that part of the tale. I edged back. "When Mr. Spy bends you over, forcing your gaze from the rifle scope you're watching through, you don't protest."

Jordan pulled a condom from his back pocket. I'd have to ask later why he had it on him, since the two of us moved past protection long ago. No. I knew why, and the realization that he was hoping for this as much as I was added to my excitement.

When he placed a palm on Liz's back and pushed, Liz took a few steps before bending forward. The movement brought her close enough to rest her hands on either side of my head. Liz dipped nearer, until I felt her breath. "Stop talking, and enjoy your own story," Liz said. She brushed her lips over mine, lightly the first time. Liz jerked forward when Jordan drove inside her. She groaned and kissed me harder.

The hunger compelled me to rub faster, and I hedged toward climax.

Liz broke our kiss with a cry when Jordan increased his pace. I didn't dare look away from the captivating image of Liz bent over me, Jordan just visible from behind, as I stroked myself.

I lost track of the world when I came, hovering somewhere between the fantasy and the vivid reality it led to. My head swam with the sensation of my fingers sliding against my skin. With the scents of Liz's perfume and Jordan's aftershave. With the intoxicating sounds of them nearing their own peaks.

I pushed myself beyond pleasure until I couldn't take anymore, and my body jerked away from my touch. The familiar and delicious sound of Jordan getting off mingled with Liz's whimpers, wrapping me in an extra layer of yummy as I floated down from climax.

When the cries in the room faded, I met Liz's gaze again, and she gave a light laugh as she collapsed on the couch. Jordan dropped on my other side, nuzzling my hair and muttering, "I'll get you water as soon as I can stand."

As far as I was concerned, this moment was perfect. So without flaw that I refused to admit it couldn't last. I'd burn this fling into my thoughts forever, so Jordan and I could reference it again and again.

That would be enough. It would have to be, because Liz wasn't ours.

TWENTY-ONE

Do you have to go home?

Chloe's question from the night before echoed in my head, as I extracted myself from the sleeping couple and their bed.

It was barely six. No sane person was up this early on a Sunday. I'd never considered myself completely sane, though. This entire scenario was a perfect example of my loose grasp on the rational. Screwing around with a two people who I felt a stronger connection to each time we met. A couple who were obviously completely head-over-heels for each other.

I wasn't cut out for no-strings any more than I was destined to find a nice guy to settled down in suburbia with. Now seemed like the right time to cut my losses and be celibate.

I looked at the sleeping couple one more time, and turned to the clothes I'd draped over the back of a chair. I wasn't wearing those panties home, and the my jeans were tantalizingly rough against my bare skin when I pulled them on.

It would be rude to leave without saying goodbye, but it would be more awkward to stick around, and I needed to get home.

My thoughts were a jumble as I padded into the living room. It wasn't as though I was falling in love with Chloe or Jordan. *Love.* Where did that even come from? I barely knew them. They were already attached. If I let things get physical with them again, it would be too hard to sever ties. I already hated the thought.

But if I could start convincing myself now that it was the best thing to do, that things like last night couldn't happen again, I could cement the resolve in my mind before it was too late.

I was grateful their balcony door slid open with little noise, and I stepped outside, trapping myself, rather than taking the front door. Chloe and Jordan were on the tenth floor, and the view up here was enough to be breathtaking without being terrifying. In the distance, a train horn sounded. Somewhere a few streets over, a car revved its engine. But the only movement I saw was a pair of pigeons nesting across the street. I loved the serenity of this city when most of its inhabitants slept or prepared for their day of worship.

"It's pretty, isn't it?"

I didn't know how Chloe had sneaked up on my. "One of my favorite sights. Have you lived here all your life?" I asked.

"In this condo? Nah. We only bought it a few years ago."

"Smartass." I laughed. "I meant in Utah."

"Yeah. Grew up on the west side. You?"

"Moved here when I was thirteen." At the time I thought it was the worst thing that had ever happened to me. *God*, how naive young-me was. The thought used to make me bitter, remembering how little I knew back then, but today I was almost okay with it. "Came from Chicago. Our hills look like your speedbumps."

"Where you can see the city skyline from an eternity away." Chloe approached the railing and rested her arms on the wrought iron. "I've been there. Stunning and flat, except for the buildings."

Silence settled between us, broken only by the occasional chirp of a bird. The sky grew lighter with creeping dawn.

"What do you want to be when you grow up?" Chloe asked, voice barely more than a whisper.

Odd question. "I'm already grown up. So I guess… Account Manager for my best friend's advertising firm?" The reply tasted like sawdust in my mouth.

Chloe traced the pattern of the railing. "I can't make this come out right, so I'm sorry in advance. You strike me as someone who wants more from life than that. It's probably a great job, and working with your friend—awesome. But… Never mind me. I don't mean anything by it."

"No, I get it." The words hit closer to home than I wanted, summoning a foreign sense of longing. "I've got a master's in Business with a focus in Accounting. I can do this with numbers that are almost artistic. Which sounds boring, I'm sure, and on its own doesn't take me far. I got a bit of a late start on reality, so I'm still feeling my way through adulthood." It was embarrassing to admit that at twenty-eight, I didn't have a clue about where I was going. I suspected Chloe wouldn't judge, though.

She looked up, a tiny smile playing on her lips. "Everyone has to start somewhere."

"When I was little, I had vast, sweeping fantasies of becoming a wife and mother. You're this brilliant executive, so that probably sounds silly to you, but don't laugh."

"I would never." Chloe sounded sincere.

You should. I brushed away the bitter thought. "When I graduated high school, I got to live the dream, and I was happier than I thought possible."

"But you're single now."

"My parents, husband, and baby girl died when I was nineteen." I almost gagged on the words. Nearly a decade later, it still hurt to talk about. An ache flared in my chest, stealing my air, and acid scorched my throat. I gripped the railing, focusing on the external chill and the corners of the metal digging into my palms, rather than the past.

"Jesus. I'm sorry. I had no idea."

People always said that. How could she have known? "I'm grateful you didn't. It's a part of my life I don't need the public digging into." Seeing it in papers when it happened had been bad enough. I

I studied the light of the rising sun reflecting off the building across from us. Listened to the distant purr of traffic on the freeway. Anything to keep me grounded in the now.

"I didn't mean to dredge up painful memories." Chloe covered my hand, and the contact jolted me from the depths of my mind.

"It's okay. I need a minute or two to process. For the most part, I dealt with it a long time ago." Besides, it was nice to talk about it with someone who didn't have a snide opinion about it. Someone besides Mercy and Ian.

People were so intrusive about everything—from offering their opinions about how I should have prevented the accident to comments like *I bet you wish you'd been there* to open, raw pity. I hated all of it. "My point is, after that, I thought I still wanted the same thing. I went through therapy and healing, and I was sure I could still find that dream.

"When I met George, I expected to be giddy about having children. Instead, the notion of losing another one outweighed the potential of seeing a young life grow up in this world. At the time, it seemed like fate that George didn't want kids either. It would have been nice to know it was because he had two." My bitterness bubbled up in a laugh. "Anyway. Beyond that, I never really thought about my future. I hit a point where I was tired of not contributing, so I got a job. I'm good at what I do, so I don't complain."

I didn't want to be in this mental space right now, but I needed a hand out. A reason to talk about anything else. "What about you? What do you want to be when you grow up? If you're not already there."

Chloe studied me, her brows furrowed, and her face

relaxed. "I'm not quite there." She was quiet, as if this were a confession.

I wanted to hug her for moving away from me as a topic without protest, and also for the familiar traces of stuckness I recognized in her.

"When I was a teenager, I was too busy fantasizing and writing about watching pretty boys having sex, to think about much else," Chloe said. "It wasn't that I did or didn't want the all-American dream of a house in the suburbs, a white picket fence, and two-point-five kids. It wasn't something that was on my radar one way or another. I was going to write a brilliant novel in my spare time, after school and on weekends. I figured my English teacher would stumble on my incredible ramblings, see what a literary genius I was, and tell a book publisher. I was going to be rich and famous before I was eighteen."

More of my nausea fled. "I like that. It's a wonderful idea."

"It was stupid." Chloe didn't look upset. She said it as if it were the most basic, boring fact. "I took it too far one day, and turned in one of my stories instead of my assigned work. I was convinced it would be my big break. She'd read my random chapter, pull me aside, and praise me. I'd be on my way to the big time. Instead, she chastised me in front of everyone, for writing stories about my classmates. I never heard the end of the teasing.

"I wanted to crawl in a hole and die. Turned out, even amid mortifying embarrassment, life moves on. Right after graduation, a little start-up software company found my fan fiction in their forums. It turned out my dream could become a reality. They offered me a writer job, I met Jordan, and I never looked back. Until he was fired yesterday. Now, when I should be worrying about him, I'm instead wondering if I didn't set my goals high enough."

I hadn't expected to see regret on Chloe. "Nothing's stopping you from doing it now. If you're talking about reaching for more, there's always time." Could I take my own advice?

"I guess. I'll ask again—what do you want to be when you grow up?"

"Someone who makes dreams come true." Where did that come from? I'd never had that thought before, but it sounded like fun. "Kind of like a fairy godmother. I know, that's not a job."

"There has to be a way to make it one."

The sun was up now, bright enough to make me squint and long for my sunglasses. The Conversation was too enthralling for me to break the flow and grab them, though. "I envy you."

"Me? Why?" Chloe's question lilted with shock.

"When I was younger—hell, even a year ago, I would have looked at you and thought you didn't know what you were doing or where you were going. A woman who lived with her boyfriend, instead of insisting on marriage. Who obviously put career first." That sounded bad. I held up my hand in response to Chloe's wounded look. "Whatever your reasons or story, I would've judged you, and I would have been wrong. You've got it made."

Her short laugh echoed with doubt. "Yeah. Sexy boyfriend, bad reputation, and pizza and video games every night. I'm living the dream."

"He's got you, too." I envied their synergy. "But you are living the dream, aren't you? You wanted someone to come along and find your writing and heap glory and work on you. Don't you have that? Plus, you make your own decisions. You have to answer to the big boss, but you're doing something you love."

"Yeah. I really am." Somewhere in the condo, a door creaked. Chloe turned to lean her back against the railing, which left her facing inside.

"In response to your question, I don't. I don't have any idea what I want to do with my life," I said.

"At least you've got the entire rest of it to figure things out."

That was a bit optimistic. "It would be nice to at least have a direction."

"Do you want to go to breakfast with us?" Chloe asked. "Jordan and I always go somewhere Sunday mornings, while the world is quiet. Come with us, and we'll plot world domination. Or our futures. Something. Anything. Everything."

I so very much did want that. "I should get home." I forced the resolution through my veins. This seemed like as good a time as any to start severing ties. The serious conversation was over, but the mood wasn't light and silly.

Chloe's smile flickered toward a frown and didn't quite recover. "Do you have half an hour? We're going to need to look at the fallout from yesterday's letter sometime, and if you're here, you can keep us in check."

"I don't want to keep you from breakfast."

Chloe grabbed my hand and tugged me inside. "Then it's settled. You'll go with us. We'll read while we're there. All three of us sitting together but staring at our phones. Like a proper American family."

"Except we also have to talk about what we're reading. In case we need additional strategy." I refused to dwell on the statement about family. "I've got a little bit of time to hang out." So much for resolve.

I gave my permission for them to look at the news, and Jordan and Chloe were all over it in a heartbeat.

The apology from Jordan went as well as could be expected. Commenters questioned his lack of sincerity and pointed out he hadn't taken any responsibility, but the right news site picked it up, ran it with the headline *Jordan Iverson Looking for Justice in Horrific Assault*, and most of the outlets copied the news from there.

Somehow, my *little bit of time* turned into most of the day. Dusk settled in before I said goodnight. I didn't hesitate to say *sure* then they asked if I was free next weekend, and walking alone to my car was more difficult than I expected. So much for limiting my emotional attachment.

It wasn't like we'd all agreed to have sex. I had new friends, they were open-minded, and they could help me meet someone of my own. Or move on to the next fling. I wasn't ready for the PTA life just yet.

TWENTY-TWO

JORDAN

I could've slept in. I could count on one hand the Monday's I'd had as an adult that were mine alone.

Sure, there had been vacations and holidays, but this was different. I was free. The entire world stretched out in front of me, beaconing with potential.

In high school, I'd worked at Walmart, and that was the last time I ever went to a job interview. I'd never had to look for another job or write a resume. How did such a thing even work?

Which was why, at five in the morning, I was awake and staring at the clock, my brain refusing to shut up enough for me to go back to sleep. Maybe a walk would help.

I dressed silently, and left with just as little noise. There was a shopping center around the corner, and the coffee shop was open. By the time I grabbed drinks and food for both of us, plus an extra surprise for her from the convenience store, and returned to the apartment, it was almost time for Chloe to be up.

Perfect timing.

I padded into the bedroom, clicked off the alarm on her phone, and knelt next to the bed. "Hey, gorgeous." I brushed the petals of the rose I'd bought across her cheek.

"That tickles." She fluttered her eyelids but didn't open her eyes.

The way her hair curtained over half her face was enthralling, and her curves under the sheets were intoxicating. "That's the point," I said softly as I repeated the gesture.

"You better have made coffee." She pried one eye open. I held the rose in front of her, and she opened the other eye with a gasp. "What is that?"

"It's a flower."

"Smartass. I love it. But why?" She pushed up onto one elbow and leaned in to smell the rose.

Liz was right, this small-gesture thing was brilliant. I'd do this a million times over, to see Chloe smile like this. Soft. Playful. I set the flower on the nightstand, nudged her to sit, and moved onto the bed next to her. "Just because. Do I need a reason? And no, I didn't make coffee. I grabbed you a large latte—light on the vanilla, heavy on the espresso. It's in the kitchen."

"My hero." Chloe shifted on the mattress and rested her head against my shoulder.

I trailed my fingers through her hair, memorizing the warmth of her body against mine. "I had an amazing time this weekend. I don't say this enough, but

I'm lucky to have you by my side." A lot of couples were torn apart by intense stress, but maybe it could be the opposite for us. The external forces would push us to band together, and move past whatever had us fighting before this mess with Stew started.

"Jordan?"

"Hmm?"

"Why did you do this?" Her voice was soft, still sleepy, but something else lay underneath. "Ten years, and you've never bought me flowers."

It was a reasonable thing to be curious about. So why did it shove aside the feathers of my pleasant mood? "Today's a new day for me. A new life. Time to do something different."

"That makes sense." She leaned more of her weight into me. "I wish I could stick around this morning and help you with your resume. It doesn't feel right, going into the office without you."

"But at least we enjoyed the last few days."

"Would it have been as incredible if Liz weren't there?"

My thoughts hitched. The question felt like a setup, but Chloe wouldn't do that to me. "The weekend doesn't exist without Liz. The press release was her idea, and that boosted both our moods. Plus, yeah, she was fun. You enjoyed having her here, didn't you?"

"Of course. But take the press release out of the equation and answer the question."

"Not possible." I was going to hold onto the pleasant parts of this moment. "I lost my job on Friday, and I was hovering on the edge of rock bottom. You being here, by my side, along with everything else, kept me from tumbling all the way in."

"Everything else." An edge crept into her voice.

I fought to keep my jaw from clenching. Too many of our fights started with this tone. "If you want to know something, ask me outright." *Don't paint me into a corner, because* fuck, *I'm tired of dancing around the subject.* "Pretend I'm a stupid, clueless gamer boy, and tell me what you're actually thinking."

Chloe pushed away from me. "You've got other things to worry about. I shouldn't have brought it up."

Nope. Nope. Double nope to infinity. "If it's on your mind now, let's talk about it now."

"Liz is my exact opposite."

I could work with that. Experience told me Chloe wasn't trying to be difficult, but I couldn't be expected to give her answers, if she wasn't sure about what she was asking. "That's an all-or-nothing kind of statement. She's the same height as you."

"That's aesthetic. It's on the surface." Chloe twirled a loose thread on the comforter, wrapping it until her fingertip turned red, before letting it go.

"So this isn't about looks. Good. Because you're both gorgeous in your own ways."

She looked up, expression unreadable. "True. Like puppies and salamanders are both cute, depending on your perspective."

I wiggled my fingers to keep them from tightening in frustration. "Don't drip-feed me information and then get upset when I try make sense of it." I couldn't lose track of whatever this was about by burying it in a tangent of a disagreement.

She rubbed her face and sighed. "You're right. I'm not being fair, and I don't want to fight."

We agreed on that. It was a good concession to start with. "I'm listening. Tell me what you're thinking, but understand I might ask you to clarify."

"That's fair. Do you see me as one of the guys?"

"Besides the obvious physical differences?" I dragged my gaze over her, not hiding my appreciation as I lingered on her waist, her chest, and then her face.

One corner of her mouth tugged up. "Yes. Besides the fact I've got tits and a vagina."

"You're not like anyone else in the universe." I tucked her hair behind her ear, holding her gaze. "Not one of the guys. Not one of the girls. You're Chloe. All yourself and you. I'm not saying your looks hurt—because, fuck, I'm lucky to have someone as stunning as you. Even without that, I'd love you as intensely. Nothing, no one, compares to you."

"That's corny." Despite her words, she was blushing.

"I'm not a poet. So sue me. Why are you asking?"

She leaned into my touch, resting her cheek against my palm. "People call me *dude* and *bro* and *man*. People call Liz *Ms. Thompson*, and *Elizabeth*."

"Those are her names."

"You're funny. I've seen the two of you talk. You look at her differently."

I was starting to get where Chloe was coming from. How dim was I that I didn't see it sooner? "People call you those things because they're comfortable with you.

Maybe they think you're one of the guys, but most of them wouldn't know what to do with a woman if they had one. They talk to her differently because she's intimidating."

"She's not."

"She is. Do you think she's ever done something like dye her own hair in the bathroom sink?"

"Probably not."

"Yes, she's attractive," I said.

Chloe clenched her jaw, and I pressed a soft kiss to her lips.

"There's never been a time in our relationship when we didn't check each other out," I reminded her. "As far as looking at her differently is concerned… First of all, I probably do. Second, you don't see what I see." I kissed her forehead, her nose, and her lips, feather-light each time. "When I close my eyes, I can describe you in vivid detail, because you're always at the front of my mind."

I needed to say more. "Would it make things better —heal more between us—if I said let's never see Liz again? I'm not taking anything off the table—exploration, whatever you want. If we need to redefine something, let's do it."

"Would you really be okay with never seeing her again?"

Sure. I'd Never miss her. The words stuck in my throat. "Is this one of those questions I'll need more information about in order to answer?"

"No."

"I like her. You like her. I don't only mean in a let's-get-nasty way, though you enjoyed it. At the end of the night, I'm here with you."

Chloe crawled forward and pressed her lips to mine, holding the kiss for several seconds before breaking away to look me in the eye. "Thank you for talking this through with me. Will we be okay?"

"Always and forever." Was it really this simple? Chloe was jealous ad didn't need to be, and we'd talked through it. I wanted to think that meant we'd be great going forward.

So why did I have my doubts?

TWENTY-THREE

Chloe

How was it already Thursday?

As I left one meeting, prep for the next scrolled through my head. I'd spent the last three and a half days covering both my team and Jordan's, and it had devoured my sense of time and space.

He and I had collaborated a lot on our projects here, and that helped me step into his role, but there was so much I wasn't familiar with. I couldn't offer more than stick figure drawings to give his—my—artists concept ideas, and attending a second set of meetings meant I wasn't getting my regular work done.

My phone buzzed with a new text from my assistant. Bri was heaven sent, keeping me on track schedule-wise. She was also grossly underutilized in this position. I'd been trying to push her into more writing, and I'd do so again… when I made it through this slog of work.

The message made me smile despite the flutter in my belly. *Vendor follow-up, R&T Advertising. She's in the lobby.*

Liz. I couldn't ignore the skip of my pulse. I felt bad about arguing with Jordan over her. Still, even though we'd made up days ago. I did enjoy spending time with Liz, and I needed to stop taking my insecurities out on him for the same.

I took the elevator down, repeating *be cool* the entire time, but when I stepped into the waiting area and saw her, I couldn't help my smile. This was a big upside to being in charge of the art team—I'd oversee this contract until it was signed, and then probably continue to be Liz's contact after. She probably wouldn't visit often, but I looked forward to each and every chance to see her again.

Was that bad?

I'd told her there was no such thing as a guilty pleasure.

She met me halfway across the lobby, and we exchanged a handshake. "You didn't have to dress up just to visit me," I teased. Her pants suit was a sharp contrast to my jeans and faded T-shirt.

"It's habit. When I walk into a public facing meeting, training tells me the suit makes a good impression."

You've done that either way. I would have spoken the words, but my stomach growled loud enough to be heard. Liz raised her brows, and heat flooded my cheeks. Maybe I shouldn't have skipped lunch. Or breakfast.

"We can make this a lunch meeting." Liz nodded toward the cafeteria off the main entrance.

"No. I'll grab something from the vending machine after I'm done here and before the next circus."

"That's ridiculous." Liz walked toward the smell of grease and cheese, glancing over her shoulder as she talked. "I'm the client, you've got this hour on your calendar for me, and I say we're eating."

I couldn't argue with that if I wanted to, especially with how loudly my stomach growled again. I sprinted to catch up to Liz. "You're the client," I said with a laugh.

"So what's good?" Liz paused inside the entrance.

The company cafeteria was made up of several stations, including those for pizza, burgers, sandwiches, and Tex-Mex. "They make a killer quesadilla," I said.

"I'm in." Liz tugged me toward one of the grills. Neither of us said much, as we waited for our food, paid, and found seats.

It was after two, and I was grateful for the relative silence. It was the last chatter I'd heard all day. Now that I was sitting, the smells of food teasing me, my restraint was gone. I was through half a quesadilla before I paused to breathe or take a drink.

Liz nibbled on one triangle, watching me with what had to be barely guarded amusement. "You're right, they're good."

"Told you." I remembered to swallow before I spoke. "We were in Portland a few years ago, and we discovered this little lunch truck outside the convention center the day before the show, while we were doing setup. Best quesadillas ever. We went back every day, and we've been trying to coax them here toward getting it right. They're close, but not quite there yet."

The memory carried more emotion that I was used

to. Jordan and I'd had so much fun that weekend. And since then, talking the cooks through trying new things, and he I would never do that again. Plus, Liz didn't want to hear all this. "That probably sounds pretty pedestrian to you."

Liz's smile was sad, but genuine. "It actually sounds amazing."

"You must have stories like that. About the little hole in the wall you discovered in Ibiza or Venice, that had been there for five generations."

Liz shook her head. "Yes, I've been both places, but it was with family. I loved my parents dearly, but my father never would've been caught dead in *a little hole in the wall*. But Mercy... She's got stories."

But it's been more than a decade. I kept the thought to myself. Whatever choices Liz made were her own, and she had said she'd spent a lot of time trying to figure out who she was.

"Why did she get to have all the fun without you?" I kept the question kind and light. Besides, I was pretty sure there was a catch of envy when she said *Mercy*, and it almost sounded like the same think I felt when I looked at Liz.

She sighed. "She walked away from all of this, the money... me... when she was eighteen, and backpacked around the world. She's seen so much. Met so many people. Loved so many people..."

Yup. That was definitely a bit of jealousy. Maybe Liz and I weren't completely different. "What's stopping you from doing the same?"

"Are you kidding? I'd never even lived on my own until a year ago. I couldn't."

"Me neither," I admitted. "I love the idea, but the logistics... I'm kind of a coward."

Liz's laugh was filled with disbelief. "You went on stage in front of hundreds of people, and insulted one of the biggest gaming companies in the world. You're not a coward." She was talking about the fake marriage proposal.

"It was Jordan's idea."

"I suspect it was both of your ideas, and you still did it."

My cheeks heated at her admiration. "How about this, then—I like my bed and my phone too much to leave them behind in favor of living a nomad life in another country."

"I feel that."

"Though... I do like the idea of finding some hole in the wall in Venice that's been there through five generations and serves the best... anything I've ever had."

Liz's smile was back. "Same. What's stopping us from going?"

Like, together? No, of course not. "Time."

"We're not even thirty. We're too young to be out of time," Liz said.

"You're so right." How was this easier with just the two of us? It was like that first night in the bar. Comfortable. Casual. At the same time, if we kept going down this path, I'd suggest a vacation in Europe in about two minutes, and that was making a lot of assumptions. "Should we talk work and get it out of the way?"

Liz's smile flickered before sliding back into place. "I suppose. Otherwise we'll run out of time before we get to it." She pulled a manila folder from her briefcase and handed it over. We spent the next several minutes swapping details and agreeing both companies were on board for the partnership.

All my meetings needed to go even half this smoothly. "I'll have Legal email you our boilerplate usage terms. Look them over, come back to us with any changes."

"Will do." Liz pushed aside her empty plate and leaned in. "Now, the important question. How are you doing, besides forgetting to eat?"

"Work is hectic. But Jordan's doing okay with his job search. Thanks to your apology, several development companies sought him out, and he has a list to consider. Dinner last night with my family went okay—"

"Which is good to hear." Liz covered my hand. "But I'm asking about you. This can't be easy on you."

Her concern warmed me and so did her touch. "I'm good. Stressed, but surviving." It was harder to talk about myself than I thought. I wasn't the one out of work. "Before I forget, Jordan can't make it this weekend. He's interviewing with a company in California, Friday, and he's looking at a couple other places while he's there."

"Would the two of you have to move? What about your job?" Liz frowned.

I didn't like the assumption that I'd be the one to give up my career. I nearly ran this place, especially now. I should've explained better. "He'd telecommute, and they'd bring him out there once or twice a month, for face-to-face meetings."

"Wish him luck for me." Liz's smile returned but no longer reached her eyes. "Maybe we should reschedule?"

"You and I can still do something. My boyfriend is gone for the weekend."

"It was only dinner. Let's save it until he gets back."

Did I miss something? One minute we were buds and now she wouldn't look at me. This wasn't because I'd shifted so rapidly away from the travel conversation, was it? No, it felt different. "Sure. We'll do it in two weeks instead." I didn't know Liz well. Opening up to Jordan was hard enough—putting thoughts that didn't make sense to me into words he'd understand—and no one knew me better than Jordan. I wasn't ready to rock the boat with Liz.

Liz glanced at her phone and stood. "I'll see you both then. For now, I should let you get back to work. I'll follow up with you in a few days, with any questions we have about the contract."

This definitely wasn't right. "Sounds great." My fake enthusiasm echoed in my eardrums, loud and brassy. Too many feelings crawled through me. Irrational jealousy. Unreasonable doubt.

Giving the feelings names didn't make them go away or any easier to accept.

TWENTY-FOUR

Liz

When I told Chloe I wanted to delay our plans, Chloe's confusion almost made me say *Never mind. Let's hook up anyway.*

The words wouldn't come, though, and neither would my explanation. Lunch with Chloe was difficult enough, just like being alone with Jordan the other night at their apartment. I couldn't do one-on-one time with either of them again outside of a professional environment. I needed the in-my-face reminder that they were a couple. Alone, they were each a temptation, and simply considering the possibilities filled me with guilt.

They probably never struggled with things like this, but seeing them together was the only way to remind myself they were off-limits.

I'd hoped the weekend would slide past like any other, and I wouldn't give the cancelled… date? Fun?… another thought. Nope. All weekend, they kept popping back into my head.

Mondays had never been a day for me to dread, but this one meant leaving a weekend of missed opportunities behind, and that carried a hint of bittersweet.

Might as well get some work done. I flipped on my laptop and let the weekend email spill in. The email from Stew Knapfer, asking for ten minutes of my time, went straight to spam, along with half-a-dozen messages offering me everything from enterprise-level data to top-tier human resource management.

A note from Jonathan stood out among it all. *Call me when you get in.*

I frowned at the terse subject with no message in the body, and the fact that it came in before I was a awake, and he was in an hour earlier time zone. I grabbed my phone and dialed.

It only managed half a ring before Jonathan answered. "Liz. Gotta love early risers." He didn't sound upset.

"I'm all about the customer service. You can always call me if there's an emergency, rather than waiting for me to get into the office."

"No emergency." His upbeat tone lifted my mood a notch. "I wanted to get to you before your calendar filled for the week, but nothing's on fire. How was your weekend?"

A little pathetic and a lot lonely. "Fantastic. Yours?"

"Busy, but worth it. Hey, I'm sorry to cut this short. I'd keep you company for hours if I could, but I've got a meeting in five. I'm going to be in your neck of the woods tomorrow—last minute plans—and I wondered if you'd grab lunch with me."

I did a quick check of my calendar. "It'll have to be at one, but if that's okay, sure. Do you want to stop by the office at all while you're here? Check in with Mercy or anyone else?"

"Nah. Thanks, though. My business there isn't related, but I have to say hi to my favorite account manager."

Why did this feel like an odd request? "Of course." Because I'd been overthinking things since I met Chloe and Jordan. I couldn't do that with every situation. "Send me then details and I'll meet you there."

"I look forward to it. Talk soon."

Despite my decision to not examine the conversation more closely, something about it still tickled my thoughts.

I'd never get anything done if I started looking at my entire world the way I was examining Jordan and Chloe. I shouldn't even be putting that much thought into them.

I stashed my regret about the missed opportunity this weekend, and turned to the rest of my email.

"THE FIRST HOTEL had lost my reservation and was booked solid. They were kind about it, though and called other nearby locations. It was late, and I was tired." Jonathan was telling me about the last vacation he took to Italy. "So when they told me they had a place but their only available room had a broken TV, I told the hotel I didn't care, and they sent a car for me."

I refused to tie the story to the conversation I'd had with Chloe. The one where I was all but ready to buy three plane tickets and see what we could all get up to. "That's miserable. At least you got some sleep finally."

Jonathan brushed his hand over mine. "You'd think that." His friendly gesture clicked off in her head, added to a list of other snippets of odd behavior through lunch. It mingled with yesterday's call and meeting up with him in L.A., but it still didn't make sense. "But no. It was an older building. Radiators. Locks that needed keys, instead of being electronic. I swear the lock was about a century old, and it took me about five minutes to jiggle it enough the tumblers let me lock it. Then I pretty much collapsed into bed. I slept for maybe an hour, before I heard scraping and stumbling, and someone joined me in bed next to me. He stunk of alcohol and was out cold the moment he lay down. Apparently I hadn't locked the door after all, and he was so wasted, he mixed up his room number."

I laughed and shook my head. "At least you made a new friend." How did this make me want to take that vacation even more?

"I don't need friends like that. You, on the other hand..." The way Jonathan trailed off struck me as odd.

The gears in my mind clicked into place. Holy shit. Was he hitting on me? Mercy and Ian both described him as friend, but had never mentioned things like light touches and hints about personal relationships.

What was I supposed to do if it was true? I tried to

be subtle about looking him over. He was attractive—dark blond hair, piercing blue eyes, and a toned build accentuated by an expensive suit. But I couldn't picture myself with him, regardless of the *he's a client* situation.

Because I wanted to be with someone else. Or rather, two someone's.

Wow, it was weird to fully admit that. I had no idea where I stood with Chloe and Jordan, except that despite trying to keep them at arm's length, I couldn't stop thinking about how much fun we had together, both in bed and elsewhere.

When did I fall for them> This was bad. So very, very bad. They hadn't signed up to be glommed onto by some random socialite, and I'd known that. How did I let myself sink into such strong feelings?

"Earth to Liz." Jonathan wiggled his fingers in front of my face. "You still with me?"

I had to say something. "I'm sorry. Yes, still here." What if I was reading him wrong?

He shifted in his seat, and when his toe nudged mine, he didn't pull away. He kept his gaze on my face, his expression unreadable.

If I was wrong, and he wasn't hitting on me, he must send mixed signals to a lot of people. "Listen, Jonathan… I enjoy working with you."

"Random, but thank you. Me too. It's why I was glad you had time for me today."

This was about to suck. "But it would be incredibly unprofessional to step outside those boundaries."

"You haven't heard my proposal yet. At least give me that." His confidence never wavered.

Nothing about that sounded like *this isn't like that*. My insides twisted into a knot. "I'm not in the market for any type of a relationship."

"A what?" He widened his eyes. "Oh, wow. Fuck. I didn't mean— Yeah, I guess I can see why you'd think that."

Shit. He wasn't hitting on me. Now was the point where I needed to crawl under a neighboring table and hide until he was gone. "I wasn't thinking anything. It was more of a general statement?" I didn't even sound convincing to myself.

He reached for me again, and pulled back, fist clenched. "I didn't mean to give you that impression. You're stunning and a lot of fun, but you're right. That would be over-the-top unprofessional. I wasn't hitting on you, though if the circumstances were different, I might."

"Then what are you talking about, with a proposal?"

"It's a business proposal outside of what we're working on now. It doesn't have anything to do with KM or R&T."

Business. I could talk business. I'd talk about the migratory patterns of swallows—African or European— if it meant taking the focus off my mistake. "I'm listening."

"I've got a couple of partners… financial, not personal"— he winked—"with whom I'm putting together an angel investment firm. We're talking to people who have experience with charities, investment work, and numbers, and you're on the list. That's why this lunch is unprofessional of me. I'm trying to woo you away from your position with Mercy, to join us."

I had no idea what to make of the offer. "You can hire account managers in California."

"I mean join us. As a partner. This is a preliminary offer. We'd go through fact finding and due diligence. I have a full proposal you can look at."

"So… you're using me for my money?" The words echoed in my chest with a hollow ping. It was a lot like George, except this time I knew up front.

"No. Or rather, yes, but not like that. I have an idea what you've been through personally. Your story is a lot more intense than mine, but this isn't like what happened with your fiancé. We're each coming to the table with our own funds. I need business partners I can trust, and you're on that very short list."

"I'm flattered, but I don't think that's something I can get into. It's not on my radar for the future." What was? The conversation with Chloe about what we wanted to be when we grew up flooded back.

He handed me a card. The logo on it was a stylized dollar symbol with a halo over it. "This is my non-KM contact information. Let me send you the proposal, and bounce the idea around in your head for a week before you tell me no."

"No. I'm sorry. I'm not in the market for that kind of"—Opportunity? That sounded weak—"investment."

He shrugged. "My loss."

The conversation wilted after that. Within a few minutes, we said our goodbyes. I wished him a safe flight back, then sank into my car, letting the silence wash over me. I gave him the right answer, so why was I still thinking about his offer?

Because apparently I had no idea who I was or what I wanted, and I couldn't let anything go, because of it.

TWENTY-FIVE

JORDAN

I flicked the scroll wheel on my mouse up and down, bouncing the screen and not registering anything. There was no point. I'd studied this information to death, and no amount of staring would change it.

Four employment offers from four different companies. All offering great money and benefits. All of them reputable game developers and distributors. Regardless of which I picked, I'd be making more than before. Every opportunity looked great on paper.

And yet, I was hesitating.

They all promised me creative freedom, but I'd had that at Rinslet, too. I had a good idea what each company culture was like from trade shows and conversations with colleagues. Digital Media was the only one of the four that I hated even considering. I'd worked for them for less than a year when they purchased Cord, way back when. It was the most miserable memory from adulthood. Their culture was restrictive, suffocating, and soul-crushing.

My exit from their company humiliated them and cemented my name in mainstream geekdom.

I hadn't been anyone then. I had more than a name now, there was executive experience to back it up, which meant negotiating power. Respect. The only reason DM's offer still sat in front of me was that accepting it felt like giving Rinslet the finger. Everyone I'd talked to had advice about approaching the situation—pit all of them against each other for more money; a nice office; a hot assistant.

I just wanted to go somewhere I could create again, and no one's answers were reassuring when I brought that up.

My email chimed and I switched screens. Where the fuck did all these alerts for my name come from? I scanned the headlines. It couldn't be true. I clicked through to one.

Sure enough, my job offers were on the internet, all of them, complete with titles and company names.

This couldn't possibly be good. It wasn't as though there were non-disclosure agreements in place, but I did have an unspoken understanding with all of them to not discuss anything. If the articles only mentioned one company, I'd assume someone there talked to the wrong blogger. With it being a full list, it looked like I'd spilled the beans. There was no way this would help my chances with any of them.

I wasn't waiting around to find out—I needed to make a decision now and curse the fucker later who forced my hand. As I spun in my chair, trying to collect my thoughts, my gaze landed on the shelves lining our walls. Artwork and figurines stared back. Limited edition collectibles I'd designed for various events. If I signed them, could I sell them for a little cash?

The ridiculous thought came out of nowhere, and was ridiculous. That wasn't a living, it was spending money for another month or two.

Maybe I could go into freelance. Pick up jobs here and there as they spoke to me.

That idea didn't sit any better with me than the four offers I couldn't pick between. Someone else's vision was still someone else's.

I needed to make a decision. I had to pick now.

Instead, I pulled up the sketch I'd just finished, and started digitizing it. Questions without answers drifted to the back of my mind to war among themselves. I fell into the familiar motions of filling in lines, smoothing out curves, and giving the flat work depth.

My phone chimed with a new text from Chloe. Shit, how was it almost six?

Working late. Miss you, her message said.

I typed a quick reply. *Don't forget to eat. See you when you're done. Love you.*

The alerts had piled up while I worked. There really wasn't anything more interesting for the tech world to talk about than me? That was hard to believe. I skimmed the headlines, but most were more of the same.

Stew's name caught my eye, and I clicked through to the post before my rationale could tell me it was a bad idea. The longer I read about how all four of my potential employers were idiots, for considering hiring a criminal and a bully like me, the higher my blood pressure rose.

"*Fucking asshole*," I screamed at the walls.

My focus was shot. That article was libel, wasn't it? I could sue for it? If I had a lawyer, which would require money, which we couldn't throw away on something like that.

Fuck.

Maybe I'd order pizza instead. Why weren't we drinkers? Would the pizza guy bring me beer?

As if summoned by the thought, someone knocked. I wasn't in the mood to be social, but we rarely had unannounced visitors, so it was either the wrong house or important.

When I looked through the peephole and saw Liz, I was surprised. I opened the door, not trying to fight the grin that rushed in to push away my irritation. "Hey. We didn't have plans did we?"

"No. I'm sorry for not calling, but I was in the neighborhood, I saw the headlines, and I wondered if I could help. Not that I have any brilliant ideas, but I'm worried about both of you." She lingered in the hallway. "How are you?"

I stepped aside, but she didn't come in. "I've had better days," I said. "You staying a while?"

"What about Chloe?"

I didn't know how to interpret the question. "She's still at the office. I don't know how she's taking it."

"I didn't mean—" Liz caught her bottom lip

between her teeth. "It's you I'm worried about, but if she's not here, I'll come back later."

"You're being obtuse." And I wasn't in the mood to try to figure anything new out. "Did you plan on staying before you knew she wasn't here? Come in and wait. We can brainstorm." My phone rang. What was this? Grand Center Fucking Station?

"I'll go." Liz started to turn.

I clasped her arm loosely enough she could break free if she wanted, but with enough grip to convey I meant what I said. "I'll be thirty seconds." I tugged her inside, moved my hand to the small of her back, and pointed her to the living room.

When I was sure she wouldn't skitter away, I answered my phone. "This is Jordan."

"Jordan, it's Cal with Hammer & Nail Games. Do you have a few minutes?"

"Of course." I slid into friendly without pause. Like I was going to tell the prospective employer *no*. "What's up?"

"I want to say again how great it was to meet with you last week. The team really liked what you had to say." Despite Cal's friendly tone, concern slid through me.

"Thanks. I enjoyed meeting everyone."

"That's why it's so hard to make this call." Cal's cheer vanished. "I'm sorry, but after careful consideration, we've determined we need to head in a different direction."

I ground my teeth until my ears rang. "I understand." My voice stayed pleasant. "May I ask why?"

"We just need a different feeling for our organization," Cal said. "You understand."

"Sure." I didn't. Not completely. But I had an inkling, and I didn't like it.

"Great. I knew you would. I'll let you get back to your evening. Best of luck."

"You too." I didn't know if he heard me before he disconnected.

Jesus. I half-set, half-dropped the phone on a nearby table. I should be grateful that I had one less decision to make, but I wasn't comforted. The timing was too convenient, coinciding with the leaked news of who was courting me.

I wandered into the living room, not really part of the world around me.

Liz stood at the far end of the room, studying some of the limited edition figures I'd designed. She looked up and frowned when she saw me. "Are you all right?"

"I'm fine." I shook off the haze. This wasn't the kind of thing I'd dump on anyone but Chloe. I needed to vent and curse and possibly shout, to feel better, and Chloe would get it.

The creases in Liz's brow made it look as though my answer didn't sate her. She gestured at a series of prints on the wall. "I meant to ask last time I was here, is this your work? It has your signature, so probably, but… *wow.*"

"It's mine." The awe warmed me, but her willingness to move to a new subject filled me with ambivalence. Did I want her to push the issue? "Concept art for the figurines beneath."

She hovered her fingers over the models, not making contact. "You're amazing. These are like…"

"Professional quality?" I finished for her with a smirk.

"Far better. Who was on the phone?" She hadn't moved to a new topic after all.

And I was relieved. "Hammer & Nail Games, retracting their offer." It hurt to say the words, but it was a relief to share, even without shouts of frustration.

"Because of the news?"

That she made the same assumption as me gave more weight to the theory. "Possibly. They wouldn't say." I crossed the room to join her, and followed her gaze across different pieces. Creating was my link to sanity. What did she see when she looked at all of this?

"Do you have to work for someone else?" Apparently Liz had crawled into my brain and plucked out a series of thoughts from today. "Can't you do this full time?"

"I wish. My work is specialized, and I'm not sure I could bring in enough based just on that."

"This is all… I already said wow, but I'll do it again. *Wow.* You're one of the best."

"No. I'm simply one of the best known." That wasn't self-doubt; it was honesty. I was brilliant at what I did, but that didn't mean I was top tier. "There aren't enough people out there willing to pay what I'd charge. The artists who make money on their art alone—a real income—are doing merchandising. They've got a recognizable and unique brand. They sell prints. Mugs. T-shirts. They have a tie-in that goes above and beyond *Jordan Iverson drew this*."

"I suppose. So do that. Make merchandise."

If only. "That takes start-up capital. Help. I mean, some people do it on their own at first, but if I walk into this, I need it to be a living up front, not just a hobby. It has to take off in the next few months. I can't stay out of work forever." Was I explaining all of this for Liz's benefit or my own? Who was I trying to convince it wasn't an option?

TWENTY-SIX

CHLOE

I forced one foot in front of the other, willing my body to keep moving rather than curl up in the hallway for a short nap. The condo was only a few feet away.

Despite the long day, and the fact that my legs and brain and everything in between felt like lead, I was doing okay. Things were coming together at work. There was still a lot to do, but I'd signed off on projects, met deadlines, and today I'd checked more things off my to-do list than I'd added.

Gold star for me.

When I went to unlock the deadbolt, it didn't offer any resistance. Weird. "I'm home," I called in a sing-song voice as I stepped inside and kicked off my shoes.

"In here."

I followed Jordan's voice to the living room, and my insides twisted at what I saw. Liz sat next to him on the couch, their heads bowed together, his printed portfolio spread across their laps. Was I upset? Happy to see Liz here? I was too tired to make sense of my own feelings.

I let my smile and good mood flow back. "Hey, stranger. I didn't realize we had company."

"I didn't exactly announce myself before I came over," Liz said. "But with the latest news. I was worried about both of you."

There was worrisome news? The twist inside was definitely unpleasant this time. I settled on the couch on Jordan's other side and intertwined my fingers with his. I'd had my head down at work all day, which meant zero time to check in, or do much of anything besides tell Jordan I'd be late. "Bad news?"

"It's not a big deal." The faint thread of tension running through Jordan's reply implied otherwise. Did Liz hear that nuance?

"Someone leaked the names of the four companies courting him," Liz said.

The fuck? "That's not nothing." I squeezed Jordan's hand.

He kissed me on the forehead. "But there's nothing to be done for it. Hammer & Nail retracted their offer a couple hours ago, and Synchronicity, Inc. right before you walked in."

"But DM is still on the table." I had to stop myself from hissing when I said their name.

Liz stood. "I should go. Let you two deal with this."

"Don't run out on my account." I leaned more of my weight against Jordan.

"I thought you wanted to talk to both of us," he said.

Liz turned her gaze to her feet as she shifted her weight from one to the other.

Smugness, guilt, and jealousy churned inside me. I was seconds away from acting like a brat, and I was too tired to stop myself. We'd already talked through how we felt about Liz. About each other. Why was I suddenly a land lamprey, suctioned to Jordan? "Stay, please." I winced at the sarcastic edge. "I mean it. I'm glad you're here." That was better. More sincere.

Liz finally looked at me. "I don't think that's a good idea."

"Because I'm home now?" I bit the tip of my tongue, but it was too late. The retort was out there.

"Because the two of you are obviously having a moment. Did I do something to piss you off?"

"I was going to ask you the same thing." I'd picked a path, I might as well see it through, rather than let whatever this was devour me. I'm just thinking back to the other day at lunch, when you weren't interested in our weekend plans unless Jordan was going to be there."

Liz snort-laughed. Who knew she was capable of something so base? "That's what you thought? I hesitated because one of you was going to be gone. It could've been you and my answer would have been the same. I didn't mean to be here alone with Jordan tonight. I came looking for both of you. This… whatever it is we're doing doesn't have any rules, but the last thing I want is to come between you. I'm looking for a balance and trying not to overstay my welcome."

Well shit. Fuck. God damn it. Wasn't I just the bitch?

"If we've invited you to stay, we mean it." Jordan's

reassurance echoed what I wanted to say, but set my teeth on edge.

"You say that, but it's not quite true. The two of you are a couple, and I make three. I'm trying to set my own boundaries, because I can't figure out the rules with both of you. I've got a best friend. She's as dear to me as anyone, and a single kiss nearly broke us. But with you, there's kissing, touching, fucking, and then stone walls. I can't do this anymore. After the mistakes I made with George, I need this—whatever it is—to be crystal clear."

"What do you want it to be?" Jordan asked.

I wasn't ready for that answer, regardless of what Liz said next. If she wanted everything, nothing, something in between.

Liz clenched her jaw. "The night we met, Chloe, why were you in the bar alone? Anyone can see you two are incredible together, and you really don't go anywhere without each other. What was different that night?"

Why couldn't I speak?

"Some things don't show on the surface." Jordan's reply clenched like a fist around my heart, squeezing until I thought I might collapse.

I'd fucked this all up so badly. Taking for granted that he went along with my requests. Pouting until he pushed me to figure out why. Never asking in return what he wanted. He'd lost his job. A dream job I'd do anything for but leave him, and I was pouting that he was friendly with the woman I kissed. I'd been selfish every step of the way.

And I still couldn't find my voice.

"Hypothetical situation," Liz said. "Say there's this couple who have been together long enough they might as well have been high school sweethearts. They have pretty charmed lives, all things considered. Each has lived their own Cinderella story. Except happily ever after doesn't exist in real life the way it does in fairy tales, and she starts to ask herself *is this all there is?* He realizes that's a good question. Oh, she has an idea—they'll experiment."

I winced at how on-the-nose Liz's *hypothetical* was.

"Swell." Liz didn't look as though it mattered. "From there, it's an easy jump to finding someone unsuspecting, not giving the new girl the whole story, and stringing her along until she becomes part of the problem."

She was struggling with this as much as I was, but from a different angle. I forced myself to speak. Finally. "It's not like that. *We're* not like that. Everyone says that, but I mean it."

"Of course not. You're both good people, from what I've seen. All three of us went into this thinking you'd never see me again. That's fair. Somewhere along the way, things changed. Maybe I'm the only one feeling it. I don't even know what it is, but the answer isn't *just walk away*, and that confuses the hell out of me. I don't think anyone set out to hurt anyone else, but I can't—" Liz dragged in a shaky breath. "What is this?"

God I felt all of that in my core. I closed the distance between us. "Meeting you was the best and worst timing ever"—I wasn't used to fumbling for words, and I didn't know where the hell I was going with this—"but everything we did, all of the time I spent with you, all three of us, it was genuine. I wish I could define it. I want to. But the one thing I know is you're right—you leaving isn't the answer."

"Look, I want to see you two together. You're amazing people, both apart and with each other. But I don't know if my sanity can take much more giving it time. My love's not for lease, and if I don't put distance between us now, I'm going to cross some sort of point of no return, where you two still get each other, and I just shatter." Liz stepped around her, strode toward the door, and was gone before I could think of a response.

"She's got a point." Jordan startled me, and I whirled to where he still sat on the couch, watching me. He didn't look angry or sympathetic or anything.

My pride surged forward, screaming for me to bite back. To tell him I didn't appreciate being ganged up on. I had to defend myself. But my heart ached too much for that. "I know."

"So what is it you want, Chloe? I'll give you anything, but if you're not interested in trying, I'm done."

No. No. NO. Words from my worst nightmares. I sank to my knees on the floor. "Not that. Anything but that. I'm trying. I am. Looking for something I can't define."

"Is it Liz?" Jordan asked. "Is that what—who— you want? Would you rather be chasing her down right now?"

"No." Unless I could have them both. But I wouldn't surrender Jordan for that chance. "I'll call her and talk through boundaries or something. Later. This is about you and me. You've been shit on pretty much non-stop for the last few weeks, and I'm giving you one more thing to worry about by pouting that I'm unhappy *because reasons.*"

"You can't put that on hold because I'm having a bad day. But it's not easy to deal with. I'm trying. I even swallowed my manliness and asked for advice, because I can't figure out what you want."

"Asked who?" I didn't want to know, did I?

"Liz."

Of course he did. "So the flower the other morning? The coffee?"

"She told me I should try little things. Like what your characters do for each other."

"But you do so much for me already." I just kept fucking things up and I still didn't understand why. Two weeks ago, the answer seemed simple. Jordan and I were all talk and no action. Defined by our public personas and expectations. We weren't true to ourselves.

The fling with Liz had scratched an itch, but it wasn't enough. I wanted more. But not if it cost me the center of my universe.

"We do for each other. That's who we are. Give and take and give some more." Jordan knelt in front of me, holding my gaze. "Do you want a ring? A house in Portland? A different person in our bed every weekend? You can have any of that, as long as we stop with this uncertainty. We say we're fine, when we're not. We have little conversations disguised as making things better, but they don't. Every time I feel like I finally understand what's going on, we crumble again."

I swallowed past the ache inside that agreed with him. "What do you want? I'm being sincere. What are you looking for?" I hadn't really asked that question since we started falling apart, and I needed to know.

"To create what I want when I want." He took my hands in his. "And I want you. But not like this. I understand doubt, confusion, and uncertainty. You don't have to pretend those don't exist. But I need our words to keep meaning something. I won't be the needle in a broken-record relationship, scratching and bouncing over the same skip repeatedly because there's a rut we can't get past. There are lesser things, of course, but those are the big ones."

I wanted to sob. Or hide. "I want to give you answers. I don't have them, but I'm trying."

"That's fair. I just need to know I'm not the only one fumbling. But we both have to be all in on this." He moved to sit, legs in front of him, and tugged me between his thighs.

I settled back against his chest when he wrapped his arms around me. "What do we do about your job offers?" I asked.

"Don't change the subject. That's not fair."

"I'm not. Well, I am, but it's because I need to put my thoughts into words. I'm not brushing things off, but I have to make sense of what's going on my head. You're right. Everything you said, I agree with. I don't need the ring—I thought I did, for a long time, but I was looking for a symbol, when our relationship is full of them. I don't need a new house or to fuck half the city. I need a little more time, and maybe a sounding board."

He kissed the back of my head. "I'm always here for that. It's one of the reasons we work."

It really was. "So while that rattles in my skull, is DM the only company left on the table?"

"DM and GlobTech, at last count. They may both be gone by morning."

I tilted my head back, lips raised, and he brushed his mouth over mine. Relief snapped inside and I put more weight against him, memorizing the rough texture of stubble against my cheek. Feasting on the familiar, comforting scent of his body wash. "Do you really want to go back to DM?"

"It's the ultimate *fuck you* to Rinslet." His laugh was forced.

"It's the ultimate *fuck you* to someone who said they want the freedom to create. If GlobTech pulls out, we'll find a different solution. Next round of contacts. Something."

He kissed along the edge of my ear. "We do come up with some pretty creative ideas when we put our heads together," his whisper was soft and hot against my skin.

"Tentacles and nuns?" I said.

"School uniforms and furries."

"Are the furries wearing the school uniforms?" I asked.

"Absolutely. White cotton panties, knee-high socks, plaid skirts."

It felt good to smile. "That's all been done before."

"But we'll do it better."

I settled more of my weight against him. A tiny pit

still sat empty in my stomach, but I'd think through it, and Jordan and I would work things out.

"This conversation doesn't end with tonight." He glided his palm down my arm, and pushed up the hem of my shirt to caress bare skin.

I pressed into his touch with a gasp when he moved higher to knead my breast. "I agree." My voice was breathy. Ongoing conversation. Definitely." I twisted in his lap, and his erection pressed back. Inspiration struck and I stood, pulling Jordan to his feet at the same time. At the question in his gaze, I cupped him through his jeans and traced his hard length. "I'm all in." I stroked his cock through denim, relishing the way his eyes fluttered closed and his lips parted ever so slightly. "I don't think I was before." I positioned him with his back to the chair. "But I am now, I promise."

I nudged his shoulder and he dropped into the seat without resistance. He chuckled. "Pushy much?"

"Sometimes." I knelt in front of him and glided my hands up his thighs. This wasn't only about make-up sex. The intimacy was reassuring. I wanted to show him—literally and symbolically—that I was here for him as much as he was for me. I freed his cock from his boxer briefs, drawing a low groan.

Keeping my grip loose, I stroked at a slow pace, pausing occasionally to run my thumb over the swollen, purple head.

"Fuck, Chi." He spoke through clenched teeth, voice jagged.

When I trailed my tongue along his skin and licked away a drop of precum, he jerked in my hand. Each time he shifted closer to me or a grunt rumbled from his throat, arousal spilled through me. Getting Jordan off turned me on in an entirely different, but just as intense way as feeling him buried inside me. I took him in my mouth and slid down his length.

He wrapped my hair around his hand and tugged my head back, not jarring himself loose from my mouth as he forced my gaze to his. "I want to watch you." Command filled his words. "See the desire in your eyes, while you suck my cock. Watch you squirm with need when I come."

And I would. The tingles racing through me converged between my legs, begging for me to move my free hand lower and play with myself at the same time I pleasured him. That wasn't what this was about, though.

I tightened my grip and increased my pace, bobbing my head in time with his cues. Despite his command, as he drew closer to climax, he closed his eyes and tilted his head back. *Jesus*, I loved that sight—Jordan lost in pleasure.

I found and kept a steady rhythm, bathing in the way his growls rolled over me and tightened in my nipples like ghost kisses.

When I moved my other hand to his sac, he tensed and tightened his grip in my hair, holding then relaxing when he came, spilling into my mouth, salty spurts hitting the back of my throat. I continued to suck and lick, slowing as he did and not pulling away until he stopped.

I ran my tongue over his cock one last time, eliciting

a final shudder, and stared at him, wide-eyed and anything-but-innocent when he looked at me.

He offered me a hand as he stood, and pulled me to my feet. His kiss was hard and hungry, as he dove his tongue into my mouth to explore. How had I ever overlooked this amazing intensity that flowed between us. He dragged a thumb over my nipple and I whimpered at the rough touch through clothing.

Had I almost lost this—him—because I expected a perfect life that was hiccup free and lived up to my every fantasy without any work?

Jordan moved his hand lower, flipping the button on my jeans and yanking down the zipper with a single harsh tug. I grabbed his wrist. "You don't owe me."

"Yes, I do." He furrowed his brow as if my words didn't make sense. "Give and take and give some more."

"If you insist…" Any further retort faded into a long groan, when he slid his fingers between my legs and parted my folds. When he brushed my clit, a tremor traveled through me, making my legs wobble.

"I love how worked up you get, sucking me off." He kissed along the edge of my ear, whispery words hot against my skin. He pulled back enough to tease, tracing a path along my slit but not touching the center of my need again. "Watching you writhe, because you're so wet, while you run your tongue over my cock."

I couldn't think enough to respond, so I nodded. My head was light, swimming through tendrils of pleasure.

He knotted his fingers in my hair and crushed his lips to mine. Never breaking the kiss, he zeroed in on my clit, rubbing without pause while he devoured my moans.

Orgasm spilled through me, stealing my balance and my thoughts. Jordan's grip was the only thing holding me upright. He continued to stroke until I grabbed his wrist to stop him, then he moved his hands to steady me, and locked his gaze on mine. "The conversation isn't over."

"I know." I needed to catch my breath before I could say more.

He searched my face. "I'll surrender almost everything for you, but not my sanity or sense of self."

"I'd never ask you to." But I almost had without realizing it. I'd do better going forward. I had to. "What about Liz?" Crap. Talk about a mood killer.

Something like regret or sadness flickered in his eyes. "I'm pretty sure she removed herself from the equation."

"I didn't mean that. I think I owe her a serious apology."

"I can't answer the what-about question. I'll stand by you when you grovel, though."

I let out a small laugh. "You phrased it that way on purpose."

"Maybe." He kissed my nose.

So many maybes. Maybe we'd be all right. Maybe Jordan would struggle to find work. Maybe my job would get a lot more miserable. I was okay with the uncertainty, as long as Jordan and I were both still trying. And as we checked each doubt off the list, the nagging inside would fade a little more.

TWENTY-SEVEN

The waiter took away my now empty plate as I focused on the conversation with Ian and Mercy. We were having lunch, catching up on work, and hanging out since we hadn't had much time for it the last couple of weeks.

We waved the waiter away when he asked if we wanted dessert, and Ian handed over his credit card with the bill.

"Everything else is good, work-wise?" Mercy asked me.

Now that she mentioned it... I summoned the topic I'd stayed away from the entire meal. I'd almost convinced myself I could talk about this without letting my frustration show, but I was out of time to swallow my muddled emotions. "There is one thing."

Mercy raised her eyebrows.

"Now that the Rinslet contract is almost through

legal, I think you should ask someone else to be their point person."

"Why?" Ian was suddenly more interested in the conversation.

I couldn't use the *too much work* excuse, because five minutes ago I'd asked for more to do. "I don't feel like I'm the right contact for this partnership. You want someone more hands on."

"You live less than five miles from their office and they've only said good things about you. Besides, none of our account managers are better at a personal touch than you." Mercy studied me. "What aren't you saying?"

So, so much. I tried to be subtle about glancing at Ian. I should've waited to bring this up until it was just me and Mercy. How much could I say without mentioning my sex life? "Remember what I told you about L.A.?" I asked Mercy.

"The couple... Oh *God*, Liz. No." Mercy pursed her lips.

Why did she have to say that out loud?

Ian looked between us. "I hate it when you two do this. Couple of what?"

"Liz is talking about—"

"Nothing." I tried to convey a pleading for discretion when I looked at Mercy.

"They were the Rinslet people." The way she said it sounded cold and clinical. But from her perspective, it was. A fling. A one-night stand. People I was never supposed to see again.

Once upon a time I would've already told her things

were way past that point. I fiddled with my straw. "Might have been."

"What were?" Ian asked.

"I have to tell him." Mercy was apologetic. "This is about business."

It wasn't supposed to be. When it started, it had nothing to do with the company. "The only thing that matters here is that my working with Rinslet is a bad idea for the future of that partnership." I kept my tone even and professional. Mostly. A hint of petulance leaked in. How stupid and childish was I for getting emotionally involved?

Ian signed the credit-card receipt and handed it back to the waiter. "Now we're at the point where you can tell me or I can guess. Which do you prefer?"

"She hooked up with a couple in L.A. Rinslet people," Mercy said.

So much for secrets between friends. I scowled.

"Not funny." Ian growled. "What's really going on."

"She's telling the truth," I said.

He scrubbed his face. "Are you fucking kidding me? You potentially destroyed a vendor relationship because you were feeling a little kinky?"

At his tone, my anger surged. "So one, they weren't vendors at the time, and two, who the hell are you to talk? You almost destroyed two companies with what the two of you did." As in, when Ian and Mercy were fucking, and competing for contracts at the same time.

Mercy frowned and Ian sighed. "That's different," he said with so much conviction I almost believed him.

"Really? How?" I needed to understand why their indiscretions were okay and mine were a crime.

"Mercy and I love each other." Ian made it sound as if the answer was obvious.

My irritation simmered near boiling at the assumption that I couldn't possibly have the same thing. I didn't, but I could. "You didn't know at the time that you were in love. The two of you were too busy being assholes and pretending you didn't care about each other. You didn't even tell anyone you were kind-of-pretend dating."

"But it all worked out." Apparently Ian could do no wrong.

Like so much of our lives.

"But KM nearly dropped a multi-million-dollar contract because of it," I reminded them. "This isn't even in the same universe of severity. I'm just asking you to get someone else to work with Rinslet." I looked at Mercy. "Back me up, Mel. I'm not being unreasonable."

Chatter from the nearby diners filled the empty space between the three of us. The longer the silence stretched, the sicker I felt.

"Ian's right," Mercy finally said.

"Of course he is." I swallowed a rambling, almost incoherent thought about the two of them being hypocrites. "Fine. You're the bosses, and you know best." I didn't try to hide my snideness. "My wish is your command."

Mercy reached for me as I pushed back from the table, but stopped short of grabbing my hand. "It was a bad idea when Ian and I did it, and we're lucky it worked out. For a lot of reasons. But it was—is—different. Forget the Rinslet aspect of this for a moment. Cut out all the business bullshit. You're talking about a couple, and there's no happy ending for all three of you there. You can't let them get under your skin, because regardless of anything else, you're on the outside of that."

Her words latched on to every one of my insecurities and threatened to evict my lunch. "Like I said, you know best." I nearly choked on the words. "I need to go."

"I'll ask someone else to work with Rinslet." Mercy's words held a pitying edge.

"Great." It was easier than I thought to summon sarcasm to hide my hurt. "I'm glad we're on the same page." I turned away before either of them could say something that would pull up the tears I was fighting, and I stalked to my car. With any luck, the thirty-minute drive down the canyon would give me time to recover.

It didn't. The entire drive, I was focused on how right Mercy was, rather than the green and mountains around me. I should have walked away from Chloe and Jordan after that first night. The fact that I kept going back was my fault. Why did I expect anything from them?

Because we all had fun together. Because I enjoyed their company.

And they were already together. There was no place for me in that equation.

When I pulled into my parking garage, confusion

lingered in my chest, mingling with grief over losing two people I shouldn't have gotten attached to, and fury at the scalding hypocrisy of two other people I thought I knew better than anyone.

As I approached my condo and saw Chloe pacing outside the door, the chaos inside grew. I summoned the most neutral expression I could manage. "How did you find my address?" I slid my key in the lock, not looking at her.

"I… may have placed a couple of calls and used the images contract as an excuse."

Wonderful. I should have had the *I'm not working with Rinslet anymore* conversation with Mercy yesterday, minus Ian's company and the painful condescension. "Do you want to come in?" The polite offer slipped out from habit. Even when I was annoyed, I couldn't ignore that I'd been trained to be a perfect hostess.

"I can't stay. I have a meeting at the top of the hour, but I wanted to do this in person. Partly because I thought you'd ignore my texts—and you'd be right to do so." Chloe drummed her fingers on her leg as she spoke.

I pursed my lips and stared at her finally, not trusting myself to speak. Who knew what would come out of my mouth next?

"Right, then." Chloe's laugh was nervous. "I'm sorry about last night. Or rather, I'm sorry it seemed like we used you. That was never our intent. I don't know if it matters, but I never faked the closeness or connection with you. Neither did Jordan. We wanted you around because you're you, not because we needed a third person to help us feel less stuck in life."

She sighed and tugged on her ponytail. "We don't have to do the sex stuff anymore—this will be the last time I ever mention it if that's what you want—but I don't have a lot of friends, and I consider you one, and I'm sorry. Have lunch with us this weekend, like we planned. We'll go somewhere public. No pressure. No…"

"Sex stuff?" I didn't have the headspace to deal with this right now. Especially with the fluttering inside that begged me to hear Chloe out and tell her I'd be there. I wanted to see them again, but this hurt. "I have work to do and so do you."

"That's fair." Chloe turned away. She paused and spun back to look at me. "Sorry, I guess I'm not done yet. You asked for boundaries, and I'm willing to set them. Either that, or tell me right now to go the fuck away."

Go the fuck away. The thought was vile. If we said right here and now *we're just friends* I'd know where we stood. The logic felt faulty, but the idea of never seeing Chloe or Jordan again felt worse. I enjoyed their company, even without the sex. I wanted them in my life, and their friendship was valuable to me. "Okay. Here's a boundary. No more sex."

"Okay." Chloe nodded.

"Just like that?" I asked. "You don't want something in return? You've got some serious hang-ups and that's fine, as long as you're dealing with them, but you need to draw some lines too." Where did that come from? My insistence both terrified me and eased my mind.

"Okay," Chloe said again. "I don't want you to feel

like you can't hang out with us unless we're both there. Partly because you've seen, Jordan will do what Jordan wants. But also, I want to hang out with you. Just the two of us. I don't really have any girlfriends, and I know you have Mercy, but maybe you have room for me, too?"

The simplicity of the request tugged at my heart. I did have Mercy, and I still adored her, but today was a painful reminder that I'd made her and Ian the center of my universe, and that wasn't healthy. I almost laughed as Mercy's words about couples rushed back. I'd have to watch myself with Chloe until we found a new comfort zone, but I was willing to try. "I'd love more early morning balcony talks, or lunches."

Chloe's smile warmed me. "Me too. Call me. Us. Whatever. Please?"

"Okay."

She walked down the hallway and waved one more time before stepping onto the elevator.

I pushed into my condo and leaned against the door, to close it. The conversation with Chloe felt good. I could live with terms like the ones we'd discussed.

I settled in front of my laptop and logged in to work. It didn't happen. Every project I opened, my eyes glazed over and I couldn't comprehend wat I was looking at. Well, crap. If I wasn't working, I might as well screw around. I opened a web browser, and one of the head-lines caught my attention.

Nope, Not reading it. I was here to screw around on social media and look at kitty pictures.

My finger had other ideas as it clicked on the head-line *Digital Media Courts New Director of Art.*

I skipped the fluff of the article as it recounted a distorted view of Jordan's past, and dove straight to the quote from DM's CTO.

We understand there's a lot of negative buzz directed at Jordan Iverson at the moment. It's unfortunate to see a talent like his go to waste, when he's come from a less-than-nurturing environment. Mentored the right way, someone like him could be polished from a rough piece of coal, to a sparkling diamond. We feel he's a great fit for our organization and hope he reaches the same conclusion, in the interest of his career.

I laughed at the condescension dripping from the words. I might not be familiar with the company, but that paragraph was enough to convince me Jordan would be miserable in a place like that.

The thought tickled something else. A memory from…

I reached for it and it flitted out of my grasp.

This was important. What was it?

The artists who make money at this are merchandising. A startup takes capital. Jordan needed that in order to do what he wanted.

I couldn't invest in him—not only was it a conflict of interest, but I didn't know nearly enough about what he wanted to do. But I knew someone who did.

If I made this call, I was overstepping boundaries. Jordan might not want my help and I risked pissing him or Chloe off. They didn't have to accept the offer, though, and I didn't want to give them false hope by telling them about it before I had more information.

And if I called, I'd owe Jonathan the courtesy of at

least hearing him out, regarding his offer the other morning.

Would that be such a bad thing?

I pulled Jonathan's business card from my purse and dialed.

TWENTY-EIGHT

Chloe

Seeing Liz left a warm glow in my chest. I wasn't sure she was completely on board with the new arrangement, but I'd meant everything I said, and at least she was still in our lives this way.

But as I rode the elevator up to my office, the quote on all the tech blogs, from DM about Jordan, made me scowl. *Arrogant assholes.* Figured they'd be petty about this. Had they only kept their offer out there for the sake of an eight-year-old grudge? Who did that on a professional level?

Right. I forgot what company I was talking about.

I stepped off the elevator, glanced up to make sure I wouldn't run into anyone, then sent Jordan a quick text. *Fuck them.*

His replay came quickly. *They're not worth the lube.*

Jordan was still Jordan, despite everything, and that made me smile.

Bri looked up as I approached my office. On the

surface, she didn't look like she belonged in an office, with blond dreadlocks, and tattoos snaking up her arms and above her collar.

But appearances were bullshit, and she was a Godsend as my assistant.

"Your one thirty is here." The corners of her mouth tugged up when she told me, and a hint of pink crept into her cheeks.

And like a quarter of the office, she was crushing on Scott. I didn't see the appeal. I got that he was attractive, but when I was growing up, he was always hanging out with Rae, and I knew he really was.

He was good guy, but he was also human, rather than the god on a pedestal most people thought of him as.

I stepped into my office, not surprised to see that Scott had already made himself comfortable. I closed the door, set my phone and purse down, and took a seat behind my desk. "I didn't mean to keep you waiting. Am I late?" I was five minutes early, but some habits of propriety were hard to break.

"Nah. I finished before I expected and thought I'd see if you were back from lunch yet." Scott leaned back in his seat, one ankle over the other knee, looking as if nothing could faze him. The lines near his eyes and the circles underneath shattered the illusion. "I'm sorry about what happened with Jordan. I asked Zach to think a little longer before making his decision."

"Things would've gone down the same way." I understood the circumstances, and they'd made the best decision for the company, but I didn't have to like it.

Scott sighed. "No offense, but..."

"But what?"

"Maybe it's a blessing in disguise."

Did he really just...

No. I'd heard him wrong.

But I hadn't. "Are you fucking kidding me?" Most people wouldn't talk to Scott like this, but I wasn't most people and my filter was shot. "Which part is the blessing? Where the public is gloating and calling him a monster? Where he was forced out of the job he made?"

"The part where he's free."

If I stared at him, unblinking, would he see what a stupid statement that was?

"I'm projecting. Don't worry about it." Exhaustion lined Scott's voice.

"Aren't you a little young for a midlife crisis?"

He raised an eyebrow. "Pretty sure I've aged an extra few decades in the last couple of years." The tiredness lingered in his tone, but he spoke with a hint of amusement.

"Drama queen." I tried to keep my tone light.

One corner of his mouth tugged up. "Only on my best days. I know your schedule is busy, so I'll cut to it. I'm surprised you had time for me."

"I don't," I teased. "But I'd never tell the boss *no* and I have a brilliant administrative assistant who makes it all work." I told Scott *no* all the time.

"That's what this meeting is about." He pulled a folder from the briefcase next to his chair and put it on his legs. "Your schedule, not your assistant. Who, by the way, hasn't gone unnoticed."

"Oh?" I knew what he meant, and it had nothing to do with her appearance. Her father had clashed with Scott in the past, but she didn't speak to the man, and wanted very much to keep her parentage a secret. I was fine with that.

He shrugged. "That's it. I know who she is. I trust that you know what you're doing. About the fact that you're spending half your time doing Jordan's job now..."

The way he trailed off had my mind jumping along possibilities. I hadn't screwed up. But had they found a replacement for Jordan? I hated the idea of working with someone else in that role. Had they left me out of interviews because of that? Then again, just because we'd custom built our jobs didn't mean I had a say in his successor.

"You've really come through, this past couple of weeks, " Scott said. "The situation was harsh, and it's one none of us wanted. You could have gone a lot of different ways. Walking out when he was fired. Refusing to take on his tasks. Sabotaging something. I would have understood any of those responses. Not forgiven them, but understood them."

"I'd never do anything like that."

He picked at the edge of the folder. "But you could have. The thing is, you stepped up instead. I'm impressed, and I'm not the only one. I've talked to Zach about this, and we'd rather not replace Jordan."

You shouldn't have fired him, then. I swallowed the retort for the sake of keeping the conversation on track. "I don't understand."

"If you're interested, we want to reorganize all those groups to report to you." He slid me the folder. "That's our offer. You're already doing the work. We've pre-approved the budget for you to hire two new managers, so you can delegate. It comes with a title change and a raise. But only if you're interested."

Shock froze me in place. Part of me grasped his meaning, but the rest refused to accept it. I didn't dare look at the paperwork. "The old title is already long and awkward. I don't think a business card will hold more letter."

"We're simplifying it. You'll be Senior Vice President of Creative."

And there it was. They wanted to promote me. Give me more money and power because they'd fired my boyfriend.

No. Because I'd earned it. Why wasn't I saying *yes*?

Because they'd fired my boyfriend.

But I wanted this. I didn't realize how badly, until he put the offer on the table.

"I get why you're hesitating." Scott nudged the folder closer to me. "This is a huge decision, and the job only gets more stressful. Take a couple of days to think about it." He stood.

"Thank you." I rose too. "Give me tonight, and I'll have an answer for you."

"You've earned, this Chloe. Every step of the way, *you* put yourself here. Whatever happens next should be for the same reasons." Scott turned and walked out of my office, closing the door behind him.

As silence rushed in, so did excitement. Senior VP?

Me? Holy shit. I let out a tiny shout, not wanting anyone to hear, but needing to release some energy. I unlocked my phone. I had to call Jordan.

They're not worth the lube. His message and name taunted me on the screen.

He was sitting at home screwed—again—by this situation, and I was about to call and tell him I'd been offered his job.

Scott's parting words echoed in my head, implying this decision should be mine and only because of me.

But it wasn't that easy.

TWENTY-NINE

JORDAN

When Liz called me and told me she had an angel investor opportunity for me, I whooped loud enough it scared away the birds roosting on the balcony.

I wanted to call Chloe. Text. Email. Something immediate. But this was news best shared in person, mostly to share the excitement and make sure she had time to celebrate with me, but also to soften the blow in case she didn't like Liz doing this on my behalf.

I was only a little worried about the latter.

So when she got home after work, I was there ready and waiting.

Her fidgeting as she stepped inside matched mine, but her frown threw me for a loop. Did she already know?

The instant she'd set her stuff down, and had her shoes off, I wrapped an arm around her waist and gave her a long, hungry kiss. "Welcome home."

"Thanks." She tensed under my touch, not pulling away but not leaning into me either.

Yeah. Not good. "Sit. Relax. Unwind from the day." I pointed her toward the couch. I have news that will make you smile." I hoped.

The noise she made was half-laugh, half-sigh. "Me too. I hope." This time it was all sigh. "No. You may not like it at all." She dropped onto the sofa.

I settled next to her. "You first." I wanted to end on a high note.

"They found your replacement at work."

Oh. A vise gripped my lungs. Of course they were looking, but it stung—rusty dagger to the heart kind of sting—to hear I could be replaced in less than two weeks. That was years of work. *Poof.* "Anyone I know?"

Chloe held up her hand and wiggled her fingers in an awkward wave.

Was that code for something? Were we playing charades now? "I don't understand."

"They want to merge our departments all under one heading of *Creative.*" She licked her lips and tugged her hair. "And... have-them-both-report-to-me."

It took me a moment to process the run-together words, but as I did, my hurt lifted. "You? Really?" I hoped my tone conveyed my excitement.

She winced. "It's a new title. A little more money. It didn't ask them for this, I promise, but..."

"You want it."

She nodded. "I really do. But not if it hurts you."

"I think it's amazing." I hugged her, and she finally relaxed against me. "I mean, it's going to be a lot more work. I don't know how it wouldn't be, but no one can do this better than you. If you want it, take it."

"Are you sure?"

I rested a hand on her cheek, holding her face and gaze. "It's not about me. I'm excited for you. But if you're okay with what's involved... Do it. You've earned it."

She pressed her lips to my palm. "It means a lot of late nights." Her soft words hummed over my skin. "At least until I hire some more people."

"We've always had those, and you always come home to me." I meant the reply to be light, but the meaning behind it hit hard. She really had. Even with the fighting. Struggling with who we were together and what we wanted. We always came home to each other. That had to count for a lot.

And if things went well for me, I'd be here a lot more often waiting, instead of my schedule missing Chloe's.

She leaned more weight against my hand, finally smiling. "What's your news?"

I'd been practicing this part of the conversation in my head since I got off the phone with Liz, but now that we were here, the words stuck in my throat. "I have a chance to pitch to an angel investor. Someone who will consider backing me, if I want to build a business around my art."

"Like selling prints and T-shirts? Stuff like that?"

"That and so much more. Figurines. A tie-in web series."

"Wow. Just... Wow." Chloe started at me, eyes wide.

"That's huge. You mentioned it would be fun, but I didn't realize you were pursuing it."

"I wasn't."

Creases appeared in her forehead. "So these angel-investor people called you out of the blue?"

Maybe I should've led with the next bit. But it was a detail. The opportunity was the real news. "No. Liz did this, on her own, and told me after. I was talking to her about it the other day, and she knows a guy and got me a meeting with him."

"That's awesome." Despite the words, Chloe's enthusiasm had faded. Her smile looked genuine, though.

"Yeah?"

"Absolutely." This time she sounded more sincere.

"There's a catch."

She gave a light laugh. "There always is when money's involved."

"I have to present him with a full business proposal. Profit and loss projections. Marketing plan. All the things that prove he'll make his investment back."

"You don't have experience in that."

"No." There was no going back now. "Liz offered to help. She's familiar with advertising, markets budgets, and finance."

"How convenient."

"And if you're going to be working longer hours, I'll be the only one spending the time with her." I braced myself for the fallout. Would it be pouting? A stoic *fine*? Something else?

Chloe's chest rose and fell with her deep breath, and

when she focused on me again, her eyes were bright and so was her smile. "This is amazing. You have to do it."

"You're okay with it?" I shouldn't question things, but I had to make sure.

She nodded. "There's a part of me that's going to be jealous still. I don't tell you that to dissuade you, but so you know. I trust you. I trust her. And you will be amazing at this. You have to do it. You have to try."

"There's one other catch." Might as well put all the potentially negative stuff on the table at once.

"Long list of exceptions for such good news." She grasped my fingers and rested both of our hands on my knee.

"This means I'm turning down the DM job."

She squeezed my hand. "You were going to do that anyway. You don't want to be there. They don't deserve you."

"There's no guarantee that this will work out." My own doubts were free to rush in now that I didn't have Chloe as an excuse to hold back. "I could spend the next two weeks doing nothing but prepping for this, instead of job hunting, and it may get me nowhere."

But the more I thought about what Liz proposed, the more I was desperate to have it. "I miss creating rather than telling other people what to create. I'm tired of taking orders from the top and passing them down the line. I want to spend my time designing, not delegating."

"You don't have to convince me. My job comes with a pay raise. We can stretch your severance out for a while, if we have to."

"Are you making double?" I asked. It was too much to hope for, but technically she was doing two people's jobs.

"Ten percent." She nudged my knee with hers. "But we'll stick to a budget. If you want this, we'll make it work."

"We've never in our lives stuck to a budget." We spent what we made, and when we got raises, we spent more. Why didn't I think of this sooner?

"Maybe it's time we learn to suck it up."

Which sounded impossible and glorious at the same time. "So we'll struggle and possibly make ourselves miserable, so I can do something that may or may not ever pay off?"

"It'll be worth it."

She had so much confidence in me. I needed to concede, because if I kept talking, I'd never forgive myself for convincing Chloe this was a bad idea. I kissed her. "Thank you. We should take this one last chance to spend big and celebrate your promotion."

"We're watching our budget." She leaned into me, tone playful. "So… ramen?"

"I was thinking expensive ramen."

She laughed and settled closer against my arm.

"Seriously, though." I trailed my fingers through her hair. How had I gotten so lucky? "Let's go someplace nice. Takashi?"

"That's about as expensive as ramen gets in this town."

"Technically, it's udon. We'll go Saturday night." This was perfect. I just needed to convince myself this wasn't a huge mistake. We were at the edge of healing us, with opportunity stretching out in both our futures, but one major tumble—like running out of money because I'd pursued my dream—and it could all still fall apart.

THIRTY

When Mercy called on Saturday afternoon to ask if we were still on for dinner, I almost told her *no*. But my irritation had faded from lunch the other day. Had I overreacted? The longer I dragged out not seeing them, the bigger a deal I made out of things and the harder it would be to repair.

I'd rather have Ian and Mercy back now.

"We'll get sushi." Mercy's tone was cajoling.

She did know how to entice me. "Okay, but you're coming down to the valley. You two get to make the drive for once."

"That's fair. Meet us at eight?"

Three hours later, we stood at the host's podium and Takashi, while Ian tried to smooth talk, and then bribe the host into something less than a ninety-minute wait. In the background, porcelain clinked against saucers and weekend chatter assaulted them.

"I'm sorry, sir." The host sounded anything but.

242

"Your name is on the list. We'll buzz you when your table is ready."

Mercy grabbed Ian's arm and pulled him back. "We'll wait."

"Or we'll go get steak." I should've known better than to suggest this place last minute. The scents of miso and soy sauce taunted me and made my stomach growl.

Ian glared at the host, as if shooting daggers from his eyes would change our situation. "You want sushi and we're here. Besides, this time of night on a Saturday, every place is going to be packed."

"But I bet there's only a five-minute wait at McDonald's." Mercy nudged him playfully.

He rolled his eyes, a smile threatening. "It's tempting. But even if they had sushi, I grantee you I wouldn't eat it."

"I'll sate the craving another time." Liz nodded toward the exit. "Shall we?"

"Reservation for Iverson." Jordan's voice made my blood run cold and then hot, and I wavered with the wave of conflicting emotions.

I wanted to look, but I didn't know if my resolve would hold up to seeing them.

"Liz?" Chloe's voice cut through my hesitation. "Hey. What are you doing here?"

Mercy looked at me, eyebrows raised in question.

"Dinner," I said. *Way to be witty, Liz.*

Jordan glanced away from the host and his gaze settled on me. "Go figure. We're here for the koi fishing."

The host cleared his throat, and Jordan ignored him.

That would either impress Ian, or piss him right the fuck off.

"Who are your friends?" Mercy asked.

Goodie. The moment I'd been waiting for. Not. I'd be polite, pass around names, and then Mercy, Ian, and I would be on our way. "Chloe, Jordan, this is my brother Ian and my best friend Mercy." I pointed as I listed names, though it was probably obvious to everyone who was who.

"A pleasure." Mercy shook their hands. "Do you work with Liz?"

God, I was going to kill her for pushing this issue. How was I going to convey, beyond names, who Chloe and Jordan were? *One-night stand gone longer, meet my disapproving but otherwise lovable family.*

"I thought Liz worked for you." Jordan didn't flinch.

"Oh, she does," Mercy said.

What was she doing? "Chloe is our contact at Rinslet, for the image licenses." You know. The person we argued about me not talking to, a few days ago. The woman you called me unprofessional over?

"I thought your name sounded familiar. So happy to finally meet you." Mercy sounded as genuine as I'd ever heard her. What was she up to? I'd think *just being friendly,* but the whole *ditzy* thing wasn't Mercy's usual mask.

"Are you on your way out?" Chloe asked. "You must have gotten in early."

"Didn't get in at all," Mercy said.

"Join us," Chloe nodded toward the dining room. "We're celebrating."

"Celebrating what?" Ian asked.

Probably Jordan's chance to pitch to Jonathan. Which was currently under NDA, and so Jordan couldn't discuss it.

"Life being good." Jordan didn't hesitate.

Chloe looped her hand around my arm, and the familiar contact jolted through me, the desire knocking my thoughts further off track.

"We can't intrude," Ian said.

"We're not. They invited us." Mercy took his hand. "Celebrations are more fun with more people."

Seriously. What was she doing?

"They only have a table for two." The pit in my gut insisted this was a bad idea.

"You can upgrade us to five, can't you, Matt?" Jordan grinned at the host.

Matt gestured toward the dining area. "I'm sure I've got something."

"We come here all the time for lunch." Chloe leaned in, voice a stage whisper.

"Love it." Mercy fell into step behind them, tugging Ian and spinning to face me. "See? Sushi."

Hurray. Now I was a fifth wheel instead of a third.

We were shown to a round table, and I ended up between Ian and Chloe. That would make it a lot harder to kick Mercy if she kept up whatever this was.

Tea was served, we placed our orders, and an awkward silence fell over the table.

Ian turned to Jordan. "I don't know what these two are up to—typical, I promise. Truth be told, we know who you are."

And now I could find a hole to crawl into, please and thank you.

"I can't pay to get my clients the kind of exposure you've gotten over the past two weeks," Ian said. "You didn't deserve the doxing with the job offers, but it's impressive coverage anyway. Who did you piss off?"

"Do you want a list?" Jordan laughed. "There's no such thing as bad publicity. Unofficial company mission statement."

This wasn't so bad. No one had mentioned yet that Jordan and Chloe were my hook-ups. "They rescued me at E3 from a blogger who wanted to talk about George. They're probably caught up in the mess because of me, but they're too polite to call me on it."

"Nothing to call you on. The guy's a dick." Chloe sipped her tea as elegantly as anyone in the room. She wiggled her pinky finger. "Teeny, tiny, needle-sized. And he had a problem with us long before now."

Ian raised his brows. "With all that free time on your hands, what are you up to now?"

Oh, God. *Sorry you were fired. How's that going for you?* How tactless was Ian right now?

"Packages," Jordan said with a straight face.

Mercy smirked and I choked back a laugh, remember the last time I'd had this conversation with Jordan and Chloe. I wasn't used to holding my tongue in front of any of these people, but I didn't know what the rules were with all of them together.

"Really." It was impossible to get a read on Ian. He was either playing along or getting irritated.

I set down my cup. "Yup. KaleidoMotion has an impressive tool."

"Perfect for individual market penetration," Chloe chimed in.

The corners of Ian's mouth twitched, and then his poker face slid back in.

Mercy grinned broadly. "I saw that when I was out there. They were demoing their package to the entire group. Risky, but sexy."

"Take a joke." I elbowed Ian.

He shook his head, but his smile finally burst through. "You're all children."

"And you're a grumpy old man," I teased.

"And you're my baby sister, who's sweet, and innocent, and doesn't talk about things like *package sizes*."

Mercy and Chloe snorted.

The waiter returned with our appetizers, setting several sizzling plates in the center of the table.

"He's right." Chloe held up her hands as if in surrender. "We're in polite company." Another round of laughs passed around the table and she pasted on an exaggerated scowl before her expression relaxed and she turned to Mercy. "If we're going to insist on talking business, I've heard brilliant things about your tracking and reporting capabilities."

Mercy reached in to grab a pot sticker. "We're the best. But it's all top secret, black-label stuff, so… I tell you, I have to—I don't know—cut off your ear or something."

"They're cute ears, though." I traced a finger along

the edge of Chloe's ear, realized what I was doing, and tried to be subtle about pulling back.

Mercy didn't miss a beat, jumping in before anyone had a chance to blink. "A kneecap, then. Those are extraneous."

Chloe shrugged. "I mean… I guess it depends on how much time you spend on your knees and why."

Ian coughed.

This was either going to be a lot of fun, or the longest night of my life.

As dinner came and dishes were cleared away, the conversation carried on. Apparently, Jordan and Chloe were friendly enough with the staff they didn't get dirty looks for occupying the table for several hours. Things wound down, and the five of us wandered to the parking lot together. After ten, even on a Saturday, the streets were half-empty. I squeezed Chloe's hand and then Jordan's. "We'll talk on Monday night?" I asked Jordan.

"Yup." Jordan and Chloe headed in the opposite direction of where I had parked.

"Monday?" Ian asked as soon as they were out of earshot. "What happened to never seeing them again?"

Right. The fight just a few days ago. "It's a business thing. For him. Besides, I think we all overreacted at lunch that day," I said.

"I don't overreact." Ian drew his lips into a thin line.

"Really? Tell us again about why you got kicked off the high-school baseball team in Chicago?"

"That was once, and it was fifteen years ago."

"Closer to twenty," Mercy said. "But no one's counting. What about that time you got pissed off enough you let your mouth run, and you and I almost never spoke again?"

"Almost never is a bit harsh. Besides, I groveled—of my own accord—and you forgave me." Ian spoke with finality, as if the topic was closed.

This lighthearted teasing felt right. The kind of casual fun I hadn't had with them since…Was it really before Ian and Mercy hooked up? I hated the thought. I looked at Ian. "Fine. You *never* overreact," I teased. "But you were a big grump that day, and I overreacted. I'm sorry."

"Me too." He pulled me into a hug.

They walked me to my car. I sat in the driver's seat for several minutes after they left. Tonight was a blast. More fun than I'd had in ages. No, that wasn't right. The last time I'd had that much fun was in L.A. At E3. In a hotel room. Talking.

The single reminder was enough to open a gaping emptiness inside. I started my car and cranked the radio. There was nothing blaring music couldn't fix.

Staring Monday, I'd go back to being professional and friend, but nothing more, with Jordan and Chloe. I struggled too much to distinguish the difference between that and flirting, if I thought even for a second that *more* was an option.

So, *more* was off the table.

THIRTY-ONE

When Liz showed up at our condo a little before four-thirty on Monday, I told her to make herself comfortable in the home office.

The way she said with her back straight, staring past me, she looked instead like she'd rather be anywhere else.

Did I miss something when I showered? Had I offended her at dinner the other night and not realized it? "Are you all right?" I asked.

"Absolutely." Her dull smile matched her tone. "We should get started. We have two weeks, and a lot to cover since we're starting from scratch."

"Why two weeks, and why from scratch? I have a portfolio."

"Fantastic." She kept her gaze on something that wasn't me. "We'll check that off the list. I talked to Jonathan, and there's a local industry show in fifteen days. He'll be in town and wants to meet with you then."

Wow. This was really happening. I had an appointment and everything. The weight of it almost made it possible to ignore the weird tension in the room. "You're the boss. What do I need to do?"

She pulled a tablet from her briefcase and swiped the screen. In a tone a computer would envy, she ticked off a list of things we needed to accomplish in the next two weeks. She met my gaze for a second, before staring past me again. "You pick where we start. Most of this can be done in any order. If you do the stuff you consider boring first, you'll have more energy for the fun at the end."

Like any other job. "I'd rather mix it up. Numbers today and tomorrow, initial design on Wednesday—back and forth like that."

"Sounds like a plan." She made some notes and then started down another list, this one of questions. The next couple of hours passed the same way, with Liz jerking away each time I made eye contact, and keeping several feet between us at all times.

Maybe she didn't like my cologne.

Something told me the answer wasn't that simple, though.

When Chloe got home, Liz greeted her just as professionally, and left moments later.

Chloe stared at the closed door, then turned to me. "Was it something I said?"

"She was like that all day." I shrugged, and guided

Chloe to the couch. I pulled her into my lap and handed her the remote.

"So… did I imagine Saturday night?" Chloe asked.

"Not unless it was a shared hallucination."

Chloe leaned into me but didn't turn on the TV. "She's more open in front of her regular friends?"

"Could be, but did you see the way she paled when her brother said he knew who we were?"

"That was kind of cute." Chloe sighed. "I miss the Liz who doesn't hold her tongue."

I did too. "She may be back, but things have changed. Maybe to what they always should have been." If we were going to fool around with someone else in the future—a thought that didn't entice me as much as I expected, if at all—we'd have to set stricter boundaries first.

Tuesday with Liz wasn't much different. Cool. Polite. Professional. With a smile and a nod for Chloe, as Liz left for the evening.

Every time I tried to ask what was going on, Liz brushed me off.

"Are you sure you're all right?"

"I'm fine." She didn't sound angry or irritated or much of anything.

"Did I do something to upset you? Did either one of us?"

Liz would shake her head. "Not at all." She sounded sincere.

By Wednesday afternoon, it was time to surrender. Whatever had Liz so aloof, she didn't seem interested in sharing. One thing I couldn't complain about—her professionalism and skill. Every suggestion she made and task she had was fantastic from my perspective.

I worked at my computer, arranging a series of portfolio thumbnails into a visually appealing layout. Totally different skillset than creating the art to begin with. "Can I get your thoughts on this?" I called over my shoulder to Liz, never looking up from my screen.

"Sure." Seconds later she rested a hand on my shoulder.

I tucked away my shock, not wanting to startle her. "I can't decide—keep it thematic or vary my selection?"

"Show me both." She leaned in closer, until her head was inches from mine and her breast nudged my arm. "This is thematic, isn't it?"

"Yes." My voice almost cracked. *Jesus.* I was a horny thirteen-year-old again, getting flustered because I touched a woman's boob.

She pressed closer and her soft perfume teased me. "Go with the variety option. You've got an impressive range. Show it off."

That's not the only thing about me that's impressive. I turned a tame smile on her. "Perfect. Thanks."

Her eyes grew wide and she stepped back, but not far. "Fiddle with the white space a little, and some of the angles. It's almost there, but not quite." She kept her hand on my shoulder as I dragged objects around the screen. "Closer. Maybe a new font?"

"Similar style or completely new direction?" The pleasant contact raced over my skin and teased me with memories of shared nights, but more important, it was reassuring. This was the way things should be.

"Completely different. Mechanical. Or modern."

Time to push the limits a hint, and hope it didn't make her backpedal. I selected a novelty font Chloe picked up years ago. It was subtle, until closer examination.

"Oh God." Liz laughed. "Are those anal beads? What's that supposed to be? A fleshlight? Probably not the best choice for this."

"Fine." I dragged out the word in an exaggerated huff and selected Comic Sans instead. "Better?"

"No." She slapped me playfully. "I preferred the dildos."

"That's what she said."

She shook her head, but her smile didn't fade. "Mechanical or modern."

With the tension evaporating, the next couple of hours flew by. When I heard Chloe get him, I was conflicted. I was happy she was here, but I didn't want to see Liz shrink back in her shell.

"My lovelies," Chloe called. Seconds later she stopped in the office doorway. "Am I interrupting?" Her smile and good mood were infectious.

Liz hopped from her chair. "Perfect timing." She grabbed Chloe's hand pointed her at the now empty seat. "We need your opinion. Sit. Don't think about it too long. Each time, do you like option A or B?" She leaned in, one hand on Chloe's shoulder, and clicked through a series of options. For the next hour or so, the three of us talked a little work, a lot of bullshit, and everything random.

After Liz left, Chloe stared at the front door for

several seconds. "Which one is body snatcher Liz? Tonight's iteration, or yesterday's?"

"I'm not any more certain than you are." Jordan settled a hand at the small of her back, and steered her toward the living room. "But like you, I'm hoping today was the real deal."

"Was she like that all day?"

"About halfway through it she relaxed."

Chloe smiled, and lines of stress vanished from around her eyes. "Fingers crossed it lasts."

***

FRIDAY AFTERNOON, Liz arrived at three.

"Not that I'm complaining," I said as we set up in the office in what had already become a familiar ritual, "But why so early?"

"I wrapped up work so we could get a little more time in on your project before the weekend." She scooted her chair close enough her arm pressed into mine.

We dove into work, and every few minutes she leaned past me without hesitation to make a comment or suggestion. The awkward pauses were gone.

A couple of hours in, Chloe called. "Atomic Comic Collection Connection," I answered with the line from Venture Brothers without thought.

"You're a dork. Also, you're in a good mood." Chloe sounded like she was as well.

"I might be. Life is good."

"Liz still there?"

"Yup." In fact, she'd just nudged my hand out of the way to take control of the mouse.

"Tell her I said *hi*."

Liz didn't look up from what she was doing, but cheerfully said, "Hello."

"I'm off early today. Well, early for me. Normal time for other people." No wonder Chloe sounded happy. "Pizza?"

"Hells yes," I said.

"Of course. What does Liz like?"

I glanced at her, ready to ask the question and have her shrug me off with an *I need to leave soon*.

Instead she met and held my gaze as she said, "Veggie, extra cheese, add sausage."

"How does that even make sense?" I laughed.

"It's easier than ordering it any other way.

"Tell her I got it," Chloe said in my ear. "See you both soon."

As I disconnected, Liz bumped my shoulder with hers and nodded at the screen. "If you invest in the correct equipment up front, and have some of the right connections—which you do through me—you can offer die-cut stickers and plastic figures from the start." She pointed to a few separate line items on her spreadsheet.

I loved the idea, but I was already using so many of her connections and so much of her favor. "There's no way I can do anything for you that equals what you're doing for me."

"I want to see you succeed. That's my goal. That's all you need to worry about is making this work." She sounded sincere.

I wanted that too. We dove back into work until Chloe got home. She poked her head into the office. "Stop working. Come eat."

"Two minutes." Liz didn't look up from what she was doing.

She finished, we saved, and headed toward the living room. My feet slowed to a confused halt in the kitchen. Chloe had set the table. I didn't remember the last time, outside of holidays with family, that we'd sat down to a formal meal in our own kitchen. For us, dinner was either on the go or in front of the TV.

At least the open pizza box in the middle of the table took some of the scary *fancy* out of the whole scene.

"I couldn't make up my mind, so I got two half and half pizzas," Chloe said. "I don't know what kind of wine pairs with pizza so you'll have to make do with Dew." She winked at Liz.

"I'd tell you which wine, but then you'd tease me for having an answer." Liz's smile was tentative. She sat when we did, as if waiting for our cues.

We dug in, and Chloe reached a fork toward Liz's plate. Liz shifted her food back, but not out of reach. "Excuse you?"

"I want a piece of sausage."

"You should have gotten your own."

I watched the exchange, amused.

"I couldn't make up my mind," Chloe said. "Besides, I've shared my sausage with you."

Liz rolled her eyes, but that didn't hide her blush.

"You're reaching, with a punk like that." She plucked a piece of meat from her slice, and held it out.

Chloe leaned in enough to snag both the sausage and Liz's finger, sucking both into her mouth before letting Liz go.

I managed to swallow my groan, but I couldn't ignore the heat that flooded me at the playful display. I wanted more of this, from Chloe and Liz. Them together. Them with me.

Was there any chance they both did too, or was this a long crawl toward a steep disappointment?

THIRTY-TWO

Chloe

Being able to come home and unwind was nice. Having Liz here, laughing and joking with us, and Jordan in such a great mood, was brilliant.

My new job was tough, and the hours were long, but I loved the challenge. It had been a long time since I enjoyed myself at work this much. But I still wanted the weekend to relax and unwind with Jordan.

And Liz.

The admission came easily in my head. I wanted her here more and more often.

"You two aren't going back to work, are you?" I batted my eyelashes and gave them my best *I'm adorable, stay with me* look.

Liz's expression fell. Not quite what I'd hoped for.

"I'm not asking for any nefarious reasons." I rushed to set her mind at ease. I was going to make you both take a break and watch movies with me."

"What do you think, bosslady Liz?" Jordan asked. "Can we afford a few hours of fun?"

Liz pushed back from the table and her chair squealed on the tile. "I'll let you two enjoy your evening. Let me grab my stuff."

I stared at her. What did I miss? Half an hour ago we were joking about sharing sausage and now she was bolting like a terrified rabbit.

"How about if we promise no James Bond?" Jordan asked.

Smart. "You can pick your poison. Romance. High action. Anything."

"I'm not doing anything else..." Liz chewed on her bottom lip. "Pacific Rim?"

"Another reason to love you." My mind ground to a halt. Did I really just say that? "I mean... I don't mean—"

"I get it." Liz's smile wavered then surged back too brightly. "Living room?"

We all moved into the other room, and she took a seat in the chair next to the couch, perched on the edge, and did a perfect impersonation of a mannequin.

The movie was one of my favorites, but my attention kept drifting to Liz. Why wouldn't she relax?

When we hit the lull after the first act, Jordan stood. "Popcorn?"

"I'm fine." Liz's expression looked more like a grimace than a reassuring smile.

Was this what Jordan had put up with all week? "Okay." I tried to keep my tone normal, despite my confusion and creeping hurt.

Jordan returned a few minutes later, bowl in hand, and offered some to Liz first. She picked out a few pieces, never looking away from the TV.

"We're not rationing it," he teased.

"I'm good."

I didn't like this, but what was I supposed to do? Liz was running hot and cold, and I didn't know why. I grabbed the popcorn from Jordan when he sat, and in a fit of frustration, tossed a piece at Liz.

That was childish. What was I doing?

Liz looked over her shoulder at me, eyebrows raised, then turned back to the movie.

Damn it.

I sank lower in the cushions. A piece of popcorn bounced off my forehead, and I looked up to see Liz struggling to keep a straight face as she stared at the TV.

I laughed. "I've got more ammo." I tossed a few more pieces at Liz's back.

She twisted her mouth, then leaped to her feet and lunched across the room, grabbing for the bowl.

"Nope. Mine." I held it over my head, but didn't make any effort to move away.

Liz caught her foot on the carpet, tripped, and knocked the bowl loose as she landed in my lap. Food flew everywhere. She stumbled away from me, face red. "God, I'm sorry." Liz picked up individual pieces and then handfuls. "I didn't mean to make a mess."

And now the moment was not only ruined, it was worse than before. How was I supposed to reassure her?

"Liz." Jordan's voice was a low whisper.

She looked at him, eyes wide, and he tossed a handful of popcorn at her with a grin.

She squealed, before her somber expression rushed back.

"It'll vacuum up," I said. "Don't worry about it."

We paused the movie to clean up, and when we were done, Jordan lifted Liz's chin, forcing her to look at him. "All better, right?"

"Yes."

"Good." He grabbed her wrist and tugged her onto the couch between him and me. "Stop sitting all the way over there. It looks lonely and you look uncomfortable."

Would she bolt?

Liz settled in.

Good.

Somewhere between the end of the first and the middle of the next movie, we had all shifted and adjusted so Liz sat with her back resting against Jordan, and her feet in my lap. It was perfect.

I didn't realize how late it was until the yawns broke out, spreading through the room like a virus.

"It's after one." I managed to stop another contagious yawn, but my eyes still watered. I nudged Liz's legs, hating to lose the warm weight and comfort. "You still awake?"

Liz tried to stifle another yawn. "Barely. I'm more tired than I thought."

"Crash here. In the guest room." I wasn't ready for her to leave. I'd rather have her in our bed, and I'd be content if we really only slept, but offering seemed like the fastest way to scare her off. "You can borrow something of mine, so you don't have to wear your clothes to bed."

Liz seemed to hold her breath for a moment, frozen in time .She finally exhaled and stood. "Home's not that far away. Thank you, though. Don't worry. I'll be back on Monday."

We helped her gather her stuff from the office, and wished her *goodnight*. When she was gone, Jordan pulled me into his arms. "You okay?" he asked.

"Completely." I'd promised to be honest with me. "No. But I don't know how to define… whatever this is."

"Yeah. Same." His tone rang in time with the confusion slinking inside me.

THIRTY-THREE

Liz

I couldn't do this.

Every time I knocked on Jordan and Chloe's door, I promised myself it would be the day where I found the middle ground between aloof and flirting. The mystical, magical place where friendship lived.

But every time one of them pushed the right button, my defenses shattered and it took *so much* effort to rebuild them.

Last Friday—a perfect week ending with popcorn, movies, and a spark that threatened to consume me if I kept it repressed—I almost caved. I was ready to say *fuck it* and spend the night, and probably the weekend. Reason saved me at the last minute, reminding me it would only hurt more to walk away later if I gave in now.

More than a week had passed since, and I had yet to enforce a single self-imposed limit, which culminated last night with the three of us feeding each other Chinese food, and me agreeing without hesitation when Jordan said, "Excuses aside, you're staying tonight, aren't you? Movies. Fun. Breakfast in the morning?"

So here I was, Saturday morning, still in their apartment. I'd tried to tell myself I stayed because Jordan needed to do a live run-through of his demo, and I'd be on standby while Chloe watched.

Did that send very non-professional thoughts racing through my head? Most definitely.

I was going to have to face a harsh reality—keeping my distance from them was the only way to protect my heart. When I was done working with Jordan, at the end of today, I'd say *goodbye*, walk away, and learn from my mistakes for next time.

After breakfast. And demo practice.

I stood on their balcony, looking over the quiet Saturday morning, and repeating the resolution until I was certain I could summon it on instinct, even if I didn't want to.

The door slid open behind me, and my heart jumped into my throat. It was Chloe. I knew without looking, not only from the faint hint of lavender, but because Chloe was more likely to be up and out here before Jordan.

She joined me at the railing. "You wear that better than I do." Her gaze lingered on my chest before she met my gaze with a playful smile.

Should I hug myself, to hide, or embrace the pleasant shiver that ran through me at the attention? I'd borrowed a top from Chloe to sleep in, and it hugged every curve I usually worked hard to disguise. "I doubt that." Where was that line I was looking for? The one that kept me removed. It had vanished. "But we could always swap and find out."

"Hmm…" Chloe furrowed her brow. "Tempting. But I say take my word for it."

Anything else I wanted to say would get me in trouble, so I turned back to the city. "Are you getting settled in the new job?" Could we have talked about this any time in the last two weeks? Yes. But I was too busy either staying removed or sinking into flirting to have normal conversations. This was what friends talked about, though. This was what I'd talk about with Mercy.

"I love it." Chloe leaned against the railing and her arm pressed into mine. "It makes me think. It challenges me."

"Sounds nice." I could say the same of what I'd spent the last two weeks doing. Not Mercy's task list. I was grateful for the job, but Mercy didn't delegate the bit stuff.

Working with Jordan, though… Who he was didn't hurt my enjoyment, but I loved the work, too. Seeing someone with his skill dive into his passion, and me being able to help me pursue that professionally.

"It is nice," Chloe said. "Can I tell you something? Just between us? I'm not keeping secrets from Jordan, but this is tricky."

My pulse hammered in my ears at the potential of any secrets Chloe might share. "Of course." That wasn't the right answer, but I wouldn't take it back.

"Technically, I stole his job, and he says it's okay, but

that doesn't seem like the kind of thing I should brag about."

Ah. That kind of secret. Better for me, but a pointed indication she trusted me. The realization simultaneously warmed and terrified me. "I understand. What is it?"

"The thing is, me moving into this new job made me think." Chloe's voice dropped in volume, as if she sank into that very thought. "Until the last month or so, I've never had to work for anything. Not really."

Wow that hit close to home, gnawing on doubts I usually ignored. "I get that. I grew up with money. My best friend handed me a hand-crafted job when I asked for it." I'd never really been challenged. Outside of broken hearts, but those weren't the same.

"Exactly. I never thought about it before—especially not when I was a kid. We were lower-middle class, so it wasn't as if we had everything, but we had enough. College would have cost me an armload of debt, but I skipped out on that stress. The Cord job came gift wrapped with my name on it. Jordan and I... It was always easy. Even when Cord crumbled, my sister came along and resurrected it and helped turn it into Rinslet. Which wasn't for my sake, but it served me. This is the first time in my life I've had to push for what I want, and I..."

Chloe pursed her lips, as if considering whether or not to finish her thought. "I don't like fighting with Jordan, and I'm glad we're past that. The rest of this, the demand it puts on me to excel—I'm thriving on it."

"I get it." It was as if Chloe had stripped my own thoughts from my head and put them to words.

"So I'm not insane?"

I shook my head. "No. Not even close."

"I had a feeling you'd get me." She rested her head on my shoulder.

God this felt so right. I hated it and I never wanted it to stop. "As long as we're sharing secrets, can I tell you something not even Mercy knows?"

"Of course."

I shouldn't tell anyone about this—NDA and all that —but I needed to talk about it and get it out of my head. "I figure you might share with Jordan, and that's okay, but promise it doesn't go beyond these walls."

Chloe held up three fingers, never pulling away. "Girl Scout's honor. Cross my heart and hope to die."

"I have a chance with the same investment firm Jordan is pitching to."

Chloe straightened and looked at me, surprise and excitement etched on her face. "Like, another project? One of your own?"

"Not quite." If I said this out loud—if I talked about it with someone besides Jonathan—it would become more real. And I wanted it to be. I almost gasped at the self-admission. "As a partner investor. I'd be a portion of the money, and one of the people making decisions."

"That sounds amazing." Chloe's enthusiasm was solid and genuine and contagious. "*So* perfect for you. After what you've done with Jordan, if you could help other people like that, and you're so good at it… *Wow.*" She paused. "But you're hesitating. Why?"

"I don't know." Or maybe the list was just too long to consider. It meant setting out on my own and walking away from the familiar. An excuse to move to L.A. Putting distance between myself and this couple I couldn't seem to walk away from. "Change is all well and good, but this terrifies me."

"Sounds like a perfect reason to say yes," Chloe said.

"I suppose you're right."

THIRTY-FOUR

Chloe

I didn't remember the last time I felt so much of a buzz. I'd blame it on the coffee, but I didn't have any more at breakfast than usual. No, the hum in my veins was a contact high from the company, and the fact that Jordan, Liz, and I occupied a table in the back of the diner for more than three hours before finally deciding to give up the space for other people.

We were back in the condo now, and I'd promised to help Jordan and Liz with some mysterious, unnamed task. "What do I have to do?" I asked.

"Sit." Jordan pointed at the couch. "Watch. Be interested."

I perched on the edge of a cushion, my curiosity climbing. "Ooh, are you stripping? I'm definitely interested in that."

Liz blushed. "Not the right audience. Or rather, his target audience won't appreciate him taking off his clothes nearly the way we do. I promise. Jordan needs to practice his presentation until he's comfortable with it. Which shouldn't be a problem, but it still needs practicing."

Yeah, it wouldn't be an issue. "Have you ever seen Jordan work a crowd?" I was biased, but I was also right that he was amazing at it.

"Yes." Apparently, Liz's blush could get deeper.

"Really?" Jordan paused in the middle of plugging in his laptop, and looked at Liz. "When?"

Liz focused her attention on the papers in her hands. "Research."

Jordan straightened up. "That's a bit vague. You can't say that and not offer details."

"I… uh… The night I met you, you said you knew how to handle the media, and everyone kept talking about *those Rinslet kids*, so I looked you up online before we had dinner that first time. All your old E3 presentations are on YouTube, starting with the fake marriage proposal."

The reminder of that first should tug at my regret—it always had in the past—but today I smiled thinking back on that day. For so long, I'd regretted that the fake proposal never became real. It didn't matter, though. I couldn't picture my life without Jordan.

Or Liz.

I shook the thought away.

"What did you think?" Jordan's question interrupted my spiraling memories.

Liz's papers seemed to grab her attention again. "You were adorable together that day." The rustle of pages muffled her words. "You still are. More important to this though, you started strong as showmen and grew. That's why I know Jordan can do this. Both of you really truly work an audience in ways I've never seen."

Liz's awe was impossible to ignore, sinking under my skin and buoying me. "Consider me your captive audience until you're done," I said.

Jordan stepped back from the laptop and pointed at the screen. "Imagine that's projected on the far wall. I will have a projector, won't I?" he asked Liz.

"Already reserved," Liz confirmed.

I listened for the next several hours as Jordan spun through multiple iterations of his demo. I was used sitting through this kind of rehearsal, but the content was completely new to me. He rolled out numbers, images, plans, and concepts I'd never dreamed of, and it left me in awe.

Sometimes Liz would stop him with feedback, and ask him to start over. Every time I questioned feasibility, he had an answer ready or let Liz feed him the information, and repeated it until it was his.

Morning turned into afternoon and I lost track of the time until Liz's phone chimed.

"Crap. I didn't realize it was already five. Hang on." Liz grabbed her phone. "It's going to be Mercy"—she seemed to be speaking to herself—"to ask if I'm on for my weekly dinner with her and Ian."

Skip out. Spend the evening with us. The request died in my throat. I wanted her company, but wouldn't ask her to give up family time for it.

Liz looked from the phone to Jordan and then me, while she fiddled with the device, rolling it over in her hand. She twisted her mouth, as if considering something.

Would she stay after all? Flutters of hope danced inside me.

Liz stood, no longer making eye contact with us. "You'll be amazing on Tuesday." Her gaze was directed at Jordan's feet as she spoke. "Thanks for letting me invade your private space for a few weeks. Let me know how things go. The three of us will hang out again sometime. If we have time. Bye." She all but scampered out the door.

What the hell?

"Did I miss something?" Jordan asked.

"If you did, so did I." I spun the last thirty seconds or so of Liz's rambling through my head. It felt as though Liz finished with a different conversation than the one we were having before her phone went off.

Jordan settled next to me on the couch. "Do you think she meant it this time? She made it sound so... final."

"I don't know." I wanted to believe Liz would be back on Monday, but she wasn't actually a permanent fixture in our lives.

"If we have our quiet home life back, that's good?" Jordan sounded as uncertain as I felt.

"I don't know," I repeated. I wasn't prepared to think about life without Liz.

THIRTY-FIVE

Liz

Not only was I indecisive, but I was a coward and a liar.

Mercy's text actually said *Just dropped Ian at the airport. Last minute meeting in Atlanta. You should hang out with your friends tonight.*

No clue why she thought that last bit was a good idea.

After I scurried out of Chloe and Jordan's condo like a scared rabbit, I replied. *You still in the valley? My place. Bring—*pizza had too many memories associated with it. So did Chinese. And sushi. And bar food. *Bring curry.*

I headed home to meet Mercy. While I waited, I flipped through the options in my wine rack. Except, even wine had memories attached to it. I should've asked Mercy for cheap beer, too. That should be safe.

I heard keys rattle in my lock, and Mercy let herself in. She held up a plastic bag filled with take-out boxes. "You ask, and I deliver."

"What kind of tip is appropriate in a case like this?" I grabbed the food and set it on the bar separating the living room from the kitchen.

"Hmm…" Mercy pulled silverware from its drawer. "Usually I'd say service is its own reward, but tonight you owe me information."

Crap. I set out two glasses of iced tea, and we each sat in bar stools half-facing each other. "Not sure what you're looking for. The price of gold dropped three points today?" I said.

"Bummer for gold investors." Mercy didn't sound impressed. "But not what I'm talking about." She dished rice onto her plate, covered it in mango and pork green curry, and handed each container to me as she finished with it. "Let's start with… I talked to Jonathan Wood-house today."

I froze mid-rice-scoop, and tried to cover my hesitation with curiosity. "Why didn't he call me? Is everything all right with KM?"

"I assume." The way Mercy studied me was unnerving. "He thanked me for being a good business partner and gave me his new company information, because he's leaving KM. I thought it was considerate of him to call me directly. Even said so. Asked if he'd already talked to you about it. He told me you already knew he was leaving and why, and you were kind enough to keep his secret."

So she didn't know yet that he'd invited me to join him. Good. I still needed to figure out the best way to bring it up. This should be the perfect segue, but the words were stuck in my throat. "Surprise. I didn't want to spill the beans on his behalf before he was ready."

"I bet." Mercy poked at her food but didn't eat any. "Why didn't you tell *me*?" Her hurt was impossible to ignore.

"He told me as a friend, not as an account manager, and…" I sighed. "I don't know where personal ends and professional begins anymore. With you. With Ian." With Jordan and Chloe. Apparently, I was shitty at drawing lines.

Mercy dropped her fork. "I thought you and I were okay now. Are we not?"

"We're not." I hated to tell her that, but now that I was talking, I didn't want to stop.

Mercy's frown cut through me. "Talk to me, Liz. What do we need? Tell me, please?"

I scrubbed my face, taking the delay to sort my thoughts into words. "I was so jealousy when you and Ian got together. I thought it was because I was attracted to you, and *God* that moment still haunts me, but that's not right. I don't know if you need me anymore, Mel, which is selfish of me to say, but I can't help it." The confession caught me off-guard, but it felt right, and it hurt.

"I'll always need you." Mercy squeezed my hand. "Always and forever. You were there for me when I lost myself, and now that I'm *settled down*, you can tell me stories about your sexy escapades with fun couples around the world."

My laugh hurt my raw throat. "You're trying to

make me feel better, and I appreciate it, but that's not the way to do it."

She raised her brows in question.

"You were right." I needed that wine after all. I grabbed a bottle of white from the rack, uncorked it, and poured us each a glass. "A hookup with a couple isn't permanent."

"I wasn't right. I was one-hundred percent wrong."

This was gutting me. "Don't do that. It's not helping."

"Suck it up and hear me out anyway. Tough love time, because you and I do need each other." Mercy's voice took on an edge. "When you told me about L.A., I was jealous. I'm telling you that because you deserve to hear the truth."

I didn't understand. "Why?"

"Lots of reasons. You moved on so quickly. From me. I mean, who wants to hear that?" Mercy's mouth tugged up at the corners. "And as I'm settling down, you're starting to live life. My feelings are misplaced. I wouldn't give up Ian for the world—I'm not saying anything like that—but... remember what you said to me the day you kissed me?"

I did. "It's a shame we didn't get to explore with each other when we were younger."

"Not only who we are, but the world," Mercy said. "I don't want to go back. We can't change the past, and I love my present. But sometimes the mind wonders."

"I get it. We both turned out fine though, and I wouldn't have survived seeing the world with you. I'm not cut out for this life. I can't even walk away from a fling."

"You're kidding about leaving them." Mercy frowned. "You're not. Wow. Okay. You can't walk away from them."

"Once again, you're not helping." There was no way I could stomach food now. I made the right decision this evening, leaving Chloe and Jordan behind. It had to be the right choice.

"I saw the three of you together at Takashi. You're brilliant with them. Flawless. They adore you."

The words slammed into me, and as much as my heart wanted to believe Mercy, my mind refused to. "You misinterpreted. They're friendly people."

Mercy shook her head. "Maybe, but I don't think so. There was more there."

"Even if that's true—and I'm not saying I believe it—they adore each other more, and I can't stand between them or shield myself from how much it hurts."

"I'm sorry. For everything. That we fell apart. That you got hurt."

"It's okay." I felt better having shared with someone. Not healed, but not quite as miserable. "You and I will be okay. At least, I'd like to believe we will. The rest, I'll get over."

"Why do you have to?" Mercy asked. "Call them. Talk this through."

"I can't. That's a kind of hope I won't cling to, because it doesn't pan out." I didn't know how to make myself any clearer.

Mercy searched my face. "You're set on letting this hurt."

"I'm set on moving on now, rather than prolonging the agony."

"I guess it's a good thing Ian had to leave last minute. You should come up to the house for the rest of the weekend and keep me company."

"You might not want that after you hear what I have to say next." As long as I was baring my soul and opening wounds, might as well put everything out there.

"We've already spilled our guts. How much worse can it get?"

"I'm giving my notice. I can't work for you anymore."

Mercy worked her jaw up and down several times, no sound coming out. "But we're better."

"That's not why." Rip the bandage off—that was the best way to do this. "I'll always love you for giving me this chance. You've done so much for me. The thing is… I knew what Jonathan was up to, because he invited me to join them. I had to think about it. A lot. And I'm going to do it."

Mercy's shock melted into a grin. She hopped from her stool and hugged me so tightly it ached. "*Oh my God. That's amazing. That's brilliant. It sucks for me, because you're irreplaceable, but you deserve more, and *yay* for you."

"Thank you." I broke the embrace. "I'm probably also going to L.A. They gave me the option to do this remotely, but I need…"

"A change of scenery. I get it."

And once I'd been out there on my own for a few months, I'd recognize how right it was to leave Chloe and Jordan behind. I'd never really moved into this place, since it was meant to be temporary. I could be packed and out of here by the end of the week. Maybe Mercy and I could take a road trip, make a mini vacation out of this entire thing.

This was the only way I could see to start moving on with my life.

THIRTY-SIX

Jordan

Chloe had taken the day off to be by my side, and I couldn't be more grateful. This trade show was nothing like the industry mega-shows Rinslet spent massive budgets on. There were maybe one-hundred-fifty attendees and the hall was only open for a few hours a day. All of ten tables framed the small room.

The cozy, personal feeling didn't calm me. I was about to shoot for a dream I hadn't dared admit I had less than a month ago, and now it felt like the world was riding on a win today.

"Iverson."

I didn't recognize the voice calling my name, but someone was jogging toward me. "Daryl." I extended my hand in greeting when I put a face to a name. "I didn't realize Synchronicity was here." I masked any bitterness in my greeting. Daryl was Synchronicity's CTO, and while they were the first to withdraw their job offer to me after the most recent bout of bad media, it was all about to work out in my favor.

Daryl shook my hand. "I'm checking out the new tech, seeing what's out there and what we want to leverage. Who are you with?"

"Myself. Can't say more yet." I gave him a tight-lipped smile.

"Right. I get that. Listen, I'm sorry about how things happened. We'd buy you now if we could do it without losing face."

"That's business." The acid spilled into my reply and I swallowed hard. "For the record, it wasn't me who leaked your offer information. I have no interest in sabotaging my own career."

"That's part of the reason I'm so sorry. Turns out some new kid in HR has a friend who's a blogger."

"Really?" Chloe said sweetly. "Don't suppose you know the blogger's name?"

"Stan? Stew? Not sure. Anyway, I hope you both enjoy the show. Can't wait to see what you're working on." Daryl nodded at them and strode toward one of the tables at the far end of the room.

"That little troll," Chloe muttered as soon as he was out of earshot.

"Daryl?"

She squeezed my hand. "Stew. Fucking prick. Not that it's a surprise, but wow, I really don't like that little bastard."

He could rot in a fiery pit of hell as far as I was concerned. "And we'll rub his nose in our success. I'll go set up and text you when I'm done." I kissed her.

Chloe gave me a huge smile. "Good luck."

I took one more deep breath, and headed to my pitch meeting.

Forty-five minutes later, I'd nailed every talking point and answered each question without hesitation. I flipped my laptop to the last slide and turned to Jonathan. "Any other questions I can answer for you?"

"No. I think you covered everything fantastically." Jonathan's impassive mask never shifted, regardless of his words. He'd been this way the entire presentation. Dude must be one hell of a poker player.

"Great. So what are our next steps? We can discuss terms. If you've got a sample contract, I can look that over."

"I appreciate the confidence"—for the first time, Jonathan's expression faltered—"and the time it took to assemble something this intricate. I'm sorry, though. I can't bite."

What? I heard him wrong. Didn't I? "Of course. I understand. Actually, no I don't. Why not?"

"Your numbers are solid, and so is your product. Someone else might jump on this, and I suggest you shop it around. Selling art and merchandise based on a name takes a huge platform, though. A brand of epic proportions. I was hoping to see that in your presentation. Your name is out there, but not enough. Not for me."

Mentally, I deflated like a punctured balloon—a sharp spike jabbed into my chest and all the air escaped. "I appreciate your honesty." I didn't. I loathed it. That level of honesty wouldn't serve me now. "Anything I can do, to change your mind?"

"No. I wish you luck, though. Liz speaks highly of you, and if she sees potential, someone else will too. Enjoy the rest of your day." Jonathan shook my hand one more time and then left.

That sucked. I'd really expected to land that.

He knew when he walked in here he was going to tell me *no*. I'd been fighting an uphill battle and didn't know it.

Who the fuck did he think he was? There were few people out there who were as good as me *and* as well-known as me. The internet cared who was making me job offers. Who the fuck could say that?

I crammed my laptop into its bag, along with the rest of my belongings. This wasn't Jonathan's fault. It was Stew's. It was the popularity contest that drove art. It was so much.

I needed to find Chloe, get out of here, and go somewhere I could blow off steam. Maybe avoid further damaging my career at the same time. *I'm done*, I sent her a quick text. *Meet me front. Take your time.*

From there, I cut a straight line to the closest doors, trying to find that balance between wearing a *don't fuck with me* look, and not giving anyone another reason to gossip about me being an asshole.

When I pushed through the doors, the summer sun hit my face, the scorch mingling with the heat of rage boiling inside me. I closed my eyes and turned toward the sky, looking for some semblance of inner calm.

Nope. Not there.

"Jordan. Buddy." The overly friendly greeting snapped something inside me.

I shot my attention at Stew, not trying to hide my fury. "This is a *bad* time." I spoke through clenched teeth and in my pockets, my hands balled into fists.

"No worries. I just wanted to say hi. Make sure you were doing okay." If Stew had any idea of the anger directed at him, it didn't show in his smile. "Rumor is you've had a rough month."

It was two in the afternoon on a Tuesday. Most of the conference was in break-out sessions, and lunch was over for any nearby office workers. Except for the little pockets of people passing by occasionally, no one cared what we were doing. I stalked forward, forcing Stew away until the blogger's back collided with a nearby wall. "What's your problem with me?" I growled.

"I don't have a problem with you. We're buddies. Pals. Colleagues. Practically best friends."

"Bullshit," I spat. "You don't like me. Never could stand me, and something happened in L.A. that gave you a way to take things a step further. What did I do to you? How did you even pull that off? The bruises, I mean. We both know I never touched you." Though, I was tempted.

"Your memory's faulty. You beat the shit out of me that night, because I wanted to talk to your dinner companion, Elizabeth Thompson. How is she?"

"I assume better off not having spent time with you." I was all-but yelling, and I couldn't find the willpower to scale the volume back. Really, though. Did you pay someone to punch you? Someone else got you before me, because you're a piece of shit, and you thought you'd blame me instead?"

"What? No. I'm not up for pain, even to drag your ass through the mud. I know a really good make-up artist in L.A. Those pictures? After the fact. I was beat up enough as a kid, by assholes like you, to know exactly which strikes leave bruises and which don't. I told the police enough of a story to keep you there for questioning until I was ready to drop the charges. They weren't going to hold you for more than that." Stew spoke quietly. Calmly. Maddeningly.

Jesus. This guy was pettier and more of a psycho than I'd realized. "And leaking my job offers? That was sticking another knife in?" I was shouting now.

"More or less. Did you like it?"

I desperately wanted to plow my fist into his stupid smug face. I'd never struck someone in my life, but this seemed like a good time to find out what it was like.

"Seriously?" Chloe's disbelief cut through the red clouding my vision. "How delusional are you?"

Stew looked past me, to her, and I almost put a hand to his throat. "I don't know why you're with him," Stew said. "Why do chicks always like the asshole?"

Chloe rested a hand on my arm, holding me in reality, but only barely. She held her phone past me, toward Stew. "Not true. I don't like you. We're streaming by the way. Since about the time you admitted you faked the entire assault. Do you want to say anything else?"

"You're a lying cunt, and I'm done here." Stew turned away with a snarl, and melted into the crowd that had formed.

I looked at Chloe in disbelief. She showed me the screen of her phone. Sure enough, she was livestreaming. She clicked the button to cut the feed. "Got him," she said softly.

I sank to the ground, face in my hands and brain still trying to catch up with what just happened. It wasn't over. It couldn't possibly be. Huzzah for showing the world what Stew did was on him, not me, but it didn't undo any of the fallout.

I still didn't have a job, and I didn't know if I could go back to a regular one, now that this new dream had been dangled in front of me.

What was I supposed to do next?

THIRTY-SEVEN

CHLOE

I snuggled into Jordan, hand on his bare chest as I tried to let the beat of his heart soothe me. Neither of us slept last night, and I was pretty sure we were both replaying an alternate ending to the Stew altercation, where Jordan hit him, just once.

After I cut the stream, of course.

Neither Jordan nor I actually wanted that, but the mental image was more comforting than it maybe should be.

"You have to get ready for work soon." Jordan's voice was soft and without emotion.

We'd taken a page from Liz's book and shut off everything last night. I had no idea what kind of fallout waited for us. For all I knew, I didn't have a job to go back to either. I doubted that was the case, but a few weeks ago, I also wouldn't have guessed Rinslet would fire Jordan. "Promise me you won't spend the day stalking news sites."

"You know I will."

"It won't help." I wanted to do it too, though.

"It'll make me feel better," Jordan said.

"No. It won't."

He trailed his fingers through my hair. "I'll probably stay offline most of the day." His voice softened. "Try and focus on the positive. You should do the same."

I nodded. "Sounds like a plan."

"Work." He nudged me into a sitting position. "Go shower, I'll make the coffee extra strong."

I turned the water on as cold as I could stand, hoping it would jar me away. My teeth were chattering by the time I stepped out of the tub and dried off, but my mind was still a fog. Though we both tossed and turned all night, we said very little. We were each other's comfort. No matter what happened next, we had that.

It seemed wrong that Liz wasn't here with us, and that was the one thought I couldn't reconcile. How could I want more? Still?

I pulled on my favorite Nintendo T-shirt and faded jeans, needing to be wrapped in security since I couldn't take Jordan to work with me. What were our next steps? I enjoyed a challenge, but this one had me stumped.

When I padded into the kitchen and saw him scanning his phone, my stomach dropped. No putting it off any longer. "Well?"

His lips were drawn in a thin line. And then one corner of his mouth twitched, and a sharp cackle slid out before he choked it off. He handed me the device. "They're talking about your livestream."

Of course they were. But… I scanned the headlines,

and disbelief mingled with exhaustion. We'd slaughtered Stew's reputation. Sites he'd worked with were distancing themselves. Taking down his stories. Insisting he'd never write for them again.

"His credibility is at zero." Jordan sounded like he was having as tough a time believing it as me.

When his phone buzzed in my hand, I jumped, then giggled. I didn't recognize the number. I handed the phone back. "I assume it's for you."

He frowned at the screen but answered. "Jordan Iverson... Yes... I have... Are you sure? I mean, of course you are. Thank you. I'll keep an eye out for it." He disconnected and let his phone clatter to the kitchen counter.

I tried to rein in my curiosity, but as the seconds ticked away and Jordan didn't speak, I caved to curiosity. "That was...?"

His blue eyes were clear and bright when he looked at me. "That was Jonathon Woodhouse. He said he misspoke yesterday about my platform. He didn't realize how wide it reached. Especially now. He wants to back me before anyone else gets to me."

"Holy shit." I flung her arms around him. "That's amazing. It's fantastic."

Jordan buried his face against my neck. "If he thinks other people are going to come forward with offers..."

"No. We're not fucking around with this, as long as what he's offering you is fair." I pulled back enough to slap him on the arm, then dove back into the hug. This was right. The way it should be.

"It's better than Liz told me to expect. He's sending a contract now."

I rested my cheek against his chest. This time, his heartbeat did soothe me. Steady. Right. Peaceful. "We're calling Liz to celebrate, aren't we?"

His arms stiffened around me.

"What's wrong?"

"You tell her. We should celebrate alone, though."

"No." I didn't like his tone. "You can't do the same thing she is. What's wrong with both of you?"

"My answer spoils the mood. You don't want that. Neither do I."

Because calling Liz as *just friends* would hurt too much. And Jordan felt the same. "I love you dearly and completely," I said. "You know that?"

"I do."

"Is it possible"—I swallowed my doubt and pushed through hesitation—"to feel that way about you, but still not be complete?"

"I'd live happily ever after with you and only you." He brushed his thumb over my cheek.

I knew him almost as well as I did myself. He felt the same way I did. "You recognize it too. We'd be happily-ever-after times two if she was with us."

"Yes. But Liz has to feel the same way."

"Then we'll have to convince her we're serious." Now that we'd vocalized the idea, I didn't want to shake it. "That she's not this extraneous add-on. That she's as much a bit of us as we are of each other. Is that weird?"

"Which part? Because it's all making sense to me."

"It's barely been a month, and I think I love her. It's

not what I feel for you; nothing will ever match that. But I think it's just as strong."

Jordan settled his hands on my hips and pulled me to him again. "I knew after a week of working with you. And I get it. I can't do this reality-living-life thing without you, but Liz is like a missing piece."

I loved the way he climbed into my head and picked out thoughts I couldn't put into words. Liz and I had something just as good, and yet completely different. Was Jordan right? Liz might not feel the same? She had walked away from us. "What if she's not interested?"

"No way to find out unless we ask." He kissed me on the forehead, the nose, and the lips. "Go to work. I'll call Liz and ask if she wants to meet for lunch."

I wouldn't be able to focus on work now, but I didn't have a choice. "All right." I pressed my lips to his one more time. "I love you. And thank you."

THIRTY-EIGHT

Jordan

When I called Liz and went straight to voicemail, I wasn't surprised. How much had she put on hold to help me?

"This is Jordan. Call me back."

Would she?

I turned my attention to the contract from Jonathan. The legalese made my eyes glaze over, but I recognized enough about the terms he was offering to know this was worth paying for a lawyer to look at, rather than saying *uh, thanks but no thanks.*

Every few minutes, throughout the morning, my attention drifted to my phone. I hadn't missed any calls or messages, but that didn't stop me from checking compulsively. When did Liz become so important? I couldn't pinpoint an exact moment, but not having her here for the last few days left an empty void inside.

I would've shoved the feeling aside for Chloe, but I was glad I didn't have to.

My phone buzzed and I grabbed it before it finished its hum.

Are we on for lunch?

I was happy to see the text from Chloe, but I did wish there was another, from a certain someone else.

It's just you and me. No answer from Liz yet, I replied.

I sent a text to Liz, and as noon sped in and she didn't respond, disappointment set in.

Lunch with Chloe was fantastic. We talked about more details of my offer. Work. Who was fucking whom in the office…

For the first time since I was laid off, bitterness didn't creep in when I talked about my former coworkers.

I sent Chloe back to work, dropped Jonathan's contract off with a lawyer, and headed back to the condo. Did I need a different route to talk to Liz? I called the R&T main number and asked for her.

"I'm sorry. Ms. Thompson doesn't work here anymore. All of her clients should have been notified. I apologize if that didn't reach you."

"I'm sure it's in my email somewhere." She quit? What the fuck? "May I speak with Mercy Rowe, then?"

"Ms. Rowe has a full schedule today."

I was going to push my luck a little. "Could you tell her—if you can get her on the line, that is—that this is Jordan Iverson?"

Would that deter her from taking the call? It depended on why I couldn't get hold of Liz.

"One moment. I'll check."

A prerecorded message played over the line, and seconds later, I heard a click. "Hey." Mercy sounded friendly. "I understand congratulations are in order. Something about a business venture?"

"The news isn't public yet. How did you know?" I clenched my jaw. It wasn't out there, was it? I couldn't handle another let-down like that.

"I know people." Mercy laughed. "What can I do for you, Mr. Iverson?"

"You're busy, so I won't keep you long. I'm looking for Liz, but reception tells me she doesn't work for you anymore."

"You haven't heard." Mercy sounded surprised.

"Heard what?"

"She gave me your news, and over the weekend gave me her notice. She's one of Woodhouse's business partners as of last night."

"Oh." The information sank int and so did reality. "Wait. Their offices are in L.A. She's not moving, is she?"

"Listen, Jordan, I can't—"

"Please. I need to talk to her, and she's not taking my calls."

Silence stretched over the line, and I was about to prod, when Mercy sighed. "I know who you are. Not as in I read the news this morning, or in the way Ian meant when he said it. I have a pretty good idea what you are to Liz."

"What am I?"

"It's not my place to tell you. But she did this for me once, so I'm returning the favor with a tiny caveat. Don't hurt Liz. She's had enough of that."

I thought about asking *or what*, but hurting Liz was

the last thing I wanted. "I swear, that's the furthest thought from my mind."

"She's packing up and getting ready to move. So she's either at her condo or the Park City house, figuring out what to take with her and what to put into storage." Mercy rattled off an address I didn't already have.

"Thank you." I tried to call Liz one more time and went straight to voice mail. It was almost five. Chloe still had to wrap things up at work. I could make the drive up the canyon, but unless Liz was up there and planning on staying the night, I could miss her. Checking her condo first made the most sense.

I knocked twice and rang the bell. She either wasn't home or was determined to ignore me. I wandered down to the lobby. If I was going to drive up to Park City, I'd wait for Chloe to be done with work, but there was no guarantee the trip would pay off. I could stroll across the street, grab a cup of coffee, and stalk Liz's front door.

If she wasn't already done with us, that seemed like a great way to make it happen.

"Jordan?" Liz's voice drew a smile from me before my mind caught up.

"Liz. We need to talk."

She shook her head and brushed past me. "There's a reason I'm not taking your calls."

So it was on purpose. I sent Chloe a quick text *At Liz's*, then followed Liz to the elevator. "Because you're going to leave without saying *goodbye*?"

"I already said goodbye, and I'm not having this conversation with you here."

"Where then?"

"Upstairs. My condo."

That was miles better than *nowhere. Go away.* Seeing her again drove home how much I'd missed her after just a few days. Even with the scowl etched on her face, her familiar scent and soft curves teased me. "Liz."

She held up a finger, silencing me, and I when we reached her floor, I walked with her to her place. I drummed my toes inside my shoes while I waited for her to unlock the door.

The instant we were inside, closed off from the rest of the world, she turned to me. "What?"

Any preplanned words evaporated. I closed the distance between us, cradled her cheeks between my palms, and kissed her. She parted her lips, and her gasp met my mouth. She dug her fingers into my chest with a groan. *Fuck,* this was incredible. No wonder Chloe liked it so much.

When they broke apart, Liz traced her fingers over my lips. "What was that?"

"I'm not super experienced in the matter, but I'm going to say it was our first kiss."

She stepped out of reach. "Not what I meant."

"I've been dying to find out what that was like."

"What's your verdict?"

"Intoxicating and addictive." I reached for her again.

She rested a palm on my chest, her arm locked. "Stop. This is why I'm leaving. Why I wasn't taking your calls, and why I wasn't going to say goodbye. I already told you, I'm not your third wheel."

"You're anything but." I probably should have led with that. "I wanted to do this with Chloe here, but you need to hear it. I love you. We love you. We want and need and have to have you in our lives."

"Wrong. We're not having this conversation with just you and me, because so help me, my imagination does enough concocting on its own, and unless I hear it from both of you, I can't—" Her voice cracked.

Making Liz cry was not part of the plan, as poorly thought out as it was. "That's fine." I kept my distance, not wanting to push her away when she was so close. "Chloe will be here in the next fifteen minutes, unless traffic is bad. Then will you listen?"

"Chloe's coming here? Now?"

"I texted her when you got home, and I guarantee she cut out of work the moment she saw that message, if it was an option. You know she'll drop everything. Even if you pretend you don't, you have that same synergy with us. We all click. She and I have since we met, and it's the same with you."

"I can't, Jordan. I'm sorry. I'm not sure what you're doing here, or why you think this is a good idea, but no. Meet her in the lobby and go."

"Liz, please. I'll wait until she gets here to say anything more, but you have to hear us out."

"I don't. There's nothing requiring me to do that."

I racked his brain for another argument, but I didn't have anything for a flat-out *no*. "All right." I reached for the door, hating the empty pit growing in my chest. Apparently, I'd used up my luck for the day.

THIRTY-NINE

Liz

I couldn't make sense of the swirl inside. Giddiness. Hurt. Frustration. Desire. It all waged war, until I wanted to scream and weep and stomp my foot and shout *it's not fair.*

Jordan faced me again, his hand hovering over the doorknob. "I don't know what's making you push us out, but I'm arrogant enough to think I know you, at least a little, so I'm going to take a guess. If you're making me leave because you don't feel the same, that's fine. I'll still go. You have to say it though. But I think it's something else. You're terrified because this is something no one does. I get that. I've been struggling with the same thought. But so what? I love you. When Chloe gets here she'll tell you the same thing. If you feel the same, don't sacrifice us because people say relationships like this don't work. We've done all right so far, and those people aren't us."

"Wait." The word forced itself past my lips.

Jordan moved away from the door, smile threatening. He'd said *love*. It wasn't a playful brush off. He didn't toss the word around, or make it sound like an *as a friend* kind of thing, the way Mercy and I were with each other. He said he and Chloe loved me. Both of them.

Hope clawed at my throat, daring me to defy what I'd heard.

"You can stay until Chloe gets here. But no promises." Except that was what I wanted. Promises. Not the lies George told. Not the lives ripped away too young, before I was even twenty. Something long-term.

"That's all I'm asking for," Jordan said. "Well, there will be more, but hearing us out is a start."

"Have a seat." I couldn't do the same, because I had memories associated with freaking sofas. I was so screwed if this didn't go well. Why did I let him stay?

Someone knocked, and Jordan called, "It's open."

I glared at him.

He shrugged.

"You always leave your door unlocked?" Chloe strode in and latched the deadbolt behind her.

I tried to hold onto my irritation and doubt, but both were fleeing rapidly. "When someone accosts me before I can lock it, yes."

"Aww." Chloe gave an exaggerated pout. "There was accosting, and I missed it?"

"There would have been, but Liz wanted to wait for you," Jordan said.

"Considerate woman. Another reason to love her."

"*Stop.*" The word came out louder than I intended. "I told you both already, I'm not a marital aid. I'm not a third wheel. I can't be your on-call toy."

"That's not what this is." Jordan took my hand between his. Every time he touched me, another fuse in my brain short circuited. "We want you in our life. I'm not talking about friendship or a booty call."

Chloe joined us and grabbed my other hand. "This isn't a *go home at the end of the night* kind of agreement. We mean... How presumptuous to say I'm hoping the rest of our lives?"

"So what? The three of us live together, one big happy family?" I liked the sound of it. So very, very much.

Chloe nodded. "Yup."

I wanted to believe this was all real, regardless of what logic said was and wasn't possible. I wanted to wrap myself in the promise of their words and stay there. But— "The real world doesn't work like that."

"The real world is broken sometimes. We're fond of making our own rules." Jordan tugged me to the couch and into his lap when he sat.

The number of times I'd seen him do this with Chloe and so badly wanted the same. The realization clenched around my heart. It felt so good to be held like this. Wrapped between them. It shouldn't be right, but it was, and I was tired of fighting it. "Is that an option? Making our own rules?"

"Of course it is. We rewrite reality every day." Chloe knelt on the couch next to me, which put us eye to eye.

"But how does it work? How will it work?" I didn't want to keep arguing, but this sounded too easy, when getting here was anything but.

"As a basic concept?" Jordan asked. "We all live together. No one is more important than anyone else. You've already become a part of us. Beyond that, we make it up as we go along." He dragged a finger down my spine, soft and teasing.

Such a vague plan was bound to have some holes. "What about jealousy." I'd seen that and never wanted to go up against Chloe again. Because of her insecurities or my own. I'd be breaking through a bond between the two of them that shouldn't be touchable.

"We'll talk it through. Or we shout it through. Either way, we confront it," Chloe said. "Everyone has disagreements."

"You two have really thought about this."

"Not really. Kind of, but this is more of an improv deal. Probably for the rest of our lives. Like most of adulthood, despite what we were raised to believe, there are no guarantees or norms." Jordan slipped his hand under my shirt and settled his palm against my lower back, not moving higher—simply tempting me.

Which brought up another big question. "What about in the bedroom?"

Chloe scrunched up her face in thought. "We probably need a bigger bed."

"Not what I meant, but even that has complications." I relaxed and rested my head against Jordan's chest, watching Chloe for even the slightest hint this wouldn't be as easy as they insisted.

Chloe flinched but then twisted on the couch and laid her head in my lap, looking up at both of us. "Why?"

"Three people in one bed?" Why was I still arguing? I wanted to accept this at face value. Last time I did that, I almost lost my inheritance, but this was different. They'd insist, and I agreed. Jordan and Chloe wouldn't oppose something like a background check, or any of those other precautions George insisted I wouldn't ask for if I really loved him.

And while I didn't know everything about them, I'd seen a lot more than I ever got to know about George.

I had a kind of faith in them that didn't make sense but continued to pan out. We were in sync. Which was part of the reason I loved them. And I did. I didn't want to fight it anymore. "I guess maybe."

"To which part?" Jordan asked.

"To the sleeping in the same bed part. I guess maybe. Don't think I didn't notice you dodged the sex question."

Chloe grinned. "You asked about the bedroom. We haven't had sex in the bedroom."

"Technically—"

"Our bedroom." Chloe cut Jordan off. "Hotel sex is different."

"Technically"—I picked up the argument, more because it was fun than for the sake of disagreeing—"we don't have a bedroom. So that's not possible. You're still not answering the question."

Jordan trailed his nose up the side of my neck, breath hot against my skin, and I whimpered. "If we're getting hung up on technicalities, it's not a complete question," he said. He nipped my earlobe, then kissed back down to my shoulder. "But I'll bite." He scraped his teeth along my skin.

With each new touch, he grew harder against the back of my thigh. Desire spilled through me.

"I figure if all three of us are in the mood, it'll be like it has been in the past." He dragged his lips along my jaw. "If only two of us are—any two of us—that's fine too."

He settled his palm against my cheek and turned my head to crush his mouth to mine. Chloe made a noise somewhere between a whine and a groan. I kissed back, diving into the need, my tongue dancing with Jordan's. My heart hammered against my ribs, and the rest of my arguments fled. When we broke apart, Jordan held my head captive, searching my face.

"Okay." I managed.

He laughed. "Okay to what?"

"All of it." I wanted another kiss. Or twenty. And more. "Loving you both. Making the three of us work. Being together, all of us, equally." They didn't have to invite me into their lives or ask me to stay. Yet here they were, prodding, poking, and insisting.

Chloe's weight left my legs, and the couch cushions shifted. I didn't have to look to know she had stood. Anticipation raced inside, pooling in my gut and traveling lower.

"You're sure?" Jordan's mouth quirked in a teasing smile, as he held my gaze. "If I wanted to watch the two of you together, while Chloe had her way with you, you wouldn't complain?"

"There might be a bit of whimpering and crying out, but no complaining." I was slick with anticipation.

FORTY

Chloe

I hesitated in Liz's bedroom doorway, unable to quell the fluttering inside. She stood near the bed looking completely tempting and—probably unintentionally—intimidating. She'd taken the lead last time. Would it be obvious how inexperienced I was? What was I supposed to do next? The logistics were a lot easier to figure out on paper, when I had time to plot and rearrange and add in extra hot bits and remove extraneous limbs after the fact.

Jordan nestled his hand against my back, and it chased away some of my tension "You know what you like and what you've always wanted to try." His whisper was quiet enough only I would hear. "Start there."

I swallowed my doubt, stepped toward Liz, and kissed her. Her lips were fuller than Jordan's. Softer. Yielding. And still swollen from making out in the living room. I nipped at Liz's bottom lip, and her gasp dove straight to my core. This might be terrifying, but it felt right. I could stick to kissing alone for hours, but when Liz raked her nails up my back, I wanted more.

I shoved Liz's baggy T-shirt up and over her head, to toss it aside. Her breasts were rounder and fuller than mine, and I trailed a finger along the enviable plumpness barely contained in a smooth satin bra. The way her chest rose and fell each time she gasped was delightful.

I lost track of who removed what, as our clothing fell into a growing pile next to the bed, until we stood in front of each other, exposed.

"So many stunning curves." I trailed a finger from Liz's collarbone, over one nipple, and down to her navel, before traveling back up the other side of her torso.

Behind me, the noises Jordan made matched Liz's, groan for sigh. Without looking, I was certain he was stroking himself through his jeans, trying to make this moment last. The knowledge flooded me with fresh desire that pooled between my legs.

I lowered my head to Liz's breast and took a swollen pink nub in my mouth. As I flicked my tongue back and forth, I swore I could feel the sensation on my own skin. I sucked harder and Liz squirmed. When I pinched her other nipple, she knotted her fingers in my hair and squirmed under my touch, despite holding me in place.

I continued to lick and tease and nip, each new mewl and sigh spurring me on. I glided my free hand down Liz's stomach, and her grip on my hair tightened when I dipped between her legs.

Her hips bucked closer to my touch. In the future, teasing and drawing the moment out would probably be a thing, but tonight I wanted her to feel how much I wanted her. I stroked along her slit, and dipped into her opening to thrust.

Liz gasped when I withdrew. I glided up to her clit to trace circles and stroke.

"Oh *God.*" She was panted, grinding against my hand.

Could I get myself off without being touched? Doing this, pushing Liz's buttons and hearing her—feeling her—writhe with pleasure, made my own body echo in kind. I squeezed my legs together, but the fresh pressure only intensified my need.

I stroked Liz, pulling back each time she bucked her hips before pressing in again. Liz covered my hand and rubbed both fingers against her swollen core. When she came, her whole body shuddered and drove into my touch. I felt her pleasure through every inch of me. Hot on my skin. Echoing in my nerves as if I were the one coming.

Liz sank to the mattress with a shaky laugh. "I didn't realize light torture was on the menu."

"There's a fine line between not drawing things out too long, but taking the time to enjoy them." I raised my fingers to my mouth, and holding Liz's gaze, licked them clean one by one. "Next time, I want a first-person taste."

Liz grabbed my hips and pulled me closer to kiss along my stomach, down to my hips, and trailing her lips over the top of my mound.

The flutters in my gut were intensely amazing, and multiplied by a million when she looked up at me and said, "Lie down."

I did as I was told, squealing in surprise when Liz straddled me and pinned my arms above my head. Having her warm, soft body pressed so close to my core was incredible. Liz dipped her mouth near my ear. "Payback time."

"Threats and promises." I squirmed under her, to feel skin on skin, not to get away.

Liz managed to open the drawer of her nightstand without moving off me, and pulled out a long, sheer scarf. With a couple of loose knots, she bound my hands to the headboard. If I tugged, I'd break free without a problem, but that didn't sound like any fun.

At the sound of a zipper, I twisted my head to the side to see Jordan working his cock free from his jeans. He gave me a hungry grin as he slowly stroked his shaft, and a new level of need surged inside me.

"Eyes on me." Liz's playful command drew my attention again. She reached into the magical drawer of surprise and produced a bullet vibrator. The hard plastic glinted in the light, and when she twisted the bottom a soft buzz teased my ears.

"Do your worst," I taunted.

She trailed the toy over my chest and nipples, barely making contact. The ghostlike vibrations traveled through every sensitive region they passed over, flowing through me and plucking threads of desire like strings. She traced my breasts, the insides of my wrists, my inner thighs—everywhere but the one place that ached for attention.

When she finally dragged the toy along my skin, teasing along my labia, a cry tore from my throat and I arched my back to get closer to the touch. Liz pulled away. With each pass over my slit, she pressed a little harder and drew a little closer to my clit, but never made contact with the swollen button.

The tinny buzzes rocked against my skin, and orgasm crept inside, hovering by a thin thread that refused to break. Liz finally moved up to my clit. The lightest lingering pressure was all it took to send climax crashing over me. My body shuddered away as pleasure threatened to overload my senses, but Liz kept the vibrator on its target.

"Please." I struggled for my voice. "I can't—"

Liz shoved two fingers inside me, adding a new and intense sensation to the blend. My head swam in the clouds as I came again.

Jordan's familiar grunts in the background amplified the stimuli flooding me. I ground against Liz until I couldn't anymore, and collapsed back on the mattress with a whimper.

"Beautiful." Liz kissed my thighs, pulling all other contact away, and moved up to claim my lips.

I worked my wrists free and held her close, memorizing every sound, sensation, tasted, and scent that filled the room. This was perfect. Not only the sex—though that was incredible, and I had a feeling it would only get better, the more we learned about each other—but this entire situation.

This amazing missing piece we'd found in Liz.

That Jordan and I trusted each other to make this leap.

That I couldn't have scripted this feeling, this love between the three of us, any better if I'd tried.

FORTY-ONE

Jordan

Chloe and Liz curled up together, and the evening light shone in from outside, dancing over their bare skin. They were more gorgeous than anything my imagination could concoct, and this was one of my new favorite sights.

I didn't want to disturb them, but I wanted to be closer, so I sat on the edge of the bed.

Chloe unwound herself enough to watch me, but never let go of Liz.

Was having two women at once most guys' fantasy? Sure. But that wasn't why I felt like the luckiest guy in the universe. They were both incredible, unique, and brilliant, in addition to being sexy.

"Were you really going to move to L.A. without saying goodbye?" Chloe spoke in the content, half-drowsy tone I loved. She was happy.

Liz frowned, but it vanished quickly. "I was heart-broken. You two had each other. I was tired of falling for the wrong people and then having to stick around and watch the results. Running away seemed easy."

"Without saying goodbye." Chloe repeated.

"I was going to send a card, congratulating Jordan on his new venture." Liz pointed toward the other side of the room. "It's handwritten and everything, and sitting on my dresser. That's kind of like goodbye."

Chloe's pout was exaggerated. "No. That's nothing like it."

"Speaking of…" I had been wondering this, and now might not be the time to ask, but since the topic was already out there— "Did you have anything to do with Jonathan changing his mind?"

"No." Liz's answer came without hesitation. "I asked him to hear you out in exchange for me considering their partner agreement, because I believe in your project. I couldn't mix how I felt with a decision like that, though. You deserved an impartial ear. Anything and everything he did with your presentation was his decision. He told you *no* based on what he saw, and he changed his mind for the same reason."

"You didn't influence him at all." I liked winning this on my own. Which wasn't true. Liz still made it possible, and Chloe supported the entire thing, but it was nice to hear my idea had its own merit.

"I'll admit it was harder for me to sign with them, knowing they'd passed on a deal as good as you. Fortunately, Jonathan made the right decision in the end, so my struggle didn't last long."

Chloe sat up and scooted until her back rested

against the wall. "And now you'll spend your time on the other side of the table from people like Jordan?"

"Mmm… Sexy pillow talk." A smile played on Liz's face, and teasing lined her sarcasm.

"You love it," I said.

Liz propped herself up on one elbow. "I love the two of you—"

"Wait. Stop. Hold on. That's the first time you said that." Chloe grinned.

"I love you?" Liz said. "Not that you gave me much of an opening before, barging into my place like it was important or something. But I do. I love you both. I'm completely and totally head-over-heels."

Fucking music to my ears. As good as when Chloe said it, and just as right. I nudged the bottom of Chloe's foot with my toes. "Let the lady finish her story."

"Thank you," Liz said. "I won't exactly be on the other side of the table. I made an amendment to my agreement, because I enjoyed the way I worked with Jordan. Beyond the I'm-in-love reasons."

"Excuse me—declarations of love are momentous." Chloe sounded indignant.

I agreed but couldn't help teasing her. "Are you going to Instagram it?"

"No. But I would like to bask for a moment."

"I'll be basking for a long time." Liz moved closer to Chloe.

"Okay. We'll all bask." I dragged out the words as if making a concession, loving every minute of the banter. "But I want to hear about how I'm so wonderful I changed Liz's career path."

Liz tossed a pillow at me. "Arrogant ass. I liked the work we did—figuring out if your idea was financially feasible; running the numbers; piecing it all together."

"And I couldn't have done it without you." Credit given where credit was due.

"I know." Liz smirked.

I lobbed the pillow back. "Now who's being arrogant?"

"It's not ego." She looked smug anyway. "It's a statement of fact. I figure you're not the only person out there with a marketable concept and no clue how to approach selling it. I made sure I've got the freedom to hear pitches from people who have the ideas and platform, but maybe not the contacts or knowledge to assemble a business plan around it. I work with them, to see if the numbers add up, and there will be times I'll pass on projects I pour a lot of time into. On top of that, if I want access to firm funds beyond my own, I have to sell the projects to the other partners."

"So you really are an angel," Chloe said with awe.

"With little pointy horns holding up my halo."

"Because you're not moving after all, because we're wonderful—" Chloe hesitated. "You are staying, aren't you?"

Liz nodded. "I'm staying."

"Good. In that case, when are you moving in with us, Liz?"

"That's a big assumption."

I watched the conversation like a tennis match, enjoying the way the two slid seamlessly from one topic to the next. Liz really did belong with us.

"It's not, really," Chloe argued. "We said we'd all be living together. Sharing a bed. Sharing our lives."

I made a show of looking around the room. "Liz's condo is nice."

"Liz's condo is sterile and pre-furnished." Liz spoke with disdain. "I never considered it home. We can change that if you want, but it'll mean a lot of redecorating."

"You were going to move out anyway. And I like home. I say you live with us, and we upgrade as needed." Chloe made it sound so simple.

I saw a tiny hitch in the plan. "That means two of us working from home. We'll need an upgrade sooner, rather than later."

"I want to work from home." Chloe's exaggerated pout returned.

I crawled across the mattress, to kiss it away.

"I bet you don't," Liz said. "You love it at the office."

"I do. Busted."

"And I'll probably have an office downtown. Half of our partners are based out of Salt Lake." Liz cast her gaze toward the comforter.

Chloe gasped in indignation. "So that was already an option, and you were still going to move away and leave us behind?"

"Heartbroken. Remember?" Liz met Chloe's tone gasp for gasp.

I settled my palm on Liz's chest, between her breasts. Her heart hammered against my skin. "Mended now?" I asked.

"Yes. It's much better."

"Good. The rest of the details will wait." I was good with figuring things out as time went on. For now, I wanted pizza, movies, and to probably christen another spot or two in someone's house as an official threesome, before the night was up. "We need you with us, though." Because it didn't matter what waited for us next. With all three of us, we could face anything.

THANK YOU FOR READING CHLOE, LIZ, and Jordan's story.

If you want another geeky, fun threesome trying to find their place in the world, check out SCREW THE BOSS.

Most things Bri does are to give her dad the middle finger, including working for one of his company's biggest competitors. Her new girlfriend is one more step toward proving she's not the child Dad wanted.

The fact that Kenzie's married makes it easy for Bri to remember their relationship isn't permanent. The fact that her husband, Scott, is Bri's sexy-as-sin boss, and doesn't have a problem with the relationship?

The scandal would shatter her dad's world.

Problem is, Kenzie and Scott are becoming more family that Bri's ever had, and she doesn't know which would be worse--losing them or letting them into her life.

- Click here to grab SCREW THE BOSS today

For some MMF geeky hotness, try LOOKING FOR IT. Sadie knows better than to hook up with her brother's best friends, but when they offer to show her how much fun her battery operated toys are with a partner, she can't refuse. But once she's had a taste of what the three of them could have together, can she go back to life with less?

- Start reading LOOKING FOR IT today